ALL THOSE THINGS
WE NEVER SAID

ALL THOSE THINGS
WE NEVER SAID

Marc Levy

Translated from the French by Chris Murray

McArthur & Company
Toronto

This edition published in 2011 by
McArthur & Company
322 King Street West, Suite 402
Toronto, Ontario
M5V 1J2
www.mcarthur-co.com

First published in English in Canada in 2010 by
McArthur & Company

First published in French as *Toutes ces choses qu'on ne s'est pas dites*
by Éditions Robert Laffont

Library and Archives Canada Cataloguing in Publication

Levy, Marc, 1961-
        All those things we never said / Marc Levy ; translated by Chris
Murray.

Translation of: Toutes ces choses qu'on ne s'est pas dites.
ISBN 978-1-55278-955-1

        I. Murray, Chris, 1979- II. Title.

PQ2672.E9488T6813 2010   843'.92   C2010-903939-4

Text design and composition by Szol Design
Cover photographs: red mailbox © Bruce Burkhardt/Corbis; letters © John
Clark/Getty Images
Back cover photographs: book © Stock4B/Getty Images; red mug © David
Vintiner /Corbis; robot © Lars Langemeier/A.B./Corbis; keys © Neil C.
Robinson/Corbis

Printed in Canada by Webcom

10 9 8 7 6 5 4 3 2 1

There are only two ways to live your life.
One is as though nothing is a miracle.
The other is as though everything is
a miracle.

ALBERT EINSTEIN

For Pauline and Louis

1.

"What do you think?"

"Turn around and let me have a look at you."

"Stanley, you've been looking me up and down for half an hour. I can't stand on this podium a minute longer."

"The hemline should be higher. It would be an absolute sin to hide those legs."

"Stanley!"

"Do you want my opinion or not? Now turn around again so I can see the front. Yes...just as I suspected. The plunging back and the plunging neckline are identical. I suppose if you spill something on it, you can wear it backward..."

"Stanley!"

"The very idea of buying a wedding dress on sale gives me hives. Why not just get it on eBay while you're at it? You asked for my opinion, and there it is."

"Excuse me if I can't afford anything better on an animator's wages."

"You're an artist, princess! God, how I hate industry jargon!"

"I work on a computer, Stanley, not with oils."

"My best friend brings to life amazing characters. Computer or not, she is an artist, not an animator. You overanalyze."

"So do we raise the hemline or leave it like this?"

"Three inches higher and we'd have to fix the shoulder and bring it in at the waist."

"Okay, I get it, you hate this dress."

"I never said that."

"But it's what you think."

"Darling, let me help you out with the cost. We can go to Anna Maier. Really, I beg you, will you please just listen to me for once in your life?"

"Ten thousand dollars for a dress? Are you insane? You can't afford it, either. Besides, it's just a wedding."

"But it's *your* wedding!"

"I know, I know," sighed Julia.

"With all the money your father has, he could have at least..."

"The last time I saw my father, I was stopped at a red light, and he was heading down Fifth Avenue. That was six months ago. End of story!"

Julia shrugged and stepped down from the fitting block. Stanley took her hand and pulled her in for a hug.

"Darling, you'd be stunning in any dress. I just want the one you choose to be perfect. Why don't you ask your fiancé to buy one for you?"

"Because Adam's parents are already paying for the reception. I'd feel much better if we could avoid my future in-laws gossiping about what a pauper the bride is."

Stanley headed across the boutique to a rack near the window. The sales staff leaning behind the counter chatted, ignoring him completely. He grabbed a white satin sheath and brought it to Julia.

"Try this on, and don't say a word!"

"It's a size 6, Stanley. I'll never fit into it."

"What did I just say?"

Julia rolled her eyes and went into the fitting room.

"It's a 6, Stanley!" she repeated on her way in.

A few minutes later, the curtain opened as abruptly as it had closed.

"At last! Something that looks like my Julia's wedding dress," exclaimed Stanley. "Get back up on that block."

"Do you have a winch and pulley? Because if I bend my knee..."

"You look gorgeous!"

"If I eat a single canapé, I'll split the seams."

"You're not supposed to eat on your wedding day. If we let it out a smidgen in the bust, you'll look like a queen. Who do I have to sleep with to get service in this store?"

"I'm the one who's supposed to be nervous, not you."

"I'm not nervous. I'm just a touch alarmed that, four days before your wedding, I'm the one who has to drag you to buy a dress!"

"You know that I'm drowning in work. And I can't talk to Adam about it. I swore to him that everything was ready a month ago."

Stanley took a pincushion that had been forgotten on the armrest of a chair and knelt at Julia's feet.

"Your husband doesn't know how lucky he is. You're magnificent."

"Stop it with the gibes at Adam. What do you have against him?"

"He reminds me of your father..."

"You're crazy. Adam is nothing like my father. He hates him."

"Adam hates your father? I guess that's a point in his favor."

"No, my father hates Adam."

"Your father hates anyone and anything that's close to you. He'd probably even hate your dog, if you had one."

"Very funny. But at least a dog would be able to bite him," Julia laughed.

"No, I think you have it the wrong way around. Your father would bite the dog!"

Stanley stood up, stepped back, and admired his work. He nodded and drew a deep breath.

"What is it now?" Julia asked.

"It's perfect. Or, rather, you're perfect. Let me adjust the belt, and you can take me to lunch."

"In the restaurant of your choice!"

"On a day like today, any place with tables outside

will do just fine. As long as there's some shade and you stop squirming, so I can finish. There...almost perfect."

"Why almost?"

"Because it's on sale, darling."

A saleswoman came over and asked if they needed help with anything. Stanley sent her packing with a flick of his wrist.

"Do you think he'll come?"

"Who?" asked Julia.

"Your father, silly!"

"Stop talking about him. I told you I haven't heard from him in months."

"That doesn't mean anything..."

"He won't come!"

"When was the last time you told him what was going on in your life?"

"I stopped updating his secretary a long time ago. I never talk to the man himself. He's always away on business or in a meeting. He doesn't have any time for me."

"But you sent him an invitation?"

"Are you done yet?"

"Almost. The two of you are like an old couple. He's jealous. All fathers are jealous, but he'll get over it one day."

"That's the first time I've heard you stick up for him. But if you think we're like an old couple, then we've been divorced for years."

The strains of "I Will Survive" could be heard from

inside of Julia's purse. Stanley gave her an inquisitive look.

"Are you going to get that?"

"Oh, it's probably Adam. Or the office..."

"Don't move or you'll ruin everything. I'll get it for you."

Stanley dove into her bag, pulled out the phone, and handed it to her. Gloria Gaynor fell silent.

"Too late," said Julia, glancing at the caller ID.

"So was it Adam or work?"

"Neither," she replied with a frown.

Stanley glared.

"Are you going to make me guess?"

"It was my father's office."

"Call back!"

"No way! He can call me himself."

"Isn't that what he just did?"

"It's what his secretary just did. It was his secretary's extension."

"Stop behaving like a child. You've been waiting for that call ever since you mailed his invitation. Four days before your wedding you should be minimizing your stress level. Do you want to risk getting a cold sore or a rash on your back? Call him back this instant!"

"Why? Just to have Wallace explain that my father sincerely regrets he will be traveling abroad and that the tickets are nonrefundable? Or, unfortunately, he is busy that day on extremely urgent business? Or some other excuse?"

"Or perhaps that he is delighted to attend his daughter's wedding and hopes that, despite their differences, she will have reserved him a seat at the head table?"

"My father doesn't care about that. If he came, he'd be happy seated near the coat check, as long as the girl taking coats was cute."

"Would you just stop hating him and call? If you don't, you'll only spend your whole wedding waiting for him to arrive, instead of enjoying the day."

"At least it would take my mind off the fact that I won't be able to eat anything for fear of bursting out of the dress you chose!"

"Have it your way, darling," hissed Stanley as he turned to leave. "Let's have lunch another day, when you're in a better mood."

Julia almost broke her neck getting down from the platform to run after him. She caught him by the shoulder. This time it was she who gave him a reassuring hug.

"I'm sorry, Stanley, I didn't mean that. Forgive me."

"About your father or about the dress that I had the bad taste to choose and tailor? I'd like to point out that neither your disastrous fall nor your parade through this shabby dive has torn a single stitch!"

"This dress is perfect. You're my best friend, and I couldn't imagine walking down the aisle without you."

Stanley took a silk handkerchief from his pocket and wiped away his friend's tears.

"Do you seriously want to be escorted to the altar on the arm of a raging queen, or is this your latest scheme to pass me off as your bastard father?"

"Don't flatter yourself. You don't look old enough to pull that off."

"To the contrary, it was a compliment. I was casting you as a much younger woman."

"Stanley, you're the one I want to walk me down the aisle! Who else but you?"

Stanley smiled tenderly, motioned to Julia's cell phone, and replied, "Call your father. I'll tell that idiot saleswoman, who wouldn't recognize a customer if one slapped her, to have your dress ready for the day after tomorrow and we'll go have lunch. Go on! I'm starving."

Stanley turned and headed toward the counter. He looked back and saw her hesitate and then pick up her phone to call. Stanley took advantage of the distraction to put the dress, the alterations, and a tip for the forty-eight-hour service all on his credit card. He slipped the receipt in his pocket and walked over to Julia, who had just finished her conversation.

"So," he asked impatiently, "is he coming?"

Julia shook her head.

"What's his excuse this time?"

Julia took a deep breath and looked Stanley in the eye.

"He's dead."

The two friends looked at each other for a moment without saying a word.

"I have to give it to him—his excuse is irreproachable," whispered Stanley.

"You really are an ass, you know that?"

"I don't know what came over me. I'm all mixed up. That's not what I meant to say. I'm very sad for you, darling."

"I don't feel a thing, Stanley, not a thing. I don't even feel like crying."

"It'll come, don't worry. It just hasn't hit you yet."

"No, really, it has."

"Do you want to call Adam?"

"No, not now. Later."

Stanley studied his friend with concern.

"You don't want to tell your future husband that your father has just died?"

"He died yesterday. In Paris. His body will be flown home, and the burial is in four days," she said in a voice that was barely audible.

Stanley counted the days on his fingers.

"This Saturday?" he said, his eyes widening.

"The same day as my wedding," murmured Julia.

Stanley turned on his heel and strode to the cash register, where he had his card refunded. Leading Julia out of the store, he declared, "Lunch is on me."

*

New York was bathed in the golden light of June. The two friends crossed Ninth Avenue and headed toward Pastis, a French brasserie and veritable institution in the recently revitalized neighborhood. Over the years, the slaughterhouses of the meatpacking district had given way to luxury stores and the city's most popular designer boutiques. Expensive hotels had sprung from the ground as if by magic. The former elevated rail-road had been transformed into a swath of green that extended to Tenth Street. What used to be a biscuit factory now housed an organic market on the ground floor, with production houses and PR firms on the floors above. Julia's office was on the sixth floor. Just to the west lay the banks of the Hudson River, which had been transformed into a promenade for cyclists, joggers, and couples lingering on park benches; it was a scene straight out of a Woody Allen movie. From Thursday evenings straight through the weekend, the area buzzed with the bridge-and-tunnel crowd, who crossed the river to hang out in the area's trendy bars and restaurants.

Seated at a table on the outdoor terrace, Stanley ordered two chai lattes.

"I should have called Adam by now," said Julia guiltily.

"To tell him that your father has died, yes, you should let him know, that's for sure... But if it's to announce that your wedding will have to be postponed, that you have to call the minister, the caterer, the guests, and, of course, his parents, I think it can wait a while. It's a gorgeous day. Give him another hour before you ruin it for him. Besides, you're in mourning—it's the best of excuses, and you should make the most of it."

"How am I supposed to explain this?"

"Darling, he should be able to understand that it's not easy to bury one's father and get married in the same afternoon... And though I suspect that the idea might tempt you, let me assure you, it's not a good one. How does something like this happen, for God's sake?"

"Believe me, Stanley, God has nothing to do with it. My father, and my father alone, chose to die when he did."

"I don't think he decided to give up the ghost in Paris yesterday evening just to ruin your wedding. Though his choice of location was impeccable."

"You don't know him like I do. He's capable of doing anything to interfere with my life."

"Drink your tea, enjoy the sunshine, and then we'll call your future ex-husband."

2.

The wheels of the Air France cargo jet squealed on the runway at JFK. From behind the tall glass facade of the main terminal, Julia watched as a long mahogany casket descended the conveyor belt from the cargo hold to the hearse parked on the tarmac. An airport security officer came into the waiting room to fetch her. She got into a minivan, which drove her to the plane in the company of her father's secretary, her fiancé, and her best friend. A customs officer handed her an envelope. It contained some paperwork, a watch, and a passport.

Julia fingered its pages. The array of stamps told the story of Anthony Walsh's last months. Saint Petersburg, Berlin, Hong Kong, Bombay, Saigon, Sydney... So many cities she had never seen. So many places she would have liked to discover with him.

While four men took care of formalities around the coffin, Julia thought back to the long trips her father was already taking when she was just a little girl.

She remembered the endless nights spent waiting and hoping for her father to come home, the countless mornings when the sidewalk on the way to school became an imaginary game of hopscotch whose perfect execution would assure his return. On rare occasions, her prayers were answered. The door of her bedroom would open, throwing an enchanted beam of light across the floor, and Anthony Walsh's silhouette would appear in the doorway. He would sit at the foot of her bed and leave a little present on the bedspread for her to find when she woke up in the morning. These were the highlights of Julia's childhood. Her father would bring her a special object that told the story of the trip he had taken, a little piece of the place he had just visited. A doll from Mexico, a calligraphy brush from China, a little wooden figurine from Hungary, a bracelet from Guatemala—these were Julia's treasures.

Her mother's health had begun to decline not long after this. Julia's first recollection of an episode had been at a Sunday outing to the movies. In the middle of the film, her mother turned and asked her why the lights were out. The holes in her mother's memory grew insidiously. At first she confused things like the kitchen and the music room, but this grew into screaming that the grand piano had disappeared. Alarm over disappearing objects worsened into forgetting the names of her family and descended into the final darkness of the day she looked

21

at Julia and exclaimed, "What is this pretty little girl doing in my house?" On a dreary December day, an ambulance came to the house, after she had set her bathrobe on fire. As they took her away, she held still, marveling at the power discovered in lighting a cigarette—this from a woman who had never smoked in her life.

Her mother almost never recognized her again. She died in a New Jersey clinic a few years later. As her mourning period faded, the tightly packed routine of Julia's adolescence set in, spending evening after dismal evening studying under the supervision of her father's private secretary. Her father's business trips lengthened and became more frequent. High school and then college passed by. Julia graduated and devoted herself to her passion: creating characters, sketching them on paper, and bringing them to life on a computer screen. Her animals became almost human. They were her companions and faithful friends, who smiled with a stroke of the pencil, whose tears she dried with her eraser.

"Miss, can you confirm this was your father's passport?"

The customs officer's voice brought Julia back to reality. She nodded. The man signed a form and stamped over Anthony Walsh's photo. It was the final mark in a passport whose stamps told a story of absence. The casket was loaded into the big black hearse. Stanley got in front, next to the driver, while

Adam attentively opened the back door for the woman he was to have married that very afternoon. Anthony Walsh's private secretary took a fold-out seat in the back, closest to the body. The funeral procession rolled forward, taking the expressway out of the airport.

As the hearse drove north, its passengers rode in silence. Wallace's gaze remained fixed on the box containing his former employer's remains. Stanley looked at his hands. Adam looked at Julia, and Julia contemplated the gray sprawl of New York City's outer reaches.

"Which way are you taking?" she asked the driver as a sign indicating the Long Island junction appeared ahead.

"Whitestone Bridge, ma'am," he responded.

"Could you take the Brooklyn Bridge, please?"

The driver signaled and changed lanes.

"That's a huge detour," whispered Adam. "He was taking the fastest route."

"The day is ruined anyway. We might as well make him happy."

"Who?" Adam asked.

"My father. Why don't we give him one last drive through Manhattan?"

"Sure," continued Adam, "but we should let the minister know we'll be late."

"Do you like dogs, Adam?" asked Stanley.

"Yes, I suppose, but they don't like me much.

Why?"

"Oh...no reason. I was just wondering," responded Stanley, rolling down his window as far as it would go.

They drove the length of Manhattan and arrived at 233rd Street an hour later.

The main gate of Woodlawn Cemetery opened. The hearse turned onto a narrow road, passed a row of mausoleums, crossed a bridge overlooking a lake, and came to a stop in a tree-lined lane where a freshly dug grave would soon welcome its future occupant.

A minister was waiting for them. The casket was placed above the hole. Adam went to greet the minister and explain the final details of the ceremony. Stanley put his arm around Julia's shoulders.

"What are you thinking about?" he asked.

"What am I thinking about as I bury my father, whom I haven't spoken to in years? You sure have a good sense of timing, Stanley."

"No, really, I'm serious. What are you thinking about right now? It's important to remember. This moment will always be part of your life, believe me."

"I was thinking about my Mom. I was wondering if she'll recognize him up there in the clouds or if she's still wandering around in a confused haze."

"You believe in God now?"

"No, but I can always hope, can't I?"

"I have to admit, and don't make fun of me, but as time goes by I believe in Him a little more each day."

Julia smiled sadly.

"I don't think that the existence of God would be good news as far as my father is concerned."

"The minister wants to know if everybody is here, before he gets started," said Adam as he returned.

"It's just the four of us," Julia replied, motioning for her father's secretary to join them. "That's the problem with people who are always traveling. Family and friends are just a handful of acquaintances scattered to the four corners of the earth... And acquaintances rarely come from far away to attend a funeral. It's not an easy time to ask for a favor. We're born alone, and we die alone."

"I think Buddha said that. Your father was a staunch Irish Catholic, honey," Adam replied.

"A Doberman. What you need is an enormous Doberman," sighed Stanley.

"What's with you and wanting me to have a dog, anyway?"

"Nothing. Never mind."

The minister came over to Julia to tell her how sorry he was to be officiating at a funeral. He would have much rather been celebrating her wedding.

"Couldn't you just kill two birds with one stone?" asked Julia. "In the end, we don't really care about all the guests. Isn't it the thought that counts, as far as the man upstairs is concerned?"

Stanley unsuccessfully stifled a giggle, and the priest responded with a disapproving look.

"Really, miss…"

"Seriously, it's not a bad idea. At least that way my father will actually attend my wedding... "

"Julia!" Adam said reproachfully.

"Okay, I get it. Survey says it's a bad idea," she conceded.

"Would you like to say a few words?" asked the priest.

"I wish I did," she said, gazing at the casket. "Perhaps you do, Wallace?" she asked her father's secretary. "After all, you were his most trusted friend."

"I don't think I'm capable of saying anything either, ma'am," responded the secretary. "And, besides, your father and I had a rather silent friendship. I would like to say a word, if you'd permit it. Not for him, but for you. Despite all of his faults, despite the fact he had a tough shell and was cranky, your father was a good man, and he loved you."

"And if my count is correct, that was more than one word," Stanley murmured as he watched Julia's eyes well with tears.

The priest recited a prayer and closed his missal. Anthony Walsh's coffin slowly descended into the grave. Julia handed a rose to her father's secretary.

He smiled and handed it back.

"You first, ma'am."

The petals scattered as the flower struck the wood. Three other roses fell in turn, and the four mourners turned back to the road.

Farther down the cemetery road, two Town Cars had replaced the hearse. Adam took Julia by the hand to lead her. She lifted her eyes to the sky.

"Not a cloud, just blue, blue, blue as far as you can see. Not too hot, and not too cold. Not a shadow or a shiver. What a perfect day for a wedding."

"There will be others, don't worry," Adam reassured her.

"Like this one?" Julia exclaimed, flinging her arms open. "With a sky like that? With this perfect temperature? With such green trees? With ducks on the lake? There won't be another day like this for the rest of the year. We'll have to wait until next spring!"

"The fall will be just as beautiful. And since when do you care about ducks?"

"Since they decided to follow me around! Did you see how many there were on the pond near my father's grave just now?"

"I wasn't paying attention," responded Adam, not knowing quite how to handle his fiancée's sudden burst of energy.

"There were dozens and dozens of mallards wearing bow ties. They landed right there, and they flew away as soon as the ceremony was over. They clearly meant to come to my wedding, and instead they came to my father's funeral."

"Julia, I hate to contradict you today, but I don't think ducks wear bow ties."

"What do you know? Do you draw ducks? I do. If I say they were wearing suits for the ceremony, you should believe me!" she cried.

"Okay, honey, your ducks were in black tie. Let's go home now."

Stanley and the secretary were waiting for them near the cars. Adam led Julia, but she stopped in front of a gravestone sunken into the sprawling lawn. She read the name and the date of birth of the person buried under her feet.

"This is my grandmother's grave. My whole family is buried in this cemetery now. I'm the last of the Walsh family line. Well, except for the hundreds of uncles, aunts, and cousins in Brooklyn, Chicago, and Ireland… But I've never met them." She took a breath. "I'm sorry for freaking out just now. I think I got a little carried away."

"It's no big deal. We were supposed to be getting married, and instead you're burying your father. It's totally normal that you're upset."

They continued down the lane, nearing the two Lincolns.

"And, you know, you're right," continued Adam, looking skyward. "It's a perfect day for a wedding. He really did screw things up to the very end."

Julia stiffened and pulled her hand from his.

"Don't look at me like that," pleaded Adam. "You said the same thing yourself at least a hundred times since we found out he was dead."

"Yes, but I can say it as much as I want. You can't. Take Stanley's car. I'll take this one."

"Julia! I'm sorry..."

"Don't be. I just want to be alone tonight. I have to put my father's affairs in order. My father, who bothered us to the bitter end, as you said."

"For God's sake, Julia, I'm not the one who said it. It was you!" cried Adam as Julia got into the first of the two sedans.

"Oh, and one last thing—the day we get married, I want ducks. Mallards, dozens of mallards!" she added, slamming the door.

Her car disappeared through the cemetery gate. Frustrated, Adam got in the second car and settled into the backseat, next to the private secretary.

"Maybe what you need is a fox terrier. They're little, but they have a nasty nip," concluded Stanley from the front seat as he signaled the driver to start the car.

3.

Julia's car inched down Fifth Avenue in an unexpected downpour. Stuck in traffic, they remained stopped for several minutes. Julia stared at the window display of an immense toy store on the corner of Fifty-Eighth Street. In the window, she recognized a giant stuffed otter with steel-blue fur.

Tilly was born on a Saturday afternoon like this one, the rain falling so hard that it created little streams of water down the window in Julia's office. Lost in her thoughts, the streaming rain transformed into rivers. The wooden window frame became the banks of an Amazonian estuary. The clump of leaves washed together by the rain formed the home of a little otter. She would soon be swept away by the flood, much to the dismay of her otter community.

The rain continued into that evening. Alone in the animation studio where she worked, Julia made the first sketches of her character. It would be impossible to count the thousands of hours she had spent in front of her computer screen, drawing, tinting, animating, and inventing every expression that would bring the blue otter to life. It would also be impossible to remember all of the late-night meetings and weekends spent telling the story of Tilly and her friends. Still, the cartoon's success had more than made up for the two years of work put in by Julia and the fifty employees under her supervision.

"This is fine," Julia told the driver. "I'll get out here and walk home."

The driver pointed out how heavy the rain was.

"It's the first thing I've liked about today," she assured him, the door already closing behind her.

The driver barely caught sight of her running toward the toy store. What did the rain matter, when Tilly seemed to be smiling through the glass and asking for a visit? Julia couldn't help herself and waved. To her surprise, a little girl standing next to the stuffed animal returned the gesture. Her mother rushed over and pulled her away. She tried to steer her toward the exit, but the girl resisted and jumped into the otter's open arms. Julia watched the girl cling to Tilly. Her mother smacked her hand, trying to make her release her grasp. Julia entered the store and walked over to them.

"Did you know that Tilly has magical powers?" Julia asked the little girl.

"If we need a salesperson, we'll let you know," replied the woman, glaring reproachfully at her daughter.

"I'm not a salesperson. I'm her mother."

"Excuse me?" the woman raised her voice. "Until some other proof comes along, I'm her mother!"

"I meant Tilly, the otter that seems to have attached itself to your daughter. I created her. Would you allow me to buy her for your daughter? It makes me sad to see Tilly all alone and lit up in this big window. The bright lights will fade her colors, and she's so proud of her steel-blue coat. You wouldn't believe the hours we spent getting her colors just right—the nape of her neck, her throat, her belly, her face... They make her smile, even though her house was washed away by the river."

"I'm afraid your Tilly will have to remain in the store. My daughter has to learn to stay close to me when we're in the city," the mother replied, yanking the girl's arm and forcing her to release the paw of the giant toy.

"Tilly would be so happy to have a friend," insisted Julia.

"You want to please a stuffed animal?" the woman asked, dumbfounded.

"It's been a rough day. It would make Tilly and me so happy, and your daughter, as well, I believe. Just one 'yes' would please the three of us. It's worth considering, don't you think?"

"No, I don't. Alice will not be getting any presents today, especially not from a stranger. Goodbye." She turned to go.

"Alice may be a good little girl now, but with the

way you treat her, don't come complaining to me in ten years!" Julia blurted out in a fit of anger.

The mother turned and glared at her.

"You may have designed a stuffed animal, but I gave birth to a child. I think you should keep your advice to yourself."

"You're right. Children aren't like toys. You can't just patch up the damage."

Outraged, the woman stalked out of the store. The mother and daughter walked away down Fifth Avenue without turning around.

"I'm sorry, Tilly," said Julia to the otter. "I wasn't very diplomatic, was I? You know it's not my strong suit. Don't worry, we'll find you a good family, you'll see. A family just for you."

The store manager had been watching the entire scene. He came over to Julia.

"What a pleasure to see you again, Miss Walsh. You haven't come in for at least a month."

"I've had a lot of work these past few weeks."

"Your creation has been a huge success. This is the tenth one we've ordered. On average, they're in the window for only four days before they're sold," he assured her, returning the stuffed animal to its place. "Though, this one has been here for two weeks, if I'm not mistaken. It's probably the weather..."

"It's not the weather," replied Julia. "This one is the original, so it's more difficult. She has to choose the family that takes her."

"Miss Walsh, you say that every time you come to see us," chuckled the manager.

"They're all one of a kind," Julia affirmed, waving goodbye.

The rain had stopped. Julia left the store and melted into the crowd as she headed downtown.

*

On Horatio Street, the trees drooped under the weight of their rain-soaked leaves. At the beginning of the evening, the sun had finally reappeared, just as it was beginning to sink into the Hudson River. The side streets of the West Village glowed in a soft purple light. Julia said hello to the owner of the Greek restaurant across the street from her apartment. Busy setting up his outdoor tables, he returned her greeting and asked if he should save her a table for that evening. Julia politely declined but promised to come to Sunday brunch the next day.

She turned her key in the front door of the little building where she lived and climbed the stairs to the second floor. Stanley sat waiting for her on the top step.

"How did you get in?"

"Zimoure, from downstairs, let me in. He was taking boxes down to the basement, and I helped him. We talked about his new shoe collection—

they're miraculous. But who can afford that kind of art these days?"

"Believe me, a lot of people can, judging by the mob loaded down with bags and boxes streaming out of his shop every weekend. Did you want something?" she asked, opening the door to her apartment.

"No, I thought you might need some company."

"Are you sure you're not the lonely one? You're mooning around like a lost puppy."

"No, it's all an act to save your image. I took it upon myself to come uninvited."

Julia took off her jacket and flung it on an armchair near the fireplace. The room was filled with the scent of the wisteria that grew along the building's brick facade.

"It's so cozy here," Stanley commented, collapsing on the sofa.

"That's one thing I can claim to have accomplished this year," remarked Julia as she opened the refrigerator.

"What's that?"

"Fixing up this dump. Do you want a beer?"

"Too many carbs. Maybe a glass of wine?"

Julia quickly set the table with a cheese platter for two, uncorked a bottle of wine, and put on a Count Basie CD. She motioned for Stanley to sit across from her. He looked at the Cabernet's label and made an admiring sound.

"Yeah, what a party…" said Julia as she sat down. "If we had two hundred guests and some hors d'oeuvres, you'd think it was my wedding."

"Can I have this dance?" asked Stanley.

Before she had a chance to reply, he pulled her to her feet and led her into a swing.

"See? It's still a party," he laughed.

"What would I do without you, Stanley?"

"You'd be lost, but I've known that for a while now."

The music ended and Stanley sat down.

"Have you called Adam since this afternoon?"

Julia had apologized to her future husband on her long walk home. Adam understood her need to be alone. He said he was the one who was sorry, for being so awkward during the funeral. His mother, whom he had talked to on the ride home from the cemetery, scolded him for being so insensitive. He was going to his parents' country house to spend what was left of the weekend with his family.

"I almost think it was a good thing that your father was buried on your wedding day," whispered Stanley as he poured himself a second glass.

"You really don't like Adam, do you?"

"I never said that!"

"Stanley, I was single for three years in a city with millions of single men. Adam is polite, generous, and attentive. He accepts my demanding schedule, and he does his best to make me happy. Most of all, he loves me. Couldn't you try to be a little more understanding?"

"I don't have anything against Adam. He's perfect. But I'd rather see you swept off your feet by a man with flaws than settling for somebody because they don't have any."

"That's easy for you to say. Why are you still single?"

"I'm not single. I'm a widower. It's not the same thing. Just because the man I loved is dead doesn't mean he's gone. You should have seen how beautiful Edward was on his hospital bed. His illness didn't take that away from him. He was making jokes right up to the end."

"What were his last words?" asked Julia as she took Stanley's hand.

"I love you."

The two friends sat in silence. Stanley got up, put on his jacket, and kissed Julia on the forehead.

"You win. I'm going to go to bed. I'm the lonely one tonight."

"No, stay. Were his last words really 'I love you'?"

"It was the least he could do—he died from cheating on me," Stanley said with a smile.

*

In the morning, Julia opened her eyes to find herself

on the couch, under the throw that Stanley had laid over her. A few moments later she found a note tucked under her mug. It read: "No matter what happens, you're my best friend, and I love you. Stanley."

4.

At ten o'clock, Julia left her apartment, having decided to spend the day at the office. She was behind on her work and saw no good coming from staying cooped up at home, organizing things that would invariably end up just as disordered as before. And it was pointless to call Stanley, who, on Sundays—unless she dragged him to brunch or promised to make him cinnamon pancakes—rarely got up before mid-afternoon.

Horatio Street was still empty. At Pastis, Julia waved in passing to a few neighbors sitting outside and then quickened her step. As she walked up Ninth Avenue, she sent Adam an affectionate text message. Two blocks farther on, she entered Chelsea Market. The elevator attendant took her to the top floor. She slid her security badge across the reader and pushed open the heavy iron door.

Three colleagues were seated at their desks, and judging from their weary faces and the empty coffee cups overflowing out of the wastebasket, it was clear that they had spent the night there. Her team had been struggling with the same issue for the past week. From the scene in front of her, it appeared that no one had yet figured out the correct algorithm for animating a squadron of dragonflies meant to defend a castle from an invading army of praying mantises. The schedule posted on the wall showed that the deadline was Monday. If the squadron didn't take off in twenty-four hours, the citadel would fall into enemy hands and production would fall drastically behind schedule. Neither of these was an option.

Julia rolled her desk chair over to her coworkers. She reviewed the progress they had made and immediately decided to activate the emergency plan. She picked up the phone and, one after another, called in the rest of her team, each time apologizing for ruining their Sunday afternoon and asking them to be in the conference room within the hour. Even if it meant crunching numbers into the night, she was determined that, by the following morning, dragonflies would invade the skies of Enowkry.

Seeing that the first team was way past exhaustion, Julia went downstairs to the market and filled two cardboard boxes with sandwiches and pastries to sustain her troops.

By noon, thirty-seven people had responded to Julia's call. The quiet morning atmosphere of the office gave way to a hive of activity. Illustrators, graphic designers, colorists, programmers, and animation experts discussed reports, analyses, and far-fetched schemes.

At five, a new team member's novel idea set off a burst of energy. A meeting was called in the large conference room. Charles was a young programmer who had been hired only eight days earlier. When Julia asked him to explain his theory, his voice trembled and he stuttered. The head programmer didn't help matters by criticizing his public-speaking skills. Exasperated, the young man decided to demonstrate what he was failing to explain and began inputting numbers on the keyboard while the team looked on. The awkward silence was broken only by occasional derisive laughter. Even the snickering fell silent, however, when a dragonfly began beating its wings in the middle of the screen and traced a perfect circle in the sky above Enowkry.

Julia was the first to congratulate him, followed by the applause of her team. Now they only had to get the other 740 armor-wearing dragonflies into the air. The young programmer's confidence swelled, and he laid out a method they might use to multiply the formula. The phone rang in the middle of his explanation. The assistant who answered the call discretely gestured to Julia that it was for her and that it seemed urgent. Julia asked the person sitting next to her to take careful notes and went to take the call in her office.

*

Julia immediately recognized the voice of Mr. Zimoure, the owner of the store on the ground floor of her building. She worried that the plumbing in her apartment had caused problems yet again. Water was no doubt streaming through the ceiling onto Mr. Zimoure's shoes, each pair costing nearly half her monthly salary (or a week's, if they were on sale). Julia had been shocked when she learned exactly how much the shoes cost, the year before, when her insurance agent cut a large check to Mr. Zimoure to cover the water damage she had caused. She had forgotten to close the valve on her archaic washing machine before leaving her apartment. But didn't everybody make a mistake once in a while?

Her insurer had insisted that the company would never again cover a problem of this nature. He had made an exception that time and had successfully convinced his company not to simply cancel her contract then and there, only because Tilly was his children's favorite cartoon character and because the Tilly DVDs were the savior of his Sunday mornings.

Reestablishing friendly neighborly relations with Mr. Zimoure had been a far more strenuous task and had required a significant effort on Julia's part. An invitation to a Thanksgiving dinner at Stanley's house, a gentle reminder during Christmas season of forgiveness, and much special attention had been necessary before the icy mood between the two neighbors thawed to its normal chilly state. Zimoure was a rather unpleasant character, had an opinion about everything, and only ever laughed at his own jokes. Julia held her breath as she waited for the damage report.

"Miss Walsh..."

"Mr. Zimoure, I would like to say how very sorry I am for whatever has happened."

"Not as much as I am, Miss Walsh. My store is packed with customers, and I have better things to do with my time than tend to your deliveries while you're not here."

Julia tried to slow her rapid heartbeat and understand what Mr. Zimoure was telling her.

"I'm sorry, what delivery?"

"That's what I'd like you to tell me."

"But I haven't ordered anything. I always have everything delivered to the office."

"Well, apparently not this time, since there's an enormous truck parked in front of my window. Miss Walsh, Sunday is my busiest day, and it could really ruin business. The two brutes who unloaded the crate claim it's for you and refuse to leave until somebody signs for it. What do you suggest we do?"

"A crate? Are you sure?"

"That's what I just said. Should I perhaps keep my customers waiting while I repeat everything for you?"

"I just don't understand, Mr. Zimoure," Julia continued. "I don't know what to tell you."

"How about you tell me when you'll be here. That way I can let these guys know how much more time we'll waste while waiting for you."

"But I really can't come right now. I'm in the middle of something at work..."

"And I suppose you think I'm here twiddling my thumbs?"

"Mr. Zimoure, I'm really not expecting a delivery. Not even a box or an envelope, and certainly not a crate! There has to be a mistake."

"Are you sure? Because on the label, which I can easily read through my shop window without my glasses since your delivery is sitting on the sidewalk right outside my store, your name is clearly printed in capital letters just above our shared address and just below the word 'fragile.' I'm sure you've simply forgotten again. It certainly wouldn't be the first time your memory has failed you."

Julia had no idea who could have sent her a crate. Could it be a present from Adam? Could it be an order for work that she had accidentally shipped to her home address? Either way, Julia couldn't abandon her team, especially after calling them into the office on a Sunday. But given Mr. Zimoure's tone, she knew she would have to find a solution as quickly as possible.

"I have an idea how we could solve our

problem, if you're willing to help."

"I do admire how you always manage to get *two* people involved. Now if you had told me you would take care of it yourself, then I would have been amazed. So what's this idea of yours? I'm all ears."

Julia confided that she had hidden an extra copy of her house key under the staircase carpet on the sixth step. He just had to count. If it wasn't the sixth, it was the seventh, or maybe the eighth. Mr. Zimoure could then open her door for the deliverymen. She was sure that, as soon as they were done, they would disappear, along with the truck that was blocking his window.

"I suppose that I will have to wait for them to leave, and lock the apartment door behind them…"

"You stole the words right out of my mouth, Mr. Zimoure."

"If this is another washing machine, Miss Walsh, I highly recommend that you have it installed by a certified plumber, if you catch my drift?"

Julia was about to reassure him that she had ordered no such thing, but her neighbor had already hung up. She stared at the phone for a minute and then returned to the task at hand.

*

As night fell, the team gathered in front of the big screen in the executive conference room. Charles was behind the computer, and the results seemed encouraging. A few more hours of work and the "battle of the dragonflies" would be finished on time. The programmers adjusted their calculations, the graphic designers tweaked the backgrounds, and Julia began to feel useless. She wandered into the break room, where she found Dray, an illustrator and friend from her college days.

As Julia stretched her back, Dray asked if she was getting a backache and advised her to go home. Julia was lucky that she lived only a couple blocks away and should take advantage of it. He promised to call and check in with her when they were finished. Julia was touched by his concern but thought she should stay with the team. Dray replied that there was no point in her pacing from office to office, which only aggravated the general feeling of exhaustion.

"Since when has my presence been a burden?" demanded Julia.

"Come on, don't overreact. Everybody's on edge. We haven't had a day off in six weeks."

Julia was supposed to have been out until the following Sunday, and Dray teased her that the staff had been looking forward to a little relief.

"We all thought you'd be on your honeymoon. Don't take it the wrong way. I'm only the messenger," Dray went on sheepishly. "It's the price you have to pay for being a boss. Ever since you were named creative director, you're not just a colleague anymore. You represent management. Look how you got everybody to come in on a Sunday with just a few phone calls."

"I thought the project was important. It was worth it, wasn't it?" Julia responded. "But, hey, since my authority seems to stifle everyone's creativity, I'll leave you to your work. Be sure to call me when you've finished. I'm not just the boss, you know. I'm also part of the team."

Julia grabbed her raincoat, double-checked that her keys were in the pocket of her jeans, and walked over to the elevator.

She dialed Adam's number as she left the building but only got his voice mail.

"It's me," she said after the beep. "I just wanted to hear your voice. It's been a gloomy Saturday and a depressing Sunday to boot. I'm not so sure it was a good idea to be alone after all. Oh well, at least I spared you my bad mood. My own team has just kicked me out of the office. I'm going to walk around for a while. Maybe you're already back from the country and in bed. I'm sure your mother must have worn you out. I wish you would have left me a message. You're probably sleeping now, so I guess there's no point in asking you to call me back. Anyway, I think I'm just rambling. See you tomorrow. Call me when you wake up. Love you."

Julia put her phone back in her purse and went

for a stroll along the river. When she got home, half an hour later, she found an envelope with her name scrawled on it taped to the front door of her building. The note said: "I lost a customer taking care of your delivery. I put the key back where it was. P.S. It was under the eleventh step, not the sixth, seventh, or eighth! Hope you had a good Sunday!" There was no signature.

"He should have just posted an open invitation to burglars!" she grumbled to herself.

As she climbed the stairs to the second floor, she thought about the delivery and was overcome with curiosity. She quickened her step and fished out the key from under the stairway carpet, annoyed that she would now have to find a new hiding place for it. Opening her door, she turned on the lights and entered her apartment.

Dominating her entire living room was an enormous wooden packing crate.

"What on earth?" she muttered out loud, abandoning her things on the coffee table.

Right below the word "fragile," the shipping label indeed bore her name and address. Julia began by walking around the gigantic wooden crate. It was too heavy for her to try moving even a few feet. And not owning either a hammer or a screwdriver, she couldn't begin to imagine how she would open it.

Since her call to Adam had gone straight to voice

mail, she resorted to her usual backup plan. She dialed Stanley's number.

"Am I bothering you?"

"Of course not," replied Stanley sarcastically. "At this hour on a Sunday night, I was waiting by the phone for you to call me to go out."

"Please tell me you didn't have a stupid six-foot-tall box delivered to my house."

"Julia, what in heaven's name are you talking about?"

"Okay, right, I thought not. Next question: How does one open a stupid six-foot-tall box?"

"Well, that depends. What is it made of?"

"Wood."

"A saw?"

"Thank you for your help. I'm sure I must have one in the bottom of my purse somewhere."

"Not to be nosy, but what's in this box?"

"Well, if I could open it, then I'd know. If you're that curious, why not jump in a taxi and come give me a hand."

"I'm in my pajamas, princess."

"I thought you were waiting to go out."

"I'm already in bed!"

"All right. I'm sorry. I'll manage by myself."

"Hold on. Give me a minute. Does it have a handle?"

"No."

"Are there hinges anywhere?"

"I don't see any."

"Well, maybe it's a piece of modern art, an unopenable box signed by a famous artist," chuckled Stanley.

Julia's silence let Stanley know that this was not a time for jokes, however cute they might be.

"Have you tried giving it a little nudge? You know, just an umph, like, to open a stuck door?"

As Stanley continued offering ideas, Julia placed her hand against the wood. She gave a little push, as Stanley had just suggested, and the side of the crate swung open.

Flabbergasted, Julia dropped the phone.

"Hello? Hello?" Stanley called into the receiver. "Are you still there?"

Stanley's voice crackled from the receiver at Julia's feet. Without taking her eyes off the case, she slowly bent down to pick it up.

"Stanley?" Julia's voice came out in a croak.

"You scared me half to death, darling. Are you all right?"

"Sort of."

"Do you want me to get dressed and come over?"

"No, don't bother."

"Did you manage to open it?"

"Yes," she responded absently. "I'll call you to-morrow."

"You're making me nervous…"

"Go back to bed, Stanley. Goodnight."

Julia hung up before Stanley could say anything else.

"Who could have sent me this?" she asked, alone in the middle of her apartment.

*

Inside the crate stood a perfect life-sized wax replica of Anthony Walsh. The resemblance was uncanny. If it opened its eyes, it would practically seem alive. Julia could barely breathe. A drop of sweat rolled down the back of her neck. She edged closer. The statue was incredible. The color and texture of its skin were astonishingly lifelike. And the shoes, the charcoal gray suit, and the white cotton shirt were all identical to the clothes Anthony Walsh had always worn. She was tempted to touch its cheek or pluck one of its hairs just to reassure herself that it wasn't him. But Julia and her father had long lost the habit and ease of any sort of physical contact. At the end, they no longer hugged, kissed each other hello, or even touched one another's hands. They avoided any gestures that might suggest tenderness. The distance that had grown between them over the years was impossible to bridge, and she wasn't prepared to attempt it with a statue.

Julia tried to come to terms with the bizarre reality that stood in front of her. Somebody had created a waxwork figure of Anthony Walsh, just like the ones in the museums in Quebec, Paris, and London, but even more realistic. It was a carbon copy of her father. Julia wanted to scream.

She studied the figure closely and noticed a little piece of paper pinned to the outside of its sleeve. A small arrow drawn in blue ink pointed to the suit jacket's breast pocket. Julia unpinned it and read three words scribbled on the back: "Turn me on." It was written in her father's unmistakable handwriting.

In the place where Anthony Walsh had always slid his signature silk pocket square, Julia saw a small remote control with one white rectangular button.

Julia thought she would faint. This had to be a bad dream. Any minute now, she would wake and laugh at having believed all this. As she had watched her father's coffin sink into the ground, she had promised herself that her period of mourning was over and that she would never lament his absence again, not after having been consumed by that very suffering for the past twenty years. Her father had abandoned her childhood, and there was no question she would allow him to come back to haunt her adult life.

She heard the sound of the dumpster clattering on the street and knew she was not dreaming. Julia was clearly awake. Standing in front of her was the improbable statue. With its eyes shut, it seemed to be waiting for her to decide whether to push the button on the remote control.

The garbage truck rumbled away. She wished it had stayed. She could have run to the window and begged the garbage men to take this nightmare out of her apartment. But the street was silent now.

Her finger gently traced the button on the remote, but she couldn't find the strength to apply any pressure.

She had to get rid of it. The wise thing to do would be to close the crate, find the label with the address of the shipping company, and call first thing in the morning. She would tell them to come take away this horrible doll and find the person responsible. Who among her friends could have come up with this prank? Who could be capable of such a sick, cruel joke?

Julia opened the window and filled her lungs with the soft night air.

Outside the world was just as she had left it. The tables at the Greek restaurant were piled up; its neon sign was turned off. A woman walking her dog crossed the intersection. The chocolate Lab wove back and forth, pulling its leash to sniff the base of the streetlamps and the foot of the wall.

Julia held her breath and let her grip tighten around the remote. She ran through her address book in her head, and only one name came back to her over and over again. She knew only one person capable of imagining something like this. Driven by her anger, she spun around, determined to confront her growing suspicion.

She pushed the button. There was a click. The statue's eyelids opened, and its face broke into a smile.

She heard her father's voice ask, "Don't you miss me just a little?"

5.

"I'm going to wake up. None of this is even remotely possible. Say it! Tell me I'm not going crazy."

"Come on, Julia, calm down," her father's voice responded.

He stepped out of his box and stretched. The accuracy of every one of his movements, even those of his facial features, was astonishing.

"You're not crazy," he continued. "You're just surprised. And I admit, given the situation, that's a completely normal way to react."

"Nothing about this is normal. You cannot be here. This is impossible!"

"That's true, I can't be here. But, then again, it's not exactly 'me' who's standing in front of you."

Julia brought her hand to her mouth and broke out into uncontrollable laughter.

"The human brain really is incredible! I almost believed it for a second. I really am just sleeping. I must have drunk something when I got home that upset my stomach. Was it the white wine? That must be it. I can't drink white wine. What an idiot, letting my own imagination get the better of me," she continued, pacing around the room. "Of all my dreams, this is by far the craziest!"

"Stop it, Julia," commanded her father gently. "You're awake. You're perfectly lucid."

"I highly doubt that. I'm looking at you and talking to you, and you're dead."

Her father looked at her in silence for a moment and gently replied, "Yes, Julia, I'm dead."

She stood frozen, staring at him. Anthony Walsh put his hand on her shoulder and gestured to the sofa.

"Why don't you sit down a moment and hear me out?"

"No!" she said, pulling away.

"Julia, please just hear me out."

"What if I don't want to? Why do things always have to be your way?"

"It's not like that anymore. All you have to do is push the button again and you'll turn me off. But then you'd never have an explanation for what is happening right now."

Julia looked at the remote she held in her hand. She thought it over a moment, then, however counterintuitive it felt, she gritted her teeth and sat down, obeying the strange machine that so eerily resembled her father.

"I'm listening," she muttered.

"I know that all of this is a bit disorienting. I also know it's been a long time since we've been in touch."

"A year and five months."

"That long?"

"And twenty-two days."

"You have a very accurate memory."

"It's not very hard to remember my own birthday. You had your secretary call me to say that we shouldn't wait for you to start dinner and that you would join us during the meal. But you never showed up."

"I don't remember that."

"Well, I do!"

"Anyway, that's not the question."

"I never asked," replied Julia dryly.

"I'm not sure where to begin."

"Everything has a beginning. Isn't that one of your catchphrases? How about you begin there, by explaining what's going on."

"All right. A few years ago, I became a shareholder in a high-tech company. After a few months, their revenues had increased, along with the value of my shares, and I found myself chairman of the board of directors."

"Yet another company absorbed by your conglomerate?"

"No, this time it was a strictly personal investment. I was just one of many shareholders, but I still had a significant stake."

"And what did this company do that you invested so much money?"

"They develop androids."

"What?!" Julia exclaimed.

"You heard me. Humanoids, if you prefer."

"What for?"

"We weren't the first company to try to create robots in human form to do the jobs real humans don't want to be bothered with."

"You've returned from the dead to vacuum my apartment?"

"Or to do the shopping, watch the house, answer the phone, and provide responses to all sorts of questions. All of these tasks are among our product's possible applications. But we developed a far more elaborate and ambitious project."

"Meaning?"

"Meaning we wanted to make it possible for loved ones to have a few extra days in the company of the deceased."

Julia was taken aback. She was having difficulty processing what he was saying.

Anthony Walsh went on: "A few extra postmortem days." He looked at her meaningfully, waiting for her to catch on.

After a few moments of silence, Julia finally exploded: "Is this a joke?"

"If you call this a joke it was a pretty successful one, judging by the look on your face when you switched me on," responded Anthony as he examined his reflection in a mirror on the wall. "I must say, they got me exactly right. Although, I don't think I ever had lines on my forehead like this. They exaggerated a little bit."

"You had them even when I was child. Unless you had a face-lift, I don't know where they would have gone."

"Thank you," replied Anthony with a smile.

Julia got up to inspect him more closely. If she was looking at a machine, she had to admit that it was a remarkable piece of work.

"This is ridiculous, not to mention technologically impossible!"

"Would you have believed the things you accomplished on your computer screen yesterday were possible only a year ago?"

Julia sat at the kitchen table and held her head in her hands.

"We invested an enormous amount of money to get to this point. All things told, I'm just a prototype. You're our first customer, though, of course, there's no charge. It's a present," Anthony Walsh added affably.

"A present? Who would be crazy enough to give that kind of present?"

"Do you know how many people say to themselves, at the end of their lives, 'If only I had known... If only I could have understood or listened… If only I could have told them… If only they knew…'"

Julia said nothing.

Anthony went on, "There is a considerable market…"

"The thing I'm talking to now, is it really you?"

"Almost. This machine contains my memory, most of my cerebral cortex. It has a highly resistant mechanism made up of millions of processors containing technology that reproduces the color and texture of my skin. It's capable of moving in almost perfect imitation of the human body."

"Why? For what?" asked Julia, stunned.

"So that we can share those few days together that we never had. So that we can steal a few hours from eternity. So that we can finally say all those things we never said."

*

Julia paced back and forth in the living room, coming up with then rejecting one crazy theory after another. She struggled to admit it to herself, but Anthony Walsh's explanation was the most plausible one yet. She went to the kitchen for a glass of water, drank it in a single gulp, and returned to Anthony Walsh's side.

"Nobody will ever believe me," she said, breaking the silence.

"Is that what you say to yourself every time you come up with one of your stories for work? Is this not the very problem you focus your energy on every time you pick up your pencil to give life to one of your characters? Didn't you tell me I was ignorant and didn't understand the power of imagination when I refused to support the career you'd chosen? How many times did you explain to me why thousands of children drag their parents into the imaginary worlds that you and your colleagues invent on computer screens? And didn't you remind me that I had never approved of your professional choice, when you were awarded that prize? You gave birth to a ridiculous Technicolor otter, and you believed in her. Are you telling me now that an improbable character has come to life before your very eyes and you won't believe in it because it looks like your father and not an animal? If your answer is yes, I told you, all you have to do is push the button!" concluded Anthony Walsh, gesturing toward the remote control that Julia had left on the table.

Julia applauded sarcastically.

"Don't think you can be insolent just because I'm dead."

"If that button were all it would take to finally close your mouth, I wouldn't hesitate."

As her father's face developed that all-too-familiar expression that belied his anger, they were interrupted by two short blasts from a car horn outside.

Julia's heart leapt to her throat. She recognized the unmistakable sound of Adam's car's gears grinding as he shifted into reverse. There was no doubt—he was parking in front of her building.

"Shit," she muttered, running to the window.

"Who is it?" her father asked.

"Adam!"

"Who?"

"The man I was supposed to marry yesterday."

"Supposed to?"

"You were buried yesterday."

"Oh yeah."

"Oh yeah." Julia rolled her eyes. "We'll discuss that later. In the meantime, get back into your box!"

"Excuse me?"

"As soon as Adam manages to parallel park, which, knowing him, will take another couple of minutes, he'll come up here. I canceled our wedding to attend your funeral. It would be better to avoid him finding you in my apartment."

"I don't see the point of keeping useless secrets. If you wanted to share your life with this man, I think I owe him my trust. I can explain the situation to him, just like I did to you."

"First of all, enough with the past tense, the wedding was only postponed. As for you explaining the situation, that's exactly the problem. I can hardly believe it myself. I don't expect him to."

"Perhaps he's more open-minded than you."

"Adam can't even work a VCR. I'm not sure how he would handle an android. For God's sake, get back in your box!"

Julia looked at her father with exasperation.

"There's no use making that face," he replied. "Just think about it. You think he's not going to notice the six-foot-high crate in the middle of your living room?"

When Julia didn't respond, Anthony added with satisfaction, "That's what I thought."

"Please," pleaded Julia, leaning to look out the window, "just hurry up and hide somewhere. He's turned the car off."

"You've got a really tiny place here," Anthony Walsh said, looking around.

"It's the size I need and the size I can afford."

"I hardly think so. If there were, I don't know, perhaps a little sitting room or a library, maybe a billiard parlor or a laundry room...then I might have some place to go and wait for you. These one-room apartments... What a strange way to live! How are you supposed to have any intimacy?"

"Most people do not have a library or a billiard parlor in their apartment."

"Maybe not the kind of people you frequent..."

Julia shot him a withering look.

"You ruined my life while you were alive, and now this three-billion-dollar machine is going to continue to do so after your death?"

"Even though I'm only a prototype, this 'machine,' as you call it, is not nearly as expensive as all that. Who could afford it?"

"Perhaps the people you frequent?" quipped Julia.

"That's my Julia. You really do have a very bad temper. Let's stop bickering and hide the father that just came back into your life. What's upstairs, an attic?"

"It's another apartment."

"Do you know your neighbor well enough for me to go ring the bell and ask for a cup of sugar, while you get rid of your fiancé?"

Julia began to frantically rifle through her kitchen drawers.

"What are you looking for?"

"The key," she whispered, hearing Adam's voice calling for her from the street.

"I hope it's for upstairs. I'm warning you, if you send me to the basement, I may very well run into your fiancé on the way."

"I own the apartment upstairs. I bought it with my bonus last year. But I still haven't had time to fix it up, so it's kind of a dump."

"What? This place is supposed to be tidy?"

"If you keep that up, I'll kill you."

"I hate to split hairs, but it's a little too late for that. And if you were a bit more organized, you'd have already found the keys hanging on the hook by the stove."

Julia grabbed the keychain and handed it to her father.

"Go up, but don't make any noise. Adam knows that nobody lives up there."

"I think you'd better go see what he wants, instead of standing here lecturing me. If he keeps bellowing your name in the street, he's going to wake up the entire neighborhood."

Julia ran to the window and leaned out over the railing of her small balcony.

"I rang the doorbell at least ten times!" shouted Adam, taking a step back on the sidewalk.

"Sorry, the buzzer is broken," Julia yelled down.

"Didn't you hear me calling you?"

"Yes. I mean, no, not until just now. I was watching TV."

"Can you let me up?"

"Sure," she responded, hesitating at the window until she heard her apartment door close behind her father.

"You don't seem real happy to see me."

"Of course I am. Why do you say that?"

"Because I'm still down here. On your message it sounded like you weren't doing so well, so I decided to stop by on my way home from the country. But if you'd rather I left…"

"No, of course not. I'll buzz you in."

She went to the intercom and pressed the button. She heard the latch open and Adam's footsteps on the stairs. She hurried to the kitchen and grabbed the remote control, then realized it would have no effect on the TV and threw it away. She found the TV remote in a drawer and prayed that the batteries were still good. The TV flickered to life just as the door opened.

"So you don't lock your front door anymore?" Adam asked as he came in.

"No, of course I do. I unlocked it for you just now," Julia improvised, silently cursing her father.

Adam took off his jacket and laid it on a chair. He noticed the blizzard of static raging on the TV screen.

"Why were you watching TV? I thought you hated it."

"Oh, I watch every once in a while," she responded, trying to gather her wits.

"This isn't the most absorbing program I've ever seen."

"Don't make fun of me. I tried to turn it off, but I must have hit the wrong button on the remote."

She saw Adam eyeing the imposing crate in the middle of the living room.

"What?" asked Julia with unconvincing innocence.

"In case you haven't noticed, there's an enormous box in the middle of your living room."

Julia offered her hastily thought up and risky explanation. It was special packaging to return a broken computer. By mistake, the deliverymen had left it at her house instead of her office.

"It must be incredibly fragile to need such a tall box."

"Yes, it's a very complex machine," Julia explained. "And very bulky and delicate."

"And they delivered it to the wrong address?" continued Adam, intrigued.

"Yes. Or, rather, I was the one who filled out the form incorrectly. I've been so worn out these past few weeks…"

"You should be careful. They could accuse you of trying to steal company property."

"Nobody's going to accuse me of anything," snapped Julia, betraying her growing impatience.

"Is there something we should talk about?"

"Why?"

"Because I had to ring your buzzer ten times and wake up the entire neighborhood by shouting your name in the street just to get you to come to your window. Because," he added gently, "you look like a wreck. Because the television was on, but the cable isn't even plugged in… Because you're not yourself, Julia."

"What? What are you implying? Are you saying I'm hiding something?" Julia snapped.

"I don't know," Adam replied, "that's for you to say. I never said you were hiding anything."

Julia flung open the bedroom door and the closet door behind her. Then she went to the kitchen and began throwing open all of the cupboards, beginning above the sink and not stopping until they were all hanging ajar.

"What in God's name are you doing?" Adam asked.

"I'm trying to see where I could have possibly hidden my lover. Isn't that what you were asking?"

"Julia!"

"What?"

The telephone interrupted their uncharacteristic squabbling. They both stared at the ringing phone, stunned. Julia finally picked it up. She listened for a long time, thanked the person for the call, and offered her congratulations before hanging up.

"Who was that?"

"The office. They finally fixed the problem that had been holding up the project. Production will go ahead on schedule."

"See?" Adam said, his tone softening. "If we had left tomorrow morning, as planned, you would have had a clean conscience during our honeymoon."

"I know, honey, I'm really sorry. If only you knew how sorry I am. Which reminds me, I have to give you the tickets—they're at my office."

"Don't worry about that—you can throw them away. Or keep them as a souvenir. They're nonrefundable and nonexchangeable."

Julia raised her eyebrow, one of her typical faces, which meant she was holding her tongue regarding a subject that annoyed her.

"Don't look at me like that," Adam defended himself. "You have to admit that most people don't cancel their honeymoon three days before they leave. And we could still go."

"Because the tickets are nonrefundable?"

"That's not what I meant," continued Adam, taking her in his arms. "Your message didn't do your mood justice. I shouldn't have come. I understand you need to be alone. Let's just leave things alone for now. I'll go home. Tomorrow is another day." He kissed her softly before letting her go.

As he was heading toward the door, a faint creak could be heard through the ceiling. Adam looked inquisitively at Julia.

"Please, Adam. It's just a rat."

"I don't know how you manage to live in this pigsty."

"I like it here. Someday I'll have enough money to live in a big apartment, you'll see."

"We were supposed to get married this weekend. You could at least say 'we.'"

"I'm sorry. That's not what I meant to say."

"How much longer do you count on shuttling back and forth between your place and mine?"

"Now is not the time to rehash that old argument. I promise, as soon as we can afford the construction, we'll connect the two floors and have plenty of space for the two of us here."

"It's only because I love you that I haven't insisted

that you leave this apartment. Sometimes you seem more attached to it than you are to me. But if you really want to stay here, why can't we live here together now?"

"What are you insinuating?" Julia demanded, changing her tone yet again. "If you're talking about my father's money, I wanted nothing to do with it when he was alive, and I'm not going to change my mind now that he's dead. I have to go to bed. I'm not going on vacation, and I have a busy day tomorrow."

"You're right. Go to bed. I'll write off your last remark and your tone to fatigue."

Adam shrugged and left. He didn't even turn to see Julia wave a feeble goodbye from the top of the stairs. The building door slammed shut behind him.

*

"Thank you for that comment about the rat," Anthony Walsh grumbled as he came back into the apartment.

"Would you have rather I said that the latest thing in android technology, created in the image of my father, was pacing above our heads? So that he'd call an ambulance and have me committed?"

"It would have been exciting," retorted Anthony, amused.

"While we're bickering," continued Julia, "I'd like to thank you for ruining my wedding."

"Well, excuse me for dying!"

"And thanks for getting me in trouble with the owner of the store downstairs. In addition to everything else, I'll now get the stink eye every time I see him for the next two months."

"The shoe salesman? What do you care about him?"

"Oh, and while we're at it, thank you for ruining the only evening off I've had all week."

"At your age I only took a break on Thanksgiving."

"I know! And finally, and here I really have to hand it to you, but thanks to you I behaved like a complete monster with Adam."

"I didn't cause your fight. You should blame yourself. I had nothing to do with it."

"How can you honestly claim that you had nothing to do with it?" shouted Julia.

"Well, okay, maybe I did play a little part. Truce?"

"Truce? For what happened tonight, yesterday, or perhaps during all our fights over the years?"

"I'm not at war with you, Julia. I may not have been around much, but I wasn't mean."

"You've got to be kidding. You always tried to control my life, even from a distance. You had no right. But what am I doing? I'm talking to a dead person!"

"You can turn me off if you want."

"It's what I probably should do. Put you back in your box and ship you off to whatever high-tech laboratory you came from."

"1-800-300-0001, code 654."

Julia looked at him inquisitively.

"It's how you get a hold of the company that made me. You just dial the number and give them the code. They can even turn me off from a distance, if you're afraid to do it yourself. Within twenty-four hours they'll come get rid of me. But think it over. How many people would like to be able to spend a few days more with a recently deceased parent? You won't get a second chance. We have six days together, and not a second longer."

"Why six?"

"It was the decision of the ethical committee."

"Meaning?"

"Well, as you can imagine, this kind of technology raises some moral issues. We thought it was important that our clients didn't get too attached to these machines, perfect though they are. There are already many ways of communicating after one's death: wills, books, voice or video recordings. Let's just say that, in this case, the method is more innovative and, above all, more interactive," enthused Anthony Walsh as though he were selling the product to a potential customer. "It's simply a question of offering the dying person a more complete medium than a piece of paper or a video to express their last wishes, while also giving the family the opportunity to take advantage of a few last days in the company of their loved one. But we couldn't risk a complete transfer of affection to a machine. We learned many valuable lessons from previous attempts. I don't know if you remember, but one manufacturer's baby dolls were so convincingly lifelike that their owners ended up treating them like real babies. We don't want to reproduce that sort of deviant behavior. We are not interested in producing a clone, however tempting it might be."

Anthony took note of Julia's skepticism.

"Apparently there's no danger of that here. So, at the end of the week, the batteries will no longer be able to recharge, the content of my memory will be erased, and the last signs of life will disappear."

"There's no way of stopping it?"

"No, they covered all the bases. If some smart aleck tries to tamper with the batteries, the memory is automatically reformatted. It's sad to say, for me anyway, but I'm like a disposable flashlight. Six days of light, and then darkness. Six days, Julia. Six short days to catch up on all of the lost time—it's up to you."

"Only you could have come up with such a twisted idea. I'm sure you were more involved than just an ordinary shareholder."

"If you decide to go along with this, and seeing as you haven't yet pressed the button on that remote control to turn me off, I'd prefer you speak to me in the present tense. We'll call it a little bonus, if you agree?"

"Six days? I haven't taken six days off in ages."

"You're a chip off the old block."

Julia shot her father a furious look.

"It was just an offhand comment. You don't have to take everything so seriously," responded Anthony.

"What am I supposed to tell Adam?"

"Just a little while ago you seemed perfectly capable of lying to him."

"I wasn't lying, I was hiding something. It's not the same thing."

"The nuance escapes me. In that case you can just keep…hiding something."

"And Stanley?"

"Your homosexual friend?"

"My best friend, period!"

"Yup, that's the one I meant," responded Anthony Walsh. "If he's really your best friend, you'll have to be more subtle."

"So you'll just hang around here all day while I'm at the office?"

"Weren't you supposed to take a few days off for your honeymoon? So you don't really need to go in to the office."

"How do you know I was supposed to leave?"

"The floor of your apartment, or the ceiling, if you prefer, is not soundproof. Always a problem with these old, run-down buildings."

"Anthony!" Julia ranted.

"Oh, I beg you, I may only be a machine, but please call me Daddy. I hate it when you call me by my name."

"For Christ's sake, I haven't called you Daddy for twenty years."

"All the more reason for us to make the most of the next six days," responded Anthony Walsh with a broad smile.

"I haven't the faintest idea what to do," muttered Julia as she returned to the window.

"Go to bed, sleep on it. You're the first person on earth to make this decision. It's worth thinking over calmly. Tomorrow morning you'll make your choice, and whatever it is, it'll be the right one. At worst, if you decide to turn me off, you'll be a little late to the office. Your marriage would have cost you a week away from work. Isn't the death of your father worth at least a few hours?"

For a long time, Julia quietly observed the strange machine looking back at her. If the man she had known as her father hadn't always been so distant, she would have thought she detected some affection in its gaze. And even though it was just a copy of what her father had been, she was tempted to say goodnight to it, but decided not to. She closed her bedroom door and stretched out across her bed.

The minutes crept by. An hour passed, and then

another. Her curtains were open, and light spread across the shelves. Through the windowpane the full moon seemed to float above the room's hardwood floors. Lying in bed, Julia's childhood memories came flooding back. There had been so many nights when she had waited for the man now on the other side of the wall to come home. She had spent so much of her adolescent insomnia reinventing her father's travels, the breeze outside her window carrying her mind to thousands of distant countries. She had spent so many evenings awake yet dreaming, a habit she had not lost through the years. How much drawing and erasing had it taken her imagination to invent and perfect characters who would come to life and satisfy her need for love, one frame at a time? Julia had always known that this escape was a vain attempt to seek clarity and comfort. The blinding daylight of reality had evaporated even the most intricately drawn illusion in a heartbeat. She still felt the pain of the lonely girl she had been.

Beside her bed slept a little Mexican pottery figurine of an otter. She had been inspired by it to create Tilly. Julia got up from her bed and took it in her hands. Her intuition had always been her best ally, and with time her imagination had only grown. Why shouldn't she believe now?

She put the figurine back, slipped on a bathrobe, and opened her bedroom door. Anthony Walsh was sitting on the living-room sofa watching the TV.

"I took the liberty of plugging in the cable. I've always loved this show."

Julia sat down next to him.

"I've never seen this episode. At least, it's not in my memory," continued her father.

Julia took the remote and put the TV on mute. Anthony rolled his eyes.

"You wanted to talk?" she said. "Let's talk."

Neither one of them spoke for at least fifteen minutes.

"Wonderful. I've never seen this episode. At least, it's not in my memory," Anthony Walsh repeated, turning up the volume again.

This time Julia turned off the TV.

"You have a bug. You just said the same thing twice in a row."

Another fifteen minutes of silence went by. Anthony's eyes stayed riveted on the darkened screen.

"I remember one of your birthdays—your ninth, I think. After dinner—it was just the two of us, at that Chinese restaurant you liked—we spent the entire evening watching TV, just like this. You were spread out on my bed, and even when the programming ended, you kept watching the static on the screen. You probably don't remember; you were too young. You finally dozed off around two in the morning. I wanted to take you back to your room, but your arms held the pillow attached to the headboard so tightly I couldn't pry you away. You were sleeping diagonally across the top of the bedspread, and you took up the entire bed. I settled into the armchair across from you, and I watched you the entire night. You couldn't possibly remember. You were only nine."

Julia said nothing. Anthony Walsh turned the TV back on.

"How do they come up with these scenarios? They must have amazing imaginations. I've always wondered about that. The funny part is that you end up getting attached to the characters and their lives."

Julia and her father stayed that way, sitting side by side, not talking. Their hands rested next to each other without moving closer. Not a single word interrupted the silence of the night. When the first light of dawn crept into the room, Julia got up noiselessly and crossed the room. At her bedroom door she turned to her father.

"Goodnight."

6.

The clock radio on the nightstand read nine o'clock. Julia opened her eyes and leapt out of bed.

"Shit!"

She hurried to the bathroom, stubbing her toe on the door frame along the way.

"Another Monday," she grumbled. "What a night." She pulled back the shower curtain and stepped into the tub, letting the water run over her skin for what seemed like a long time. A while later, while she was brushing her teeth and looking at her reflection in the mirror above the sink, she got a case of the giggles. She wrapped the towel around her waist, rolled another around her hair, and went to make her morning cup of tea. As she crossed her bedroom, she told herself she would call Stanley as soon as she finished her first sip. Sharing her strange dream with him would bring repercussions; he would probably want her to set an appointment with a shrink. Still, there was no way she could keep it from him. She never managed to spend even half a day without calling him or stopping by for a visit.

Such an incredible dream needed to be shared with her best friend.

Julia smiled and was about to open her bedroom door when a clatter of dishes made her jump.

Her heart started to pound. She dropped the wet towels on the floor, threw on a pair of jeans and a polo shirt, and tried to untangle her hair in a rush. Looking at her reflection in the mirror, she decided a little dab of blush wouldn't hurt. Julia cracked open the door to the living room and whispered worriedly.

"Adam? Stanley?"

"I didn't know whether you took coffee or tea, but I made some coffee," her father called out from the kitchen, victoriously brandishing a steaming coffeepot. "Good and strong like I like it!" he added jovially.

Julia looked at the old wooden table. A place had been set for her. Two jars of jam were impeccably aligned with a jar of honey. The butter dish stood at a 90-degree angle to the cereal box. A carton of milk stood directly across from the sugar bowl.

"Stop it!"

"What? What have I done now?"

"This ridiculous act of being the perfect father. You never made breakfast for me before. You're not going to start now that you're…"

"No, no! Not the past tense. It's the only condition I asked for. Only the present… I'm afraid the future is beyond even my means."

"It's the rule that *you* agreed to. And I drink tea in the morning."

Anthony poured some coffee for Julia.

"Do you take milk?" he asked.

Julia turned on the water and filled the kettle.

"So have you made up your mind?" asked Anthony Walsh, taking two pieces of bread out of the toaster.

"If the point of all this is for the two of us to talk to each other, last night wasn't very convincing," replied Julia softly.

"I enjoyed the time we spent together. Didn't you?"

"It wasn't my ninth birthday; it was my tenth. It was our first weekend without Mom. It was a Sunday, and she had been taken to the hospital that Thursday. The Chinese restaurant was called Wang's. It closed last year. Early the next morning, while I was sleeping, you packed your bags and left to catch a plane without saying goodbye."

"I had a meeting in Seattle at the beginning of the afternoon. Or was it Boston? God, I can't remember anymore. I came back on Thursday. Or was it Friday?"

"What's the point of all this?" asked Julia as she sat down at the table.

"In just a few sentences we've already said a lot, don't you think? Your tea will never be ready if you don't turn on the stove."

Julia inhaled the aroma steaming up from her mug of coffee.

"I don't think I've ever tasted coffee in my entire life," she said, taking a sip of the brew.

"Then how do you know that you don't like it?" asked Anthony Walsh, watching his daughter as she took a large gulp.

"Because!" she said, grimacing as she put the mug down.

"You get used to the bitterness, and then you come to enjoy its sensual side," Anthony said.

"I should go to work," replied Julia as she opened the jar of honey.

"Have you made up your mind yet? This indecision is very frustrating. I have a right to know, don't I?"

"I don't know what to tell you. Don't ask the impossible. You and your colleagues forgot about some other ethical issues."

"Please share. I'm curious."

"Turning somebody's life upside down when they never asked for it…"

"Somebody?" Anthony retorted, his voice tightening.

"Don't twist my words. I don't know what to tell you. Do what you want. Call them and give them the code and let them decide for me."

"Six days, Julia. Six days so you can mourn your father and not some stranger. Are you sure you don't want to make that decision yourself?"

"Six days for you, you mean."

"I'm not alive anymore. What could I possibly get out of it? When you think about it, it's pretty ironic," continued Anthony Walsh, amused. "That's another thing we never thought of. It's unheard of! Up until this incredible invention, it was unimaginable that one could actually break the news of one's own death to one's daughter and see her reaction. How extraordinary! Okay, I see you don't think it's very amusing. I guess it isn't that funny after all."

"No, it isn't."

"I do have some bad news for you, though. I can't call them myself. It isn't possible. The only person who can break off the program is the beneficiary. Besides, I've already forgotten the password I gave to you. It was erased from my memory. I hope you wrote it down just in case..."

"1-800-300-0001, code 654."

"Oh, so you memorized it. Very good."

Julia got up and put her mug in the sink. She turned around, looked at her father for a long time, and took the telephone off its hook on the kitchen wall.

"It's me," she said to her coworker Dray. "I'm going to take your advice, in a way... I'm taking today and tomorrow off. Maybe more, I don't know yet. I'll keep in touch. Send me an email every evening to let me know how the project is going, and be sure to call me if you have any problems. Oh, one last thing—be sure to watch over Charles, the new guy. We owe him big time. Try to help him become part of the team. I'm counting on you, Dray."

Julia put the phone back on its hook without taking her eyes off her father.

"It's good to look after your team," approved Anthony Walsh. "I always say that a company is supported by three pillars: teamwork, teamwork, teamwork."

"Two days! I'm giving us two days, you understand? It's up to you whether you want them or not. In forty-eight hours you're going to give me back my life, and you'll…"

"Six days!"

"Two!"

"Six!" Anthony Walsh continued bargaining.

The telephone rang, interrupting their negotiations. Anthony picked up, only to have Julia grab the receiver and muffle it, signaling to her father to be as quiet as possible. Adam said he was concerned that he couldn't get in touch with her at work. He explained how angry he was with himself for having been so untrusting and oversensitive with her the previous night. Julia apologized for having been short-tempered and thanked him for listening to her voicemail and coming by. Even if it hadn't been the best moment, showing up unexpectedly under her window had been very romantic.

Adam offered to pick her up after work. While Anthony Walsh did the dishes, making as much noise as possible, Julia explained that her father's death had affected her more than she dared admit. Her sleep had been filled with nightmares, and she was exhausted. It would be impossible to endure a second similar night. What she needed was a calm afternoon and to go to bed early. They would see each other tomorrow at the latest. By then she would be more like herself, more like the woman he wanted to marry.

"Exactly like I said. A chip off the old block," repeated Anthony Walsh as she hung up.

She glared at him.

"What now?"

"You've never washed a plate in your life."

"What do you know? Besides, doing the dishes is part of my new program," he replied cheerfully.

Julia left him to his work and turned without responding, taking the keychain from its hook.

"Where are you going?" asked her father.

"I'm going upstairs to set up a room for you. It's out of the question for you to spend the night pacing around in my living room. I have some sleep to catch up on..."

"If it's the TV, I can turn down the volume."

"You're sleeping upstairs tonight. Take it or leave it."

"You're not really going to put me in the attic, are you?"

"Give me one good reason I shouldn't."

"There are rats. You even said so," replied her father, sounding like a chastised child.

As Julia headed out the door, her father called after her with a firm voice.

"We'll never get anywhere staying here!"

Julia closed the door behind her and went upstairs. Anthony Walsh checked the time on the oven clock. He hesitated a moment and then looked for the white remote control, which he found where Julia had left it on the counter.

He heard his daughter's footsteps in the apartment above, the sound of furniture being moved around and the opening and closing of a window. When she came back down, her father was back inside the packing crate, holding the remote control.

"What are you doing?" she asked.

"I'm going to turn myself off. It's perhaps better for both of us this way, especially you. I can see that I'm in your way."

"I thought you couldn't do it yourself," she said, grabbing the remote.

"I said you were the only one who could call the company and give them the code. I think I'm capable of pushing a button," he grumbled, stepping back out of the crate.

"Do what you want," she responded, handing back the remote. "You're wearing me out."

Anthony Walsh set it on the coffee table and

returned, taking up a position in front of his daughter.

"Where were you supposed to go on your honeymoon?"

"Montreal. Why?"

"He didn't make much of an effort, did he?" commented her father.

"What do you have against Canada?"

"Nothing at all! Montreal is a very charming city. I've even had some lovely times there. But that's not the point," he coughed.

"What is the point, then?"

"It's just that…"

"That what?"

"A honeymoon that's just a one-hour flight away isn't exactly a change of scenery. Why not just drive there in a Winnebago and save money on the hotel?"

"What if it was my idea to go? What if I love Montreal? What if we both have special memories there? What would you know about that?"

"You wouldn't be my daughter if you had chosen to spend your wedding night an hour from your apartment, that's all," affirmed Anthony ironically. "I'd love to believe that you're mad about maple syrup, but there are limits…"

"You'll always be blinded by your preconceived ideas, won't you?"

"I think it's a little late for me to change now. But let's say you decided to spend the most memorable evening of your life in a town you already know. So long, discovery! See you later, romance! Innkeeper, give us the same old room as last time. After all, this is just a night like any other. Serve us the usual food. My future, I mean, new husband hates a change in routine."

Anthony Walsh burst into laughter.

"Are you done?" Julia was fuming now.

"Yes," he said, excusing himself. "God! Being dead isn't half bad. You can say whatever is on your mind. It's a kick!"

"You're right—we're getting nowhere," said Julia, cutting short her father's mirth.

"Not here, anyway. We need neutral ground."

Julia looked perplexed.

"How about we stop playing hide-and-seek in this apartment? There's not enough space, even with that room upstairs where you've been trying to stash me away. We're wasting precious minutes together bickering like spoiled children, and we'll never get them back."

"What do you suggest?"

"A little trip. No calls from the office, no unexpected visits from Adam, no evenings watching TV like two zombies. We'll go on walks together and talk to each other. That's why I came back. A moment, a few days for the two of us. Just the two of us."

"You're asking me to give you something you

were never willing to give me."

"Stop fighting me, Julia. You'll have the rest of eternity to fight. My side in this argument only exists in your memory now. Six days is all we have left. That's what I'm asking you for."

"And where are we going on this little trip?"

"Montreal."

Julia couldn't repress a smile.

"To Montreal?"

"Well, the tickets are nonrefundable… We can always try to change the names of one of the passengers."

Julia pulled back her hair and put on a coat. When Anthony realized that she was leaving, he stood in her way, blocking the door.

"Don't be like that. Adam said you could just throw them out!"

"He suggested I keep them as a souvenir. Maybe you were so busy eavesdropping you missed the sarcasm. I don't think he meant I should go with somebody else."

"I'm your father. I'm not just anybody."

"Get out of my way, please."

"Where are you going?" asked Anthony Walsh as he stepped aside.

"To get some air."

"Are you mad at me?"

The only response was his daughter's footsteps heading down the stairs.

*

Julia climbed into a taxi that had slowed down at the corner of Greenwich Street. She didn't need to look up at her building to know that her father was watching as the cab pulled away toward Ninth Avenue. As soon as it disappeared through the intersection, he picked up the phone and made two calls.

Julia had the driver drop her off in SoHo. Normally she would have gone on foot—it was only a fifteen-minute walk, and she knew the neighborhood by heart—but she had been so desperate to get away from her apartment that she would have stolen a bicycle if somebody had left one unattended on the corner. She pushed open the door of the cozy antique shop. Seated in a baroque armchair, Stanley looked up from his reading when he heard the little bell ring.

"Garbo in *Queen Christina* couldn't have done better!"

"What are you talking about?"

"Your entrance, princess. It was regal and terrifying all at once."

"This isn't a good day to make fun of me."

"No day, no matter how beautiful, should go by without a dose of humor. Aren't you supposed to be at work?"

Julia walked over to an old bookcase and studied a delicately gilded clock perched on the top shelf.

"You're playing hooky to check what time it was in the eighteenth century?" questioned Stanley, pushing his glasses up from the point of his nose.

"It's very pretty."

"So am I. Is something wrong?"

"Oh, nothing. I just stopped by to see you, that's all."

"And I'm about to give up Louis XVI for Pop Art," Stanley replied, putting down his book.

He got up and took a seat on the corner of a mahogany table.

"Is my pretty girl having a bad day?"

"Something like that, yeah."

Julia rested her head on Stanley's shoulder.

"It really is bad, isn't it?" he said, giving her a hug. "I'll make you some tea a friend sent me from Vietnam. It cleanses the soul, you'll see. Its virtues are beyond suspicion, unlike those of my friend."

Stanley took a teapot from a shelf. He put a kettle of water to boil on the hot plate he kept on the antique desk that served as his counter. After a few minutes of infusion, the miracle tea filled two porcelain cups taken from an old armoire. Julia inhaled its jasmine-scented perfume and took a sip.

"I'm all ears. Don't try to resist. This divine potion is known to draw forth the most fiercely guarded of secrets."

"Would you go on a honeymoon with me?"

"If I had married you, why not? But you'd have

to be a Julian, not a Julia. Otherwise I fear our honeymoon would be rather dull."

"Stanley, if you closed your store for just a week and you let me elope with you…"

"What a romantic idea. Where would we go?"

"To Montreal."

"Never."

"What? You have something against Quebec, too?"

"I didn't endure six months of close starvation to lose ten pounds just to gain them back in a few days. Montreal's restaurants are irresistible, as are its waiters. Plus, I hate the thought of being your plan B."

"Why do you say that?"

"Who refused to go before I did?"

"That doesn't matter. Anyway, you'd never believe me."

"How about you begin by explaining what's bothering you?"

"Even if I told you the entire story from beginning to end, you'd never believe me."

"You're right. I'm an idiot. When was the last time you took a half day at the beginning of the week?"

Julia remained mute. Stanley continued.

"You show up in my store on a Monday morning, stinking of coffee. You hate coffee. Under your very patchily applied makeup lies a sweet little puss that's had, at most, ten minutes of sleep. At the last minute you ask me to be your traveling companion, instead of your fiancé. What's going on? Did you sleep with another man last night?"

"Of course not!" exclaimed Julia.

"I'll rephrase my question. What are you running from?"

"Nothing."

"All right, princess. I have work to do, so if you don't trust me enough to confide in me, I'll get back to taking inventory," Stanley replied, pretending to head to the back of his shop.

"You're a terrible liar. You were falling asleep with a book in your hand when I came in," said Julia, laughing.

"And not a moment too soon!" Stanley smiled affectionately at his best friend. "I was growing weary of your gloomy face. Would you like to take a walk? The neighborhood shops open soon, and I'm sure you must need a new pair of shoes."

"If you saw all the shoes I never wear hibernating in my closet…"

"I'm not talking about shoes for your feet, darling. I'm talking about shoes for the *soul*."

Julia got up and walked back over to the old bookcase. She picked up the little gilded clock. Its glass face was missing. She traced the circumference with the tip of her finger.

"It's really very pretty," she said, nudging back the minute hand.

In response, the hour hand also began to move backward.

"It would be wonderful if we could go back in time…"

Stanley observed Julia.

"Turn back time? You wouldn't want to give that antique back its youth. Look at it this way—it gives us the beauty of its age," he replied, taking the clock from Julia and putting it back on the shelf. "Will you just tell me what's on your mind already?"

"If somebody offered you a trip, to trace the footsteps of your father's life, would you accept?"

"Why not? If I had to go to the end of the world just to find a bit of my mother's life, I'd already be in the plane, hassling the stewardess, instead of wasting my time sitting around with an old queen. Even if the old queen was my best friend. If you get the chance to go on a trip like that, you shouldn't hesitate."

"What if it's too late?"

"Too late only happens when everything's over. Even though he's gone, your father is still a part of your life."

"You have no idea."

"No matter what you tell yourself, you miss him."

"Over the years I got used to him being gone. I really learned to live without him."

"Darling, even children who never knew their

parents feel the need to find their roots sooner or later. It's often difficult for those who raised and loved them, but it's human nature. It's tough to get through life when you don't know where you come from. No matter what sort of journey you have to undertake, if it finally allows you to know who your father was, if it allows you to reconcile yourself with your past and his, you should do it."

"We didn't have a lot of memories together, you know."

"Maybe you have more than you think. For once, forget that pride that I love and take a chance. If you don't do it for yourself, do it for one of my best friends. I'll introduce you to her someday. She's a wonderful mother."

"Who's that?" Julia asked with a tinge of jealousy.

"You, in a few years."

"You're the best, Stanley." Julia planted a kiss on his cheek.

"I have nothing to do with it, darling. It's the tea."

"Tell your friend in Vietnam that his tea has an incredible effect," added Julia on her way out the door.

"If you like it that much, I'll buy a few boxes for when you get back. I got it at the corner grocery."

7.

Julia climbed the stairs two at a time and opened the door of her apartment. The living room was empty. She called out several times, but nobody answered. After searching the other rooms, she was certain that the apartment was empty. She noticed that a photograph of Anthony Walsh in a little silver frame now sat in the middle of the mantelpiece.

Her father's voice asked her where she had been, and she jumped with fright.

"God, you scared me! Where did you disappear to?"

"I'm touched that you care. I went for a walk. I was bored sitting here all alone."

"What's that?" Julia asked, pointing out the picture on the mantle.

"I was settling into my bedroom upstairs, since that's where I'll be exiled tonight, and I happened to find it…under a dust bunny. I didn't think I'd sleep well with a photo of myself in the room. I thought it looked good there, but you can move it somewhere else if you want."

"Do you still want to go on this trip?" asked Julia, ignoring his comment.

"As a matter of fact, I just got back from the travel agency down the street. The Internet will never replace good old-fashioned customer service. There was a very pretty girl working there—in fact, she reminded me of you. But she smiled more… What was I saying?"

"A pretty girl…"

"Right. Anyway, for me, she was willing to make an exception. I thought she was retyping the complete works of Hemingway, but after pecking at her keyboard for half an hour, she managed to reprint the ticket in my name. While I was at it, I had her upgrade us."

"You really are something else. What on earth made you think that I'd go along with all this?"

"I didn't think anything. But if you're bent on pasting the tickets in your souvenir scrapbook, they might as well be first class. It's a question of family honor, my dear."

As Julia headed toward her bedroom, Anthony Walsh asked where she was going.

"To pack a bag for two nights," she responded, insisting on the number. "Isn't that what you wanted?"

"Might be wise to pack a little extra, since our trip is for six days. The dates on the tickets were unchangeable. I begged and begged, but the girl I was telling you about was very stubborn."

"Two days!" shouted Julia from the bathroom.

"Okay, do what you like. If worse comes to worst we can buy you a new pair of pants in Montreal. I don't know if you've noticed, but the jeans you are wearing are ripped. I can see your knee." Anthony Walsh walked over to the packing crate and lifted what revealed itself to be a false bottom. A black leather suitcase had been placed in the space below.

"They thought ahead and packed everything I might need to remain elegantly dressed for the duration of my battery life," he said to Julia, not without a certain sense of satisfaction. "In your absence, I took the liberty of reclaiming my passport, as well as my watch," he added, proudly extending his wrist. "You don't have any objection to me wearing it for the time being, do you? It will be yours soon enough."

Julia popped her head out of the bedroom. "I'd be very grateful if you'd stop poking around in my things."

"My dear, 'poking around' in your apartment is an affair for experienced spelunkers only. I found my things in a manila envelope abandoned in the middle of your messy attic."

Julia zipped her bag shut and put it in the entryway. Now she only had to go justify her upcoming absence to Adam.

"What do you plan on telling him?" Anthony Walsh asked.

"I think that's between the two of us," Julia responded.

"I'm not worried about him; it's your side of the story that interests me."

"Oh really? Is that also part of your new program?"

"Whatever the excuse you come up with, I highly recommend you don't tell him where we're going."

"I suppose I should take the advice of a man with such vast experience in secrets."

"Simply take it for what it is. Now hurry up and go. We have to be on our way to the airport in two hours."

*

The yellow cab dropped Julia off at 1350 Sixth Avenue. She shot into the towering glass building of the New York publisher where Adam worked in the children's book department. Her cell phone didn't get reception in the lobby, so she presented herself at the front desk and asked the security officer to connect her with Mr. Coverman.

"Is everything all right?" asked Adam when he heard Julia's voice.

"Are you in a meeting?"

"Yes, we're going over a mock-up. We'll be done in fifteen minutes. Do you want me to make a reservation at our Italian place for eight o'clock?"

Adam noticed the number on the screen of his phone.

"You're in the building?"

"At reception."

"I'm really sorry, but we're very busy with the presentation of the new publications..."

"We have to talk," Julia said, interrupting him.

"Can't it wait until this evening?"

"I can't have dinner with you, Adam."

"I'm coming down," he responded as he hung up.

Julia waited for him in the lobby.

"There's a café downstairs," suggested Adam.

"Why don't we just go for a walk in the park instead? We'll be more comfortable outside."

"That bad, huh?" he asked as they left the building.

Julia didn't answer. They walked up Sixth Avenue, and three blocks later they entered Central Park.

The tree-shaded walkways were deserted, apart from a few joggers wearing headphones, wholly concentrated on the rhythm of their feet and sealed off from the world around them. A gray squirrel came toward them and stood up on its hind feet, hoping there might be some food for him. Julia plunged her hand into the pocket of her trench coat and knelt to offer him a handful of nuts.

The brave little animal approached, then hesitated a moment, greedily eyeing the unexpected bounty. It finally overcame its fear and snatched a nut, running a few feet away to shell it under Julia's melancholy gaze.

"Since when do you carry nuts in your pocket?" asked Adam.

"I knew we would come here, so I bought some before I got in the taxi," Julia replied as she offered a second nut to the squirrel. His compatriots were beginning to gather around.

"I don't think you asked me to leave my meeting to show off your talents as an animal tamer…"

Julia tossed the rest of the nuts on the grass and signaled that they should continue their walk. Adam followed her.

"I'm going away," she said, her voice tinged with sadness.

"You're leaving me?" Adam asked worriedly.

"No, silly. I'm just going away for a few days."

"How many?"

"Two… Or, at most, six."

"Two or six?"

"I don't know yet."

"Julia, you show up unannounced at my office and ask me to come with you, looking as though your world were collapsing around you. Please don't make me pull the words out one at a time."

"Sorry if I'm wasting your precious time." Julia's tone became defensive.

Adam stopped her, putting his hands gently on

her shoulders. "You're angry. You have every right, but don't be angry with me. I'm not the enemy, Julia. I'm just happy being the guy who loves you, even if it isn't always easy. Don't make me pay for things that I didn't do."

Julia's face softened. "My father's secretary called me this morning. I have to take care of some out-of-town business."

"Where?"

"In Vermont, near the Canadian border."

"Okay, so why don't we go there this weekend, the two of us?"

"Because it's urgent. It can't wait."

"Does this have something to do with the travel agency that just contacted me?"

"What did they say?" Julia asked, her voice unsteady.

"Somebody came by to see them. And for a reason that I didn't entirely understand, they refunded my ticket, but not yours. They didn't want to explain. I was on my way into a meeting and didn't have time to ask for details."

"It's probably my father's secretary's doing. He's very good at his job."

"You're going to Canada?"

"Near the border. I told you."

"You really want to go?"

"I think so, yes," she responded darkly.

Adam took Julia in his arms and held her tightly.

"Go wherever you need to go. I won't ask any more questions. I don't want to take the risk of coming off as the guy who didn't trust you twice in a row. Besides, I know you'd never stay away from work for very long. Walk me back to my office?"

"I think I'll stay here a while longer."

"With your squirrels?"

"Yes, with my squirrels."

He kissed her on the forehead, took a few steps backward, and waved goodbye as he turned and walked away on the tree-lined path.

"Adam?" Julia called to him.

"Yes?"

"It's a shame that you have that meeting. I really would have liked to…"

"I know, but the two of us haven't had much luck these past few days."

Adam blew her a kiss.

"Gotta run. Call me when you get to Vermont, okay?"

Julia watched him walk away.

*

"How did it go?" asked Anthony Walsh, delighted with his daughter's return.

"Couldn't have gone better."

"Why the long face, then? You look like you came from a funeral. Better late than never, I suppose…"

"God, I wonder why. Maybe because I just lied to the man I love for the first time?"

"You mean the second. You're forgetting yesterday… Or, if you'd rather, we can chalk yesterday up as a false start and say it didn't count."

"Even better! I've betrayed Adam twice in two days! And he's being so sensitive by letting me go, no questions asked. In the taxi on the way back, I felt like the kind of woman I always swore I would never become."

"Let's not exaggerate."

"Oh no? What's more revolting than lying to somebody who trusts you so much that they don't even ask you any questions?"

"Being so caught up in your work that you don't pay attention to the other person's life?"

"You've got nerve to make a remark like that…"

"Yes, but as you observed, it comes from somebody who knows what he's talking about. I think the car is waiting downstairs… We shouldn't dawdle. With all of the security checks these days, we'll spend more time in the airport than we will in the airplane."

While Anthony Walsh took their bags downstairs, Julia looked over her apartment. Before leaving she turned the photo of her father on the mantle to face the wall and closed the door behind her.

*

An hour later the limo pulled up outside the terminal at JFK.

"We could have taken a taxi," said Julia, looking through her window at the planes parked on the tarmac.

"Yes, but even you must admit that these cars are much more comfortable. Besides, I found my credit cards in your apartment. From what I understand, you don't want your inheritance, so allow me to waste it for you. So many dead people must dream of having the chance to spend the fortunes they worked their whole lives to accumulate… This really is an unprecedented opportunity, when you think about it. And stop looking so gloomy. You'll see Adam again in a few days, and you'll be even more in love. Why don't you make the most of these moments with your father? When was the last time we went on vacation together?"

"I was seven, and Mom was still alive. She and I spent our time sitting around a hotel pool while you spent yours in a phone booth taking care of business," Julia replied, getting out of the limo.

"It's not my fault they hadn't invented cell phones yet!" grumbled Anthony Walsh as he opened his door.

*

The international terminal was packed. Anthony rolled his eyes and went to the end of a long line of passengers that snaked its way to the ticket counter. Once they had their boarding passes, a precious reward for their patience, the waiting began again at the security checkpoint.

"Look how irritated everyone is. All this hassle ruins the pleasure of traveling. And how can you blame them? Who wouldn't become impatient standing like this for hours, chasing down restless toddlers who can't possibly sit still for this long wait. Who would honestly suspect that that woman in front of us would hide explosives in her baby's food? Dynamite applesauce perhaps?"

"Believe me, anything's possible."

"Oh come on. A bit of common sense is all I'm asking for. Think of the English, who took their tea during the Blitz!"

"Under falling bombs?" whispered Julia, embarrassed that Anthony was talking so loudly. "You still complain about everything, don't you? What if I told the security officer that the man I'm traveling with is not exactly my father? What if I explained the details of our situation? He'd have the right to forget about common sense then, don't you think? I know whatever remnant of common sense I once had disappeared when you stepped out of your box."

Anthony shrugged and moved forward in line. It was almost his turn to walk through the metal detector. The implications of what Julia had just said hit her. She tugged on his arm.

"Come on," she whispered, practically in a panic. "Let's get out of here. It was a stupid idea to take the plane. Let's rent a car. I'll drive, and we'll be in Montreal in six hours. I promise we'll even talk along the way. It's easier to talk in a car anyway."

"What's gotten into you, my dear?"

"Don't you get it?" she hissed in his ear. "They'll find you out in two seconds. You're stuffed with electronics. You'll set the metal detectors screaming. The police will jump on you, arrest you, search and X-ray you from head to toe, and then take you apart to understand how you work!"

Anthony smiled and stepped toward the security officer. He opened his passport and unfolded a letter tucked inside the cover, which he handed over to the guard.

After reading it over, the security officer asked Anthony to step aside while he summoned his supervisor. Once the supervisor had read the letter, he adopted a very respectful attitude. Anthony Walsh was directed around the metal detector and was courteously patted down, before being allowed to go on.

Julia, on the other hand, wasn't spared the extensive security search imposed on all the other passengers. She was told to take off her shoes and belt. They confiscated her hair clip because it was too long and pointy, as well as a pair of fingernail clippers she had forgotten in her bag and a matching nail file that exceeded the acceptable length by an inch. The supervisor lectured her for her carelessness.

Didn't the screens display the list of objects forbidden aboard the plane? Julia quipped that it would be easier to list those that were authorized. The officer's tone shifted to that of a drill sergeant. He asked if she had a problem with the regulations. Julia hastily reassured him that she did not. Her flight took off in only forty-five minutes, and she didn't wait for an answer before hurrying to claim her bag and join Anthony, who had been observing her from afar. He looked amused.

"And why, may I ask, did you have the right to special treatment?"

Anthony waved the letter he still held in his hand, then handed it over to his daughter to read.

"You have a pacemaker?"

"For ten years."

"Why?"

"Because I had a small heart attack, and it became a necessity."

"When did this happen?" Julia was a little stunned.

"If I tell you that it happened on the anniversary of your mother's death, I'm certain you'll just accuse me of being overly dramatic."

"Why didn't anybody call me?"

"Maybe because you were too busy living your life to leave a phone number?"

"Nobody told me anything about this."

"We would have had to know how to reach you... Oh, let's not make a big deal out of this. For the first few months I was livid that I had to depend on a machine. When I think that today my entire body is a machine...Shall we go? We don't want to miss our flight," said Anthony Walsh, searching for their flight on the departures monitor. "Ugh, of course. We're delayed for an hour. Would it be asking too much for planes to be on time?"

Julia took advantage of the extra time to nose around the airport bookstore. From behind a magazine display she observed Anthony, who was unaware that he was being watched. He was sitting in the waiting area, facing the runways, and staring off into the distance. For the first time Julia felt that she missed her father. She decided to call Stanley.

"I'm at the airport," she said in a low voice.

"Do you take off soon?" asked her friend, his voice nearly inaudible.

"Are you with a customer? Is this a bad time?"

"I was about to ask you the same question."

"Of course not. I'm the one who called you!" Julia replied.

"Well, then why are *you* whispering?"

"I was whispering?" Julia cleared her throat and looked around, feeling a little foolish.

"You know, you should stop by the store more often. You're my good-luck charm. I sold that eighteenth-century clock an hour after you left. It had been sitting there gathering dust for two years."

"If it was really eighteenth century, another couple of months wouldn't have made a difference."

"Well, you never know, do you…" He paused a moment, then continued, "I don't know who you're with, and I don't care. But don't treat me like an idiot who can't tell when something is up."

"It's not what you think!"

"You can't begin to imagine what I think."

"I'm going to miss you."

Stanley sighed. "Take advantage of the next few days, princess. Travel can really clear your mind."

He hung up before Julia could have the last word. Stanley stared at the disconnected phone and muttered to himself, "I don't care who he is, but you better not let some Canadian steal you away. A day without you is horribly dull—I'm already bored out of my mind."

8.

At 5:30 p.m., American Airlines flight 4742 landed at Pierre Trudeau Airport in Montreal. Julia and Anthony went through customs without a hitch. A driver was waiting for them outside. Traffic was light, and half an hour later they were already crossing through the financial district. Anthony pointed out a glass skyscraper.

"I remember when that was being built," he said wistfully. "It's the same age as you."

"Is there a particular reason you're telling me this?"

"You said you liked this city, so I'm giving you something to remember. Some day you'll be walking in this neighborhood and you'll know that your father spent a few months of his life working in that skyscraper. This street will seem less anonymous."

"Wonderful," she said dryly.

"Aren't you going to ask what I did there?"

"Business as usual, I suppose?"

"No. Back then I was the proud owner of a little newsstand. You weren't born with a silver spoon in your mouth, you know. That came later."

"Did you work there long?" asked Julia, slightly astonished.

"Well, one day I had the idea to sell coffee, too. That's when business really started to pick up," Anthony continued with a twinkle in his eye. "People would stagger into the lobby, frozen stiff from the winter wind. You should have seen them throw themselves at me for the coffee, hot chocolate, tea…even at twice the usual price. Eventually I added sandwiches to the menu. Your mother would get up at the crack of dawn to make them. The kitchen in our apartment became a regular sandwich factory."

"You and Mom lived in Montreal?"

"Surrounded by lettuce, cold cuts, and Saran wrap. When I started to offer delivery to the offices upstairs and to the building that had just gone up next door, I had to hire my first employee."

"Who was that?"

"Your mother. She tended the newsstand while I made deliveries. She was so pretty people would stop by and place several orders a day just to be able to look at her. God, we had fun back then. She memorized the faces and preferences of every customer. The accountant in office 1407, who had a little crush on her, got extra cheese, but she had it out for the director of human resources on the eleventh floor, so he got all of the wilted lettuce and the leftover mustard on his sandwiches."

Their car pulled up in front of the hotel, and the bellboy guided them to the front desk.

"We don't have a reservation," she said, handing her passport to the receptionist.

The man behind the desk recognized the name next to the photo then checked his computer screen.

"Actually, you do have a reservation. And a very nice one at that."

Julia looked at him with astonishment. Anthony inched backward.

"Mr. and Mrs. Walsh…Coverman," the receptionist continued. "And unless I'm mistaken, it looks like you're staying with us the entire week."

"You didn't!" Julia whispered in horror to her father, who did his best to look innocent.

The receptionist came to Anthony's rescue.

"You have the, uh…" suddenly noticing the difference in age between his guests, he stumbled a bit, "honeymoon suite."

"You could have at least chosen a different hotel," Julia hissed in her father's ear.

"It was one of those package deals!" said Anthony, defending himself. "Your future husband went the whole hog, airfare plus lodging. We're lucky he didn't choose the hotel meal plan. I promise it won't cost him a thing. We'll put it on my credit card. And since everything that's mine is now yours, you're the one treating me!" He chuckled.

"That's not exactly what concerns me."

"What is it then?"

"Honeymoon suite?"

"Don't worry, I checked it out with the travel agency. There are two bedrooms linked by a living area. In the penthouse. I hope you're not afraid of heights."

As Julia continued to lecture her father, the concierge proffered their room key and wished them an excellent stay.

The bellboy escorted them toward the elevators, but Julia turned and walked quickly back to the receptionist.

"It's not what you think! He's my father."

"But I didn't think anything, madame," he replied, embarrassed.

"Yes, you thought something all right, but it's not true." Julia's cheeks were pink with embarrassment.

"Mademoiselle, I assure you, I've seen it all," he said, leaning over the counter so nobody would hear. "Your secret's safe with me," he said in a tone that was meant to be reassuring.

Her embarrassment morphed quickly into anger, and Julia was just about to spit a catty comeback when Anthony took her by the arm and forcefully steered her away from the front desk.

"You worry too much about what other people think."

"So?"

"Come on, the bellboy is holding the elevator.

We're not the only ones in this hotel, you know."

*

The suite fit Anthony's description exactly. The bedrooms were separated by a sitting room, and their windows looked out over the old city center. Julia barely had time to put her things down before somebody knocked at the door. A room-service waiter was standing behind a cart laden with Champagne on ice, two crystal flutes, and a box of chocolates.

"What on earth is this?" demanded Julia.

"With the compliments of the hotel, madame," he replied. "It's part of our honeymoon package."

Julia gave him a withering look and picked up the card sitting delicately on the white linen tablecloth. The director of the hotel sincerely thanked Mr. and Mrs. Walsh-Coverman for choosing the establishment to celebrate their marriage. The entire staff would be at their disposal to make their honeymoon an unforgettable one. Julia tore the card into little pieces, which she carefully put back on the cart, and slammed the door in the waiter's face.

"But, madame, it's included in the price of your room!" she heard from the hall outside.

Julia gave no response. The cart's wheels creaked as it was trundled back toward the elevator. Julia snatched open her door again and strode over to the waiter. She grabbed the box of chocolates and spun back around. The door of room 702 slammed a second time, making the young man jump. He shook his head in disbelief as he punched the button for the elevator.

"What was that?" asked Anthony Walsh, coming out of his bedroom.

"Nothing," replied Julia, calmly sitting on the window ledge of the living area.

"Great view, isn't it?" observed Anthony Walsh, gazing out at the Saint Lawrence River in the distance. "The weather is beautiful today. Would you like to go for a walk?"

"Anything to get out of here."

"I'm not the one who chose this hotel," Anthony Walsh retorted as he wrapped a cardigan around his daughter's shoulders.

*

With their uneven paving stones and quaint architecture, the streets of Old Montreal had an old-world charm to rival that of many European cities. Anthony and Julia began their walk at the Place d'Armes. Anthony Walsh took it upon himself to recount the biography of Montreal's founder in painstaking detail as they stood at the foot of the statue erected in his name above a little fountain. Julia yawned and left him in mid-recitation to check out a candy vendor a few yards away.

She returned with a bagful of sweets, which she offered her father to taste. Anthony summarily rejected the sugary treats, screwing up his face in disgust. Julia looked back and forth between the bronze statue of Lord Maisonneuve high on its podium and her father with an expression of self-satisfied approval.

"What?" Anthony asked.

"The resemblance is uncanny. You two make quite a pair. I think you would have gotten along famously."

She led him in the direction of the Rue Notre-Dame. Anthony made her stop at the façade of number 130, explaining that it was the oldest building in the city. He told her it still housed a few of the priests that were once the island city's leaders.

Julia yawned anew and pushed onward in the direction of the Notre-Dame de Montréal cathedral. Fearing what would come next, she begged her father to spare her the guided tour inside.

"You have no idea what you're missing," he called to her as she tried to speed past. "The ceiling is painted to look like a starry night sky… It's incredible!"

"And now I know," she answered from a distance.

"Your mother and I baptized you here!" Anthony had to shout after her.

Julia suddenly stopped, did an about-face, and came back to her father's side.

"Fine, we'll go in and see this starry ceiling," she said, capitulating.

The sight of the painted ceiling was remarkably beautiful. Framed by sumptuously carved wooden ornaments, the ceiling seemed to be covered in lapis lazuli. Enthralled, Julia walked toward the altar.

"I never imagined it would be so beautiful," she murmured.

"I'm glad to hear it," Anthony replied triumphantly.

He led her over to the chapel of the Sacred Heart.

"You really had me baptized here?" she asked.

"Of course not. Your mother was an atheist; she would never have allowed it!"

"What? Why did you say that then?"

"Because I didn't want you to miss out on all this beauty," Anthony responded as they retraced their footsteps back toward the massive wooden doors at the front of the church.

As they crossed the Rue Saint Jacques, Julia almost felt like she was back in downtown Manhattan, surrounded by the white facades and colonnades of Wall Street. The sky began to grow dusky, and the streetlights of the Rue Saint Hélène flickered to life. A little farther on they arrived at a small square with tree-lined paths bordered by green grass. All of a sudden, Anthony lunged for a bench to steady himself, almost falling to the ground in the process. Julia hurried over to his side.

"It's nothing," he said. "Just another bug, something wrong with my knee."

Julia helped him sit down.

"Does it hurt?"

"No, no pain," he said with a grimace. "Dying has its advantages."

"Well, then why are you making that face? You really look like you're in pain."

"I must be programmed that way. If a person hurt themselves and showed no outward signs of pain, it would seem suspicious, don't you think?"

"Okay, okay. I don't need to hear all the details. Is there anything I can do?"

Anthony took a little black notebook and pencil from his pocket and handed them to Julia.

"Can you note that on day two the right leg seemed to malfunction? You have to be sure to give them this notebook on Sunday. It could help them improve future models."

Julia said nothing. Her hand shook as she tried to write down what her father had said. Anthony noticed and took the pencil from her hands.

"It's really not that important. I can walk normally now." He got up and took a couple of steps. "The minor anomaly seems to have corrected itself. No point in writing it down."

A horse-drawn carriage rolled onto the Place d'Youville. Julia declared that she had always dreamt of taking a carriage ride. She had watched them go by a thousand times in Central Park without ever having dared, and now was the time. She caught the coachman's eye and gave a little wave. Anthony looked horrified, but she made it clear to him that this was no time for discussion. He rolled his eyes as he pulled himself up into his seat.

"Ridiculous. We look absolutely ridiculous," he muttered under his breath.

"I thought you said we shouldn't care about what other people think."

"There are limits…"

"You wanted to travel together, didn't you? Well, this is traveling."

Clearly uncomfortable, Anthony watched the horse's rear end as it swung with each step.

"I'm warning you, if that pachyderm's tail makes the slightest upward movement, I'm getting out."

"Horses don't belong to the same family of animals as elephants," Julia replied, correcting him.

"With an ass like that, anyone could make that mistake."

*

The carriage pulled up in front of the Café des Eclusiers, on the Old Port. They climbed down and looked around, but enormous grain silos along the waterside blocked the view of the opposite shore. Their colossal curving forms thrust upward out of the water and seemed to be climbing into the darkness.

"Let's go this way," said Anthony gloomily, turning away from the river. "I've never liked those ugly concrete monsters. I can't believe they still haven't knocked them down."

"I suppose they're protected," Julia responded. "Maybe they'll get a certain charm as they age…"

"I certainly won't be around to see that day, and I bet you won't either."

He led his daughter down the Old Port promenade. As they wandered along the green stretches that bordered the Saint Lawrence River, Julia walked a few paces ahead of her father. A flock of seagulls taking off caused her to lift her head skyward to watch them. The evening breeze blew loose a lock of her hair. As she tucked it back behind her ear, she caught sight of her father out of the corner of her eye.

"What are you looking at?" she asked.

"You."

"And what were you thinking about?"

"I was thinking about how beautiful you are. How you look like your mother," he replied with a faint smile.

Julia looked at him flatly. "I'm hungry," was her only response.

"We should be able to find a place you're certain to like just a little farther on. This area is full of little restaurants, each more revolting than the last…"

"And, according to you, which is the most horrible?"

"Don't worry, I've got faith in us as a team. If we put our heads together, I'm sure we'll find it!"

Along the way, Julia and Anthony loitered in front of the shop windows where the promenade intersected with the Quai des Evénements. The former dock extended out into the Saint Lawrence River.

Julia suddenly caught sight of a familiar silhouette bobbing in the crowd. "Look at that man over there!" she exclaimed, pointing.

"Which one?" Anthony's gaze followed her finger.

"The guy in the black suit coat, over there by the ice-cream stand."

"I don't see him."

She pulled her father by the arm, forcing him to walk quickly.

Anthony shrugged himself free. "What's got into you?"

"Hurry up, I'm losing him!"

Julia let herself be swept into the crowd of tourists walking out onto the jetty.

"What on earth is it?" complained Anthony as he struggled to keep up with her.

"Come on!" she called back over her shoulder, refusing to wait for him.

Anthony sat down on a bench, determined not to

walk another step. Julia left him behind, almost running toward the mysterious man who had caught her attention and made her lose sight of everything else. A few moments later, she returned to her father's side, disappointed.

"I lost him." She dropped down onto the bench next to him.

"Will you tell me what this is about?"

"Over there, near those vendors… I thought I saw Wallace, your secretary."

"My secretary is completely ordinary. He looks like everyone, and everyone looks like him. Your eyes must have tricked you."

"Well, then why wouldn't you follow me?"

"My knee…" Anthony responded plaintively.

"I thought you didn't feel anything."

"It's just the damned programming again. Give me a break, please. I can't control everything. I'm a very complicated machine. Anyway, even if Wallace were here, he has the right to be. He's a free man now. He's retired."

"I suppose so, but it would still be a strange coincidence."

"It's a small world. I'm sure you just confused him with someone else. Didn't you say you were hungry?"

Julia helped her father to his feet.

"I think I'm fine now," he said, giving his leg a shake. "See, I'm back to normal. Let's stroll around a little longer and get something to eat."

*

With the return of warm spring weather, the Old Port promenade overflowed with souvenir and trinket vendors.

"Come on, let's go over there," said Anthony, leading his daughter out onto the jetty.

"I thought we were going to have dinner."

Anthony noticed a ravishing young woman sketching a ten-dollar portrait.

"She's really very good," Anthony said, observing her work.

A few sketches clipped to the fence behind her testified to her talent, which was confirmed by the tourist's portrait to which she was just adding the final touches. Julia ignored the entire scene. When she was hungry, she had little patience for anything else. For her, hunger was an urgent matter. Her appetite had always astounded the men in her life, both coworkers and former boyfriends. Once Adam had made the mistake of challenging her to a pancake-eating contest. Julia had been eagerly attacking her seventh when Adam, who had faded after five, was already contemplating the early stages of an unforgettable case of indigestion. And to make matters worse, she never gained a pound.

"Can we go?" she insisted.

"Hold on," Anthony responded, taking the place of the tourist who had just gotten up.

Julia rolled her eyes.

"What are you doing now?" she asked impatiently.

"I'm going to have my portrait done," Anthony retorted in an uncharacteristically playful tone. He turned to the artist, who was already sharpening her charcoal pencil. "Full or profile?"

"How about three-quarters?" suggested the young woman.

"Left side or right?" continued Anthony, turning in the folding chair to show both views. "People always say I look more distinguished from this angle. What do you think? Julia? What do you think?"

"Nothing. I have no opinion," she said, turning away.

"With all of those gummy bears you swallowed a few minutes ago, you can't be hungry!"

The portrait artist gave Julia a sympathetic smile.

"My father," Julia gestured to the seated Anthony. "We haven't seen each other for years. He was too busy doing his own thing. Last time we took a walk together we went to a petting zoo. He's decided to pick up our relationship right where we left off. Whatever you do, don't let him know I'm in my thirties; he'll die of shock."

The young woman chuckled and set down her pencil.

"I'll ruin his portrait if you keep making me laugh!"

"See?" continued Anthony. "You're distracting this young lady's work. Why don't you look over her other drawings. This won't take long."

"He doesn't care about the drawing, you know. He's only sitting there because he thinks you're pretty!" declared Julia.

Anthony gestured for his daughter to lean in closer. She looked skeptical but did as asked.

He whispered, "How many women would dream of seeing their father get his portrait drawn three days after his death?"

Incapable of coming up with a clever reply, Julia walked away. Anthony held his pose and watched his daughter as she looked over the selection of old sketches the artist had hung up to attract customers.

Suddenly Julia froze. Her eyes widened and her throat constricted so that she couldn't breathe. The floodgates of her memory poured open at the sight of one particular drawing. One of the faces clipped to the fence—the one with the shaded cleft in the chin, the lightly exaggerated lines of the cheekbones, the gaze that seemed to lock eyes with her from the paper, and the noble, almost insolent brow—sent her years into the past, awakening a torrent of forgotten feelings…

"Thomas?" she stammered.

9.

Julia turned eighteen on September 1, 1989. To celebrate her coming of age and her new independence, she chose to ditch the college where Anthony had enrolled her in order to study abroad with an international exchange program. She intended to study something entirely different from what her father had planned for her. Over the years, she had earned money from tutoring, and she supplemented those savings with her winnings from late-night card games and a generous scholarship. She had needed her father's secretary's cooperation to get her school's scholarship fund to ignore her father's fortune. Despite Wallace's protestations ("Miss, if your father knew what I was doing…"), he finally signed the paperwork that certified that Anthony Walsh had long stopped supporting his daughter. When presented in combination with her pay slips, the university had been convinced and her scholarship approved.

She was able to retrieve her passport on the sly from her father's Park Avenue house during a brief and stormy visit. After she slammed the door behind her, she took the bus to JFK, and in the early morning hours of October 6, 1989, Julia landed in Paris.

In her mind's eye, she could still see the student apartment where she had lived. By the window, with its view of the Left Bank's rooftops, stood a rickety table, a metal folding chair, and a lamp—a holdover from another century. The bed had sweet-scented but scratchy sheets… She couldn't recall the names of the two girls who lived across the landing, but she clearly remembered walking down the Boulevard Saint-Michel to her classes at the École des Beaux-Arts and the dingy bar on the corner of Boulevard Arago, with its customers smoking and drinking café-cognac, even in the morning hours. She had been so happy with her newfound independence that her studies flowed by smoothly, uninterrupted even by romance. Julia drew continuously through the days and nights. She sat sketching on nearly every bench in the Jardin de Luxembourg, walked down all of its tree-lined paths, and stretched out on all of its "keep-off-the-grass" lawns to observe the clumsy gait of the birds, the only ones authorized to be there. October flew past and the last days of her first Parisian autumn evaporated into the gray of early November.

She thought back to that ordinary evening she spent in the Café Arago among students from the Sorbonne who fervently discussed the latest news from Germany. Since the beginning of September, thousands of East Germans had crossed the border with Hungary, attempting to reach the West. Just the evening before, a million citizens had demonstrated in the streets of East Berlin.

"This is an unprecedented historical event," one of the students cried out.

His name was Antoine.

The memories flooded back.

"We have to go there!" another declared.

He was called Mathias. I remember… He chain-smoked. He would fly off the handle at the drop of a hat. He never stopped talking, and when he had nothing to say, he would hum a little tune. I've never met somebody so afraid of silence.

A group of interested students had formed. It was decided that they would leave by car for Germany that very night. If they drove in shifts, they could reach Berlin by noon.

Julia couldn't say what had pushed her to raise her hand in the Café Arago that evening. Some force had simply but surely drawn her to the table of students from the Sorbonne.

"Can I come with you?" she asked as she approached the group.

I remember every word.

"I know how to drive, and I'm well-rested. I slept the whole day today."

I lied.

"I could stay behind the wheel for hours."

Antoine checked with the others. *Had it been Antoine or Mathias?* The group was swept up in the drama of the epic journey that was beginning to take form, and they called for a quick vote on whether they should include her.

"We should have an American representative along with us," Mathias added, seeing Antoine hesitate.

He was finally swayed and raised his hand, along with the others.

"When she returns to her home country, she'll be able to testify to France's sympathy for contemporary revolutions."

They pushed back their chairs to make room, and Julia found herself surrounded by new friends. A little while later they stood on the Boulevard Arago and said their goodbyes to those who were staying behind. She planted farewell kisses on the cheeks of countless faces—she didn't recognize half of them, but as she was now part of the group, she had to pay her respects to those they were leaving behind. There was no time to lose; they had a six-hundred-mile drive ahead of them. The night of November 7, as they drove along the Seine, Julia never imagined that she was saying goodbye to Paris and that she would never again see the view of the Left Bank rooftops from her studio.

Senlis, Compiègne, Amiens, Cambrai. Signs

marked with the names of mysterious towns she had never heard of rolled past their car in succession.

Julia took the wheel around midnight, in Valenciennes, just before entering Belgium.

Julia's American passport aroused the border guard's curiosity, but her student card from the École des Beaux-Arts allowed the group to continue their road trip without incident.

Mathias was always singing, and it got on Antoine's nerves. Julia just tried to decipher the lyrics, which she couldn't always understand. It kept her awake.

The memory made Julia smile…as more reminiscences came back to her. They stopped at a rest area along the highway. *We counted our money and decided to buy some baguettes and ham.* One of the two purchased a bottle of Coke in honor of her nationality, but, in the end, she drank only a sip.

Her traveling companions spoke French too quickly and used many expressions whose meanings she couldn't decipher. She had mistakenly thought that her six years of French class in high school had made her bilingual. *Why had Daddy insisted I learn French? Was it in honor of his days in Montreal?*

They took the wrong exit outside of Mons, at La Louvière, and had to endure a harrowing drive through Brussels. They stopped to ask a local for directions to Liège. Julia understood nothing of the man's thick Belgian accent, but it kept Mathias laughing for a long time. Antoine recalculated their traveling time. The detour had cost them an hour. Mathias begged her to drive faster. The revolution wouldn't wait for them! They checked the map and turned around, deciding that the northern route would take too long. They decided to go south, through Düsseldorf.

First, they crossed through the Flemish-speaking part of Belgium. As the French signs evaporated, Julia marveled that three different languages were spoken just a few miles apart. "A quaint country of waffles and lace," concluded Mathias dismissively, urging her to hit the gas. Just before Liège the car swerved unexpectedly, after Julia's eyelids had grown heavy with fatigue.

They stopped to gather their wits on the shoulder of the highway. Antoine gave her a lecture, and she was relegated to the backseat.

Her punishment certainly did not cause her any suffering. Out cold, Julia had no memory of crossing the border. Mathias, who held a diplomatic passport, thanks to his ambassador father, had persuaded the West German border guards to let his "stepsister," who had just come in on a flight from America, sleep.

The officer had been understanding and nodded them on after a cursory glance at the three passports stowed in the glove compartment.

Without consulting Julia, the two boys decided

to make a pit stop. It was clear that everyone could use a real breakfast in a real café. And so, on the morning of November 8, just as they were driving into Dortmund, Julia awoke in Germany for the first time in her life. Little did she know that her world would be turned upside down the very next day.

Julia got behind the wheel again just past Bielefeld, near Hanover. Antoine had been against it, but neither he nor Mathias was in any condition to continue driving, and Berlin was still far away. The two boys fell asleep quickly, and Julia was able to enjoy a few moments of silence. As the car approached Helmstadt, the tone of the journey darkened. In the distance, barbed-wire fences marked the border with East Germany. Mathias awoke and told Julia to pull over onto the shoulder right away.

They plotted their strategy, deciding on the roles they would play when crossing the border. Mathias would drive, Antoine would sit in the passenger seat, and Julia would stay in back. All of their hopes rested on Mathias's precious diplomatic passport. Mathias insisted they rehearse their lines. There was to be no talk of their real objective. When they were asked why they were coming to the East, Mathias would say he was visiting his father, who was a diplomat in Berlin. Julia would play up the fact that she was American and also claim to be visiting her diplomat father. "What about me?" Antoine asked. "You'll just try to keep your mouth shut," replied

Mathias, turning the key in the ignition.

A thick forest of fir trees stretched right up to the edge of the highway. In a clearing ahead stood the leviathan forms of the checkpoint compound. The buildings were more on the scale of a train station than a border crossing. Their car wove between two semi trucks. A guard motioned for them to change lanes, and Mathias's smile evaporated.

Above the treetops of the vast forest towered two enormous pylons studded with searchlights. Four watchtowers, nearly as high as the searchlights, stood across from them. A sign marked "Marienborn Border Checkpoint" loomed over the metal gates that opened and shut behind each vehicle.

At the first inspection point, they were told to open the trunk. As the officers rifled through Antoine and Mathias's bags, Julia realized she had forgotten to bring anything at all. They were told to move ahead. A little farther on they drove through a corridor flanked by white corrugated-metal buildings, where their passports would be inspected. An officer ordered Mathias to stand aside from the others. Antoine began to grumble that their trip was utter insanity, that he had said so from the beginning. Mathias reminded him about the promise to be silent he had made just before the border. Julia glanced anxiously at Mathias, as if to ask what he expected her to do now. The guard asked Mathias to follow him.

Mathias took our passports. I remember it like it was yesterday. He followed the customs officer. Antoine and I waited. Even though we were alone in that gloomy sheet-metal shed, we followed his orders—we didn't utter a word. Mathias came back with a soldier behind him. Neither Antoine nor I could have possibly guessed what was about to happen. The young soldier looked us over one at a time. He gave the passports back to Mathias and gestured for us to continue ahead. I'd never been so afraid in my life. I'd never before felt that terrible sensation of something invading my personal space, slipping under my skin, and chilling me to the bone. Our car slowly rolled ahead to the next checkpoint, where we stopped under the roof of an enormous building. Mathias left us again, taken to another place. When he finally came back, his smile made us understand that we were free to continue to Berlin. We were told to stay on the highway until we reached our final destination.

*

A cool breeze blew in across the promenade from the Old Port of Montreal, making Julia shiver. Her eyes remained riveted to the face in the charcoal drawing. The portrait was drawn on paper far whiter than the corrugated buildings that had once stood on the border dividing Germany in two.

*

Thomas, I was making my way toward you. We had no idea what was to come, and you were still alive.

It took at least another hour before Mathias started to sing again. Aside from a few trucks, the only cars they encountered were little East German Trabants. It was as though all East Germans owned the same car so as not to compete with their neighbors. In comparison, their Peugeot 504 made quite an impression. The other drivers gawked in wonder as they passed.

They drove past Schermen, Theessen, Köpernitz, Magdeburg, and, finally, Potsdam, just thirty miles from Berlin. When they entered Berlin's suburbs, Antoine insisted that he be allowed to drive. Julia burst into laughter, reminding him it had been *her* compatriots that had liberated the city forty-five years earlier.

"And they're still there," responded Antoine in a bitter tone.

"Alongside the French," Julia reminded him, dryly.

"The two of you are wearing me out," concluded Mathias.

Once again they fell silent, until they reached the gates of the Western enclave in the middle of East Germany. Nobody spoke until they had crossed into the city. Then suddenly Mathias exclaimed, "*Ich bin ein Berliner!*"

10.

They arrived in Berlin completely behind schedule. The afternoon of November 8 was already drawing to a close, but nobody cared about the time they had lost along the way. They were exhausted but didn't realize it. The excitement in the air was palpable; they could feel that something was afoot, just as Antoine had predicted. Four days earlier, a million East Germans had gathered together to demonstrate. The wall loomed over everything with its thousands of soldiers and guard dogs patrolling day and night. There were families, friends, and neighbors isolated from one another for twenty-eight years by twenty-seven miles of concrete, barbed wire, and watchtowers built suddenly and brutally during the dismal summer that had marked the beginning of the Cold War. People who had once lived together waited, without daring to believe it was possible, for the moment they would be reunited.

Seated at a bar, the three friends eavesdropped on the conversations taking place around them. Antoine

did his best to translate for Mathias and Julia, con-
centrating to put his high school German to use. People were saying that the communist regime could not
hold out much longer. Some even thought it was just
a matter of time before the borders would be opened.

Everything had changed since Gorbachev's visit
to East Germany in October. A journalist from the
Taggespiegel, who had stopped in to grab a quick
beer, admitted that his newspaper was buzzing with
activity. He let slip that the headlines, which normally would already have gone to print, were still
on hold. Something important was about to happen,
but he could not say more.

At nightfall, their long journey finally caught up
with them. Julia couldn't stop yawning and got a
case of the hiccups. Mathias tried everything to stop
them. First, he tried scaring her, but each attempt just
made her burst into laughter, intensifying the jolts
that made her body jump with each hiccup. Antoine
got involved. They contorted themselves and did
gymnastics. They made her drink a glass of water
while being held upside down with her arms spread.
The cure was supposedly foolproof, but it still didn't
work, and her hiccups returned all the stronger. A
few regulars at the bar proposed other solutions:
Drinking a pint in one gulp might work. Maybe she
should hold her breath as long as possible. Another
person suggested she lie on the ground and bring her
knees to her chest. Everybody had an idea. Finally a

friendly doctor having a beer at the bar told Julia in nearly flawless English that she should just get some rest. The dark circles under her eyes gave away her exhaustion—sleep would be the best medicine. The three friends decided to search for a youth hostel.

Antoine tried to ask the bartender where they could find a place to stay, but he was exhausted as well, and the man couldn't understand a word of his question. They finally found two free rooms in a little hotel close by. The boys would share, and Julia would have the other room to herself. They crawled up the stairs to the fourth floor and collapsed into bed. Mathias had fallen asleep, sprawled across the entire bed, before Antoine could voice any protest so he ended up spending the night on a down comforter on the floor.

*

The portrait artist was having trouble finishing her sketch. She had asked Anthony to hold still three times already, but he took no notice of her. Each time the young woman tried to capture his likeness, he twisted his head around to look at his daughter. Julia was still staring at the sample portraits. Her expression was absent; her mind seemed to be elsewhere. She had not taken her eyes from the display board since Anthony had sat down. He called her name, but she didn't answer.

*

It was almost noon on November 9 when the three travelers met up in the lobby of the little hotel. That afternoon, they explored Berlin. *A few hours, Thomas... I'll meet you for the first time in just a few more hours.*

Their first stop was the Siegessäule Victory Column. Mathias thought it was far handsomer than the one that stood in Place Vendôme, in Paris. Antoine insisted that any comparison was pointless. Julia asked if they always bickered like that. The two boys looked at her with astonishment—for them it was just a simple conversation, and they didn't understand what she was talking about. They walked on through the Ku'Damm shopping district. They wandered hundreds of streets, rode dozens of streetcars, until Julia insisted she couldn't take another step. In the middle of the afternoon, the three of them collected their thoughts in front of the memorial church that the locals referred to as *Der hohle Zahn,* or "the hollow tooth." Bombs had destroyed most of the building during the Second World War, and it had been preserved as a memorial. What remained of the church did indeed resemble a jagged incisor.

At 6:30 p.m., Julia and her friends found themselves at the edge of a park, which they decided to cross on foot.

A short while later, an East German government

spokesperson made a declaration that would change the course of history, or at least the end of the twentieth century. East Germans were to be allowed to come and go as they pleased. They would be free to cross into the West without being fired upon by soldiers or attacked by dogs. Hundreds of men, women, and children had died trying to get to the other side of the wall during the bleak Cold War years, cut down by the bullets of its zealous guardians, and now the East Berliners were free to go. A journalist asked the spokesperson when the decision would go into effect. Misunderstanding the question, the bureaucrat responded: "Immediately!"

All of the radio and television stations broadcast the news. It echoed incessantly throughout the East and the West.

Thousands of West Germans gathered at the checkpoints. Thousands of East Germans did the same. Two French students and one American girl were carried along by the mass of humanity rushing toward freedom.

At 10:30 p.m., the border crossings on both the East and the West were overwhelmed by thousands of citizens hungry for liberty. The soldiers guarding the checkpoints found themselves at the foot of the wall. The barriers at Bornheimer Strasse came down, and Germany took a step closer to reunification.

You ran through the city, making your way through the streets, rushing toward freedom, and I walked toward you without knowing or understanding the force that pushed me onward. The wall's fall wasn't my victory, and Germany wasn't my country. Berlin's streets were strange to me.

I also started running, running to escape the crush of the mob. Antoine and Mathias tried to shield me. We ran along the interminable concrete wall that hopeful artists had painted and repainted. Some of your fellow citizens who couldn't bear to wait at the checkpoints began to climb over the top. Together with you on this side of the world, we waited and watched, holding our breath. All around me people opened their arms to cushion falls or to hoist one another up on shoulders, to see those running toward them, prisoners of the Iron Curtain for only a few moments longer. Our voices cried out and joined together, to encourage you, to assuage your fear, to tell you we were waiting on the other side. Suddenly I changed. The American girl who had fled New York, the child of a country that had warred against yours—I was swept up and, in turn, became German, too. In the innocence of my adolescence I also dared to whisper, "Ich bin ein Berliner," and I wept. I wept like a child, Thomas...

*

That evening, lost in the middle of a very different crowd of people, among the wandering tourists on a boat landing in Montreal, Julia cried. The tears slid anew down her cheeks as she stared at a charcoal-sketched portrait.

Anthony Walsh couldn't take his eyes off of her. He called to her again.

"Julia? Are you all right?"

His daughter was too far away to hear. At that moment, they were twenty years apart.

*

The crowd became increasingly agitated. People started to chip away at the wall with whatever tools they had on hand—screwdrivers, rocks, pocketknives—all pathetic in the face of concrete, but this obstacle was destined to give way. Just twenty feet away from me something incredible had started to happen. A world-renowned cellist, who happened to be in Berlin, heard about the events and came to join us, to join you. He sat down with his instrument and began to play. Was it really that same evening, or the day after? It doesn't matter. His music also helped pull down the wall. Melodies of freedom floated through the air toward you. I wasn't the only one crying, you know. I saw many tears that night. Those of a mother and daughter holding tightly to one another, overwhelmed to find each other again after twenty-eight years of separation. I saw gray-haired fathers recognize their sons among thousands of oth-

ers. *I saw so many Berliners for whom tears were the only release from all the suffering they had endured. And suddenly, in the middle of it all, there you were, on top of the wall, with your dusty face and your beautiful eyes. You were the first man I had ever seen from the East, and I was the first girl you had ever seen from the West.*

You stayed crouched atop the wall for a long time, our eyes riveted on one another. We were in a daze. A new world spread itself before you, and you stared at me as though we were connected by an invisible thread. I cried like an imbecile, and you smiled down at me. You swung your leg over the wall and jumped. I did what others had done and opened my arms to you. You fell on top of me, and we rolled across a ground that had never felt your footsteps. You apologized in German, and I said hello in English. You stood up and dusted off my shoulders as though you had done so a hundred times before. You continued speaking, but I couldn't understand a word. From time to time you nodded. I laughed at how ridiculous we were. You extended your hand, and you spoke the name that I was to repeat so many times, a name that I haven't said in such a long time. Thomas.

*

On the docks a woman bumped into her without stopping to apologize. Julia didn't notice. An illegal street vendor hawking jewelry waved a string of wooden beads in her face. She slowly shook her head, deaf to the litany of sales pitches he recited like a prayer. Anthony got up and gave ten dollars to the portraitist. She gave him the sketch. She had captured his expression; the resemblance was striking. Satisfied with the result, he pulled another ten dollars from his pocket and doubled the asking price. He went to Julia's side.

"What have you been staring at over here for the past ten minutes?"

*

Thomas, Thomas, Thomas. I'd forgotten how good it feels to say your name. I'd forgotten your voice, your dimples, and your smile, until I saw this portrait that made me remember you. I wish you had never left to cover that war. If I had known what would happen the day you told me that you wanted to become a reporter—if I had known how things would end, I would have told you it was a bad idea.

You would have insisted that telling the truth about the world is the best job out there, even if photography can be cruel, even though the truth can haunt one's thoughts, even if it brings nightmares. Your voice would have grown serious and declared that, had the press known the truth about what was happening behind the wall, our leaders would have knocked it down much earlier. But they all knew, Thomas. They knew the details of your lives. They spent their time spying on you. Those who governed in the West weren't courageous enough. You would have said that only someone who had grown up in a place where people are free to think as they like and say what they like, without fear of reprisals, could give up taking risks. We would have argued all night and into the next morning. If you only knew how much I miss our old arguments, Thomas.

Unable to come up with a winning argument, I would have ended up giving in, like I did the day I left. How could I hold you back, you who had always longed for freedom? You were right, Thomas. You had one of the best jobs in the world. Did you finally meet Massoud? Did he give you that interview, now that you're both up in heaven? Was it worth it? He died a few years after you. Thousands of people followed his funeral procession through the Panchir Valley, but no one ever found your remains. What would my life be now if that land mine hadn't destroyed your convoy? If I hadn't been a coward? If I hadn't abandoned you just a short time before?

*

Anthony placed his hand on Julia's shoulder.

"Who are you talking to?"

"To nobody," she replied, startled.

"Julia, your lips are trembling."

"Go away. Leave me alone," she whispered.

*

There was a moment of awkwardness, a fragile instant. I introduced you to Antoine and Mathias, insisting so heavily on the word "friends" that I think I must have said it six times so that you would understand. It was ridiculous. You could barely speak English back then. Maybe you understood. You smiled at them, and Mathias gave you a congratulatory hug. Antoine was content to shake hands, but he was just as overwhelmed as his friend. The four of us set off into the town. You were looking for somebody. I thought it was a woman, but it turned out to be your childhood friend. He had managed to make it over the wall with his family, and you hadn't seen him for ten years. How were we supposed to find your friend among the thousands of people hugging, singing, drinking, and dancing in the streets? You turned and told me, "The world is big, but friendship is bigger." I don't know if it was your accent or the innocence of your observation, but Antoine made fun of you. I thought the idea was wonderful. Could it be that the pain of your life had preserved the childlike innocence that had been extinguished by our Western freedoms? We decided to help you in your search, and together we combed the

147

streets of West Berlin. You walked with a purpose, as though you were going to meet somebody in a specific place. Along the way, examining every face, you pushed through the milling crowd, but you constantly turned to look behind you. The sun had already set when Antoine stopped in the middle of a square and shouted, "Could we at least know the name of the guy we've been looking for like idiots the whole day?" You didn't understand what he was asking. Antoine shouted even louder, "Prénom! Name! Vorname!" You lost your temper and screamed back the name of the friend you were looking for. "Knapp!" To make you understand that he hadn't been angry at you, Antoine began to shout, "Knapp! Knapp!"

Doubled over with laughter, Mathias joined in. I also began calling out, "Knapp! Knapp!" You looked at us like we were crazy, laughed at us, and then began shouting, "Knapp, Knapp" yourself. We were practically dancing, singing our heads off to the name of the friend you hadn't seen in ten years.

A face turned toward us from the middle of the enormous crowd. A man your age was looking at you. I saw your eyes meet, and I was almost jealous.

Like two wolves separated from the pack encountering one another in the forest, you stood completely still, staring at one another. Then Knapp spoke your name, "Thomas?" You held your friend in your arms. The joy on both your faces was utterly *sublime. Antoine was crying, and Mathias was comforting him. If they had been separated just as long, the happiness of their reunion would be the same, swore Mathias. Antoine's sobs doubled in intensity as he responded that it would be impossible, because they hadn't known each other as long. You lay your head on the shoulder of your best friend. You saw that I was watching, and you immediately straightened up. You repeated, "The world is big, but friendship is bigger." Antoine wept uncontrollably.*

We sat at wooden tables outside of a bar. The cold pricked our cheeks, but we didn't mind. Together, you and Knapp sat off to the side. Ten years of life to catch up on called for a lot of talking, and just as much silence. We all stayed together for the rest of the night and into the following day. The next morning, you told Knapp that you had to go back. You couldn't stay any longer. Your grandmother lived in the East, and you couldn't leave her alone. You were her only family. She would have been a hundred years old this winter. I hope the two of you have found each other again, wherever you are now. God, I loved your grandmother so much! I remember her knocking on our bedroom door, so pretty with her long white hair in braids. You promised your friend you'd come back again soon, as long as life did not move backward, as long as freedom was here to stay. Knapp reassured you that the gates would never close again, and you replied, "Perhaps, but if I had to wait ten years to see you once more, I'd still think about you every day."

You rose and thanked us for the gift we had given you. We had done nothing really, but Mathias told you that it was his pleasure, that he was delighted to have been of use. Antoine suggested that we walk you back to the former checkpoint between the East and the West.

We set off, following all of the people who, like you, returned to the East because, revolution or not, their families and their homes were still on the other side of the city.

Along the way, you took my hand in yours. I said nothing, and we walked like that for miles.

*

"Julia, you're shivering. You'll catch your death of cold. Let's go. If you'd like, we'll buy the drawing, and you can look at it as long as you want, somewhere warm."

"No. It's priceless. We have to leave it here. Please…just a few more minutes and we'll go."

*

Here and there around the former checkpoint people were hacking away at the wall. We almost said good-bye there. You shook hands with Knapp first. "Call

*me soon, as soon as possible," he urged, handing
you his card. Was it because your best friend was a
journalist that you decided you wanted to become
one, too? Was it some pact the two of you had made
during your youth? I must have asked you a hundred
times, but you never answered directly. You would
just give me one of those mysterious smiles, the ones
you reserved for the moments when I annoyed you.
You exchanged handshakes with Antoine and Mathias and then turned to me.*

*If you knew, Thomas, how afraid I was at that
moment. How afraid I was of never knowing the
touch of your lips. You came into my life out of
nowhere. You brought your hand to my cheek, held
my face in your hands, and gently placed a kiss on
each of my eyelids. "Thank you," was all you said,
before you were already walking away. Knapp
watched the two of us. The expression on his face
surprised me. He looked as though he wanted me to
say something, as though he wanted me to find the
words that would erase forever the years that had
separated the two of you and held you at a distance
from one another. Those long years had shaped the
two of you so differently. He would return to work at
his newspaper, and you would return to the East.*

*I cried out, "Take me with you! I want to meet
this grandmother you're leaving for," and I didn't
wait for a response. I took back your hand, and I
swear nothing in the world could have separated my*

grip from yours at that moment. Knapp shrugged, and in response to your speechlessness, he said, "The roads are open now. Come back whenever you like!"

Antoine tried to convince me otherwise. He said it was craziness. Perhaps it was, but I had never felt this intoxicating feeling before. Mathias elbowed Antoine in the ribs: How was it his business? He ran over and hugged me. "Call us when you come back to Paris," he said, scribbling his phone number on a scrap of paper. In turn, I hugged them both, and the two of us set off. I never went back to Paris, Thomas.

I followed you. At dawn on November 11, we took advantage of the general state of chaos and crossed the border. At that moment, I was possibly the first American girl to enter East Berlin... If I was not the first, I was certainly the happiest.

I kept my promise, you know. Do you remember that day in the gloomy café, where you made me swear that, if fate separated us, I should try to be happy, no matter the cost? I knew you said it because my love was suffocating you, because you had lived without freedom for too long to accept me attaching my life to yours. Even though I hated the idea of tainting my happiness, I gave you my word.

I'm going to get married, Thomas. At least, I was supposed to get married on Saturday. My wedding was postponed. It's a long story, but it has taken me this far. Maybe I was supposed to see your face one last time. Kiss your grandmother in heaven for me.

*

"This is ridiculous, Julia. If you could just see your-self—you're acting like you're the one running low on batteries. You've been standing here muttering for the past fifteen minutes…"

Julia wandered away without responding. Anthony Walsh quickened his pace to catch up with her.

"Can you please tell me what's going on?" he insisted as he arrived at her side.

Julia remained silent.

"Look," he continued, offering his portrait. "It's really good. Here, it's for you," he added happily.

Julia ignored him and continued to walk back toward their hotel.

"Okay, I'll give it to you later. Clearly, this isn't a good time."

And since Julia still said nothing, Anthony Walsh continued: "That drawing you were staring at reminded me of somebody. I suppose it has nothing to do with the way you've been acting. I don't know why, but I feel like I've seen that face somewhere before."

"It's because you punched that face the day you came to take me away from Berlin. That was the face of the man I loved when I was eighteen years old, the man you ripped me away from when you forced me to come back to New York with you!"

153

11.

The restaurant was nearly full. An attentive waiter brought them two flutes of Champagne. Anthony didn't touch his, but Julia downed hers in a single gulp. She chased it with her father's Champagne and motioned to the waiter for a refill. By the time the menus arrived, she was already feeling the effects.

"I think you've had enough," advised Anthony as she ordered a fourth glass.

"Why? It's bubbly, and it tastes good."

"You're drunk, Julia."

"Not yet," she said, giggling.

"Try to tone it down a bit. If you want to ruin our first dinner out together, you don't need to make yourself sick. We can go back to the hotel. Just tell me."

"No way! I'm hungry."

"Then order room service."

"I think I'm a little too old for you to speak to me in that tone."

"You're right, Julia. We're both too old for this. You're acting like when you were a little girl and wanted to push my buttons."

"When you think about it, it was the first choice I ever made for myself…"

"What are you talking about?"

"Thomas!"

"True, it was your first independent choice. But you made many other choices for yourself afterward, didn't you?"

"You always wanted to control my life."

"It's a common condition found in fathers. But your accusation doesn't hold water, when you keep insisting I was absent from your life."

"If only! To the contrary, you were far too present. Just not in person."

"Keep it down. You're drunk. It's embarrassing."

"Embarrassing? You don't think it was embarrassing when you showed up at our apartment in Berlin? When you screamed at the grandmother of the man I loved until you terrified her into telling you where we were? When you kicked in the door to the bedroom where we were sleeping and broke Thomas's jaw? I'd say all that was far more embarrassing."

"I admit, I was out of line."

"Oh, you admit it, do you? Would you admit it was embarrassing to drag me by my hair to your car? How about when you pushed me through the airport, shaking me like a rag doll? Or when you buckled me into my seat yourself? Were you afraid I would jump out of the plane midflight? And back in New York, do you think it might have been embarrassing when you threw me in my room and locked the door, like I was some kind of criminal?"

"There are moments when I wonder if maybe it wasn't such a bad thing to have died last week…"

"Spare me."

"Oh, I wasn't responding to your sparkling monologue. I was thinking of something else."

"And what would that be?"

"The way you've been acting since you saw that drawing."

Julia's eyes widened.

"What could that possibly have to do with you dying last week?"

"It's funny, isn't it? You could say that I inadvertently kept you from getting married on Saturday," Anthony Walsh concluded with a broad smile.

"And why does that make you so happy?"

"That your wedding was called off? Up until now I was actually quite sorry about it, but now I'm beginning to feel differently…"

Made nervous by the loud conversation of his two customers, the waiter interrupted them to ask what they'd like to have. Julia ordered a steak.

"How would you like that cooked?" asked the waiter.

"Bloody, I'd imagine," replied Anthony Walsh.

"And you sir?"

"Are there any lithium batteries on the menu this evening?" asked Julia pointedly.

The waiter remained speechless. Anthony explained he didn't want anything to eat.

"Getting married is one thing," he continued to his daughter. "But allow me to say that sharing your entire life with a person is something else entirely. It takes a lot of love, a lot of space. It's something that both people have to be comfortable with... Neither person should feel constrained."

"Who are you to judge my relationship with Adam? You don't know the first thing about him."

"I'm not talking about Adam. I'm talking about you. I'm talking about how much of yourself you're ready to give to him. If your heart is clouded by the memory of another man, the happiness of your future life together is at risk."

"You'd know something about that, wouldn't you?"

"Your mother is dead, Julia. I can't do anything about it, even if you keep blaming it on me."

"Thomas is dead, too. And though you can't do anything about that either, I'll still blame you. Adam and I have all the space in the world."

Anthony Walsh coughed. A few beads of perspiration pearled on his brow.

"You're sweating," said Julia with surprise.

"A minor malfunction. It'll pass," he said, delicately dabbing his temples with his napkin. "You were only eighteen, Julia. For God's sake, you wanted to spend the rest of your life with a communist you had known only a few weeks!"

"Four months!"

"Sixteen weeks, then."

"And he was from East Germany. That does not make him a communist."

"You're right. That's so much better," retorted Anthony sarcastically.

"If there's one thing I'll never forget, it's why I sometimes used to hate you so much!"

"We had an agreement: no past tense. Don't be afraid to talk to me in the present. I may be dead, but I'm still your father, or, at least, what's left of him..."

The waiter brought Julia's food. She asked him to refill her glass, but Anthony covered it with his hand.

"I think we still have a lot to say to each other."

The waiter left them alone without asking any questions.

"You were living in East Berlin, and I hadn't heard from you in months. What was next? Moscow?"

"How did you find me?"

"Somebody was kind enough to send me a copy of the interview of you that was printed in that German newspaper."

"Who?"

"Wallace. It was his way of making up for the fact that he had gone behind my back to help you study abroad."

"You knew about that?"

"Or maybe he was just as worried as I was and had decided it was time to put an end to your caprice, before you actually put yourself in danger."

"I was never in danger. I loved Thomas."

"At that age, it's easy to confuse self-love with falling in love. You were supposed to be studying pre-law in New York, and you dropped everything to take drawing classes in Paris. And once you were there, it wasn't long before you turned around and left for Berlin. Then you ran off with the first man you fell for and kissed art school goodbye to become a journalist. If I remember correctly, he also wanted to be a journalist. What a curious coincidence."

"How was that any of your business?"

"I was the one who had told Wallace to give you your passport the day you asked for it, Julia. I was in the next room when you came to take it from my desk drawer."

"Why didn't you just give it to me yourself?"

"We weren't getting along terribly well back then, if you recall. If I had given you your passport, it would probably have compromised your sense of adventure. Didn't your trip seem all the more exciting because you were rebelling against me?"

"You really thought that?"

"I told Wallace where your passport was. I really was in the next room. And to tell you the truth, the whole situation hurt my pride."

"Hurt? You?"

"And Adam?"

"Adam has nothing to do with any of this."

"I'd like to remind you that, as strange as it is, if it weren't for my death, you'd be his wife right now. Let me rephrase my question. But please close your eyes first."

Julia couldn't understand why her father was asking her to do so, but finally she gave in to his insistence.

"Close them tightly. I want you to see nothing but complete darkness."

"What are you getting at?"

"Just do what I ask, for once. It will only take a second."

Julia scrunched up her eyes, shutting out the light.

"Now eat."

Amused, she did as she was told. Her hand patted the tablecloth until she found her fork. Clumsily, she tried to pierce the piece of meat on her plate. With no idea of what she was bringing to her lips, she opened her mouth.

"Did your food taste different because you couldn't see it?"

"Maybe," she replied, keeping her eyes closed.

"Now do something else for me. Whatever you do, don't open your eyes."

"Okay, I'm listening," she said with a hushed voice.

"Think about a time when you were completely happy."

Anthony watched his daughter's face.

I remember we were taking a walk together on the Museuminsel. When you had introduced me to your grandmother, the first thing she asked was what I did in life. The conversation was difficult. You tried to translate what I said with your rudimentary English. I told her I was a student at the École des Beaux-Arts in Paris. She smiled and went to her dresser to find a postcard of a painting by Vladimir Radskin, a Russian artist she liked. Then she told us to go out and get some air and take advantage of the beautiful day. You hadn't told her anything about your incredible trip to the West or the way we had met. When we were saying our goodbyes at the front door, she asked if you had seen Knapp. You hesitated for a moment, but the look on your face gave away the truth. She smiled and said she was happy for you.

As soon as we were outside, you took me by the hand. Each time I asked where we were going, you answered, "Come on." We went over the little bridge that spanned the Spree and onto the island.

I had never seen so many buildings dedicated

solely to art. I had thought that your country was only gray, but here everything was in color. You led me to the entrance of the Altes Museum. The building itself was square, but inside was a sort of rotunda. I had never before seen architecture like that. It was strange, almost unbelievable. You brought me to the center of the rotunda and then started to walk around me in circles, making me turn faster and faster, until I became dizzy. You stopped our crazy waltz and held me in your arms. You said that was German Romanticism, a circle inside a square, the marriage between two completely different forms. Then you took me to the Pergamon Museum.

"So," asked Anthony, "did you think of a time when you were completely happy?"

"Yes," Julia replied, her eyes still shut.

"Who was there with you?"

She opened her eyes.

"You don't have to tell me, Julia. It belongs to you. I'm not going to try to live your life for you anymore."

"Why did you make me do that?"

"Every time I close my eyes, I see your mother's face."

"I believe that Thomas appeared to me in that portrait, like a ghost or a shadow, to say that I can now move on. I can get married without regret, and I can stop thinking about him. It was a sign."

Anthony coughed.

"For God's sake, it was just a drawing. If I throw my napkin and it does or doesn't make it to the umbrella stand by the door, that doesn't mean it will or will not rain. Whether the last drop of wine falls in the glass of that woman at the table over there has nothing to do with whether she'll marry the ass she's having dinner with. Don't look at me like that! If that idiot hadn't been trying to impress his girlfriend so loudly, I wouldn't have heard every word of their conversation since we sat down."

"You're just saying this because you don't believe in signs. You've always needed to be in control of everything."

"There are no such things as signs, Julia. I used to throw thousands of balls of crumpled-up paper at my office wastebasket, convinced that if I made the shot my wishes would come true. But the call I was waiting for never came. So I pushed the idea further, believing that three or four perfect shots would make it happen. After two years of dedicated practice, I could land a ream of paper in the center of a wastebasket thirty feet away. It changed nothing.

"During a business dinner with three important clients, while one of them droned on about the various countries where we had our branches, I wondered where the person I loved most was waiting for me. I imagined the streets she would walk down when she left home in the morning. As we were leaving the restaurant, one of the clients, a Chinese man—and don't ask me to remember his name—told us a wonderful legend. He said that if you jump in a puddle reflecting the full moon, its spirit will bring you the person you miss most. You should have seen the face of my colleague when I jumped into the gutter. My client's suit was soaked, and he had water dripping from the brim of his hat. Instead of excusing myself, I told him that his trick didn't work—the woman I missed was still gone.

"So don't talk to me about idiotic signs that people cling to against all reason once they've lost their faith in God."

"Don't say that!" cried Julia. "When I was little, I would have jumped in a thousand puddles to make you come home in the evening. It's too late to tell me that kind of story now. My childhood is long gone!"

Anthony Walsh looked sadly at his daughter. Julia remained angry. She pushed back her chair and left the restaurant.

"Please excuse my daughter," he said to the waiter as he left a few banknotes on the table. "I think your champagne disagrees with her."

They walked in silence through the narrow streets of Old Montreal, back to the hotel. Julia had trouble walking straight and, from time to time, tripped on the uneven paving stones. Anthony held out his arm to steady her, but she shunned his gesture without even touching him, preferring to find her balance on her own.

"I'm a happy woman!" she said as she staggered along. "Happy and perfectly fulfilled... I love my job, I love my apartment, I have a wonderful best friend, and I'm going to get married to the man I love. I couldn't be better!"

Julia's ankle buckled, but she caught herself in the nick of time and slid down to the ground against a lamppost.

"Shit!" she grumbled, sitting on the sidewalk.

She ignored her father's hand, so he knelt down and sat next to her. The street was empty. The two of them stayed there, their backs against the street-lamp. After ten minutes had passed, Anthony took a little bag from his coat pocket.

"What is that?" she asked.

"Candy."

Julia rolled her eyes and turned her head.

"I think there are still a few gummy bears strolling around in the bottom... Last I heard, they were playing jump rope with a licorice stick."

Julia showed no reaction, until Anthony started to put the bag back in his pocket, then she suddenly grabbed it from his hands.

"When you were a little girl, you adopted a stray cat," Anthony recounted as Julia scarfed down the candy. "You loved him very much, and he liked you, but he left eight days later." He paused, before adding, "Do you want to go back to the hotel now?"

"No," Julia replied, her mouth full.

A carriage pulled by a reddish-brown horse rolled past. Anthony hailed it.

*

They arrived back at the hotel an hour later. Julia crossed the lobby and took the elevator to the right. Anthony took the one on the left. They crossed paths again in the hallway on the top floor and walked side by side down the hall to the door of the honeymoon suite. Anthony stepped aside and let his daughter pass. She went directly to her bedroom, and he went to his.

Julia threw herself onto her bed and rummaged around in her purse for her cell phone. She looked at the time before calling Adam. It went to voice mail. She listened to his message but hung up before hearing the ominous beep. She called Stanley.

"You sound like you're in rare form."

"I miss you, you know that?"

"I had no idea. So how's your trip going?"

"I think I'm coming back tomorrow."

"So soon? Did you find what you were looking for?"

"Yes, basically."

"Adam just left my place," announced Stanley abruptly.

"He was at your place?"

"That's what I just said. Have you been drinking?"

"A little bit."

"Doing that well, are you?"

"Yes, I said I was fine! Why do you all think that I'm not okay?"

"You all? I'm alone now, as I just told you."

"So what did Adam want?"

"To talk about you, I imagine. Unless he's switching teams, in which case he's wasting his time. He's not at all my type."

"Adam came to talk to you about me?"

"No, he came with the hope that I would talk to him about you. It's the sort of thing people do when they miss somebody they love."

Stanley could hear Julia breathing.

"He's sad, princess. As you know, I'm not Adam's biggest fan, but I never like to see a man suffer."

"What's he sad about?" she asked, sincerely concerned.

"Either you've lost your senses or you really are drunk. He's in complete despair because, two days after the cancellation of his wedding, his fiancée— God, it's unbearable when he calls you that; it's so last century—his fiancée has disappeared without an explanation or even a forwarding address. Does that make sense to you, or do I need to FedEx you a cup of detox tea and a bottle of aspirin?"

"First of all, I didn't disappear out of the blue. I stopped by his work to tell him where I was going."

"Vermont, darling. You told him you were going to Vermont. You call that an address?"

"What's wrong with Vermont?" asked Julia.

"Nothing, except that I messed up."

"What did you do?" asked Julia, holding her breath.

"I accidentally let slip that you were in Montreal. How was I supposed to know you told him Vermont? Next time you decide to lie, tell me! I could give you lessons. And we could have coordinated our stories."

"Shit!"

"You took the word right out of my mouth."

"The two of you had dinner together?"

"Oh, it was nothing. I just whipped up a little something…"

"Stanley!"

"I couldn't let him starve to death. I don't know who you're with or what you're up to, and I understand that it's none of my business, but please call Adam—it's the least you could do."

"It's not at all what you think, Stanley."

"Who told you what I think? If it makes you feel better, I promised him that your disappearance had nothing to do with the two of you as a couple. I told him that you had gone on a trip to learn more about your father. See? It takes a certain talent to lie like me."

"I swear to you, it's not a lie."

"I told him you were really shaken by your father's death and that it was important for your future together that you take care of unfinished business from your past. Nobody needs ghosts haunting their marriage, right?"

Julia said nothing.

"So how is the investigation into Papa Walsh's past coming along?" continued Stanley.

"I've rediscovered all the things I hated about him."

"Perfect. What else?"

"Maybe a few of the things that made me love him."

"So why are you coming home tomorrow?"

"I don't know. It's probably better for me to come back to Adam."

"Better because…?"

"I went for a walk earlier this evening, and there was this portrait artist…"

Julia told Stanley about her discovery in the Old Port of Montreal. For once, her friend was at a loss for witty interjections.

"Don't you think I should come home now? I haven't been very happy away from New York. And, besides, if I don't come home tomorrow, who'll be your good-luck charm?"

"Do you really want my advice? Get a piece of paper and write down everything that crosses your mind. Then do exactly the opposite. Goodnight, princess."

Stanley hung up. When Julia got up to go to the bathroom, she didn't hear her father's footsteps shuffling back into his room.

12.

The sky blushed pink as dawn broke over Montreal. Sunlight gently flooded into the sitting room between the suite's bedrooms. There was a knock at the door. Anthony opened it, and a waiter wheeled a tea cart into the middle of the room. The young man offered to set the breakfast table, but Anthony slipped him a few dollars and took over. As the waiter left, he made sure that the door closed silently behind him. He hesitated between the coffee table and a side table by the windows with a sweeping view of the town. He opted for the view, and with the utmost care, he arranged the tablecloth, plate, silverware, a small pitcher of orange juice, a bowl of cereal, a basket of pastries, and a single rose standing proudly in a bud vase. He stood back, then adjusted the flower (it looked off center to him) and moved the milk jug (it would be better next to the bread basket). On Julia's plate he placed a rolled-up piece of paper tied with a red ribbon, then covered it with a napkin. He moved back a few feet to assess the harmony of his arrangement. Then, tightening the knot in his tie, he knocked gently on his daughter's bedroom door and announced that madame's breakfast was served. Julia groaned and asked what time it was.

"Time to get up. The school bus will be here in fifteen minutes, and you're going to miss it again!"

Buried up to her nose in blankets, Julia opened one eye and stretched. It had been a long time since she had slept so soundly. She ran her fingers through her hair but kept her eyes scrunched shut until they adjusted to the daylight. She got up in one movement and then sat on the edge of the bed, overcome by dizziness. The alarm clock on the bedside table read eight o'clock.

"Why so early?" she grumbled as she stumbled into the bathroom.

While Julia was taking her shower, Anthony Walsh sat waiting in an armchair in the little sitting room. He contemplated the red ribbon peeking out over the edge of the plate and sighed.

*

The Air Canada flight had taken off from Newark at 7:10 a.m. Not long afterward, the captain's voice crackled over the loudspeakers, announcing the beginning of the plane's descent into Montreal. They would be arriving at the gate on time. The head flight attendant took over the communication and directed the passengers to prepare for landing. Adam stretched as much as was possible and put his tray table in the upright and locked position. He looked out the window. The plane was flying over the Saint Lawrence River. The suburbs of Montreal appeared up ahead, and the outlines of Mont Royal could be seen in the distance. The MD-80 banked, and Adam tightened his seat belt. The lights along the runway were already visible through the window.

*

Julia knotted the sash of her bathrobe and walked into the living room. She looked at the table set for breakfast and smiled at Anthony, who pulled out her chair for her.

"I ordered Earl Grey," he said, filling her cup. "The waiter gave me the choice of breakfast tea, black tea, yellow tea, white tea, Lapsang souchong, jasmine, and about forty others, before I threatened to commit suicide if he continued."

"Earl Grey is perfect," replied Julia, unfolding her napkin.

She saw the paper tied up with the red ribbon and turned to give her father an inquisitive look.

Anthony took it from her hands.

"Open it after breakfast."

"What is it?" asked Julia.

"Those," he said, pointing to the pastries.

"The long twisty ones are called croissants, the rectangular ones with the brown stuff sticking out are pains au chocolat, and the spiral-shaped things with the dry fruit on top are pains aux raisins."

"I was referring to the diploma you're hiding behind your back."

"I told you—after breakfast."

"Well, then why did you put it on my plate?"

"I changed my mind. It's better if you look at it later."

Julia waited until Anthony had turned around. In a single gesture, she neatly snatched the paper out of his hands.

She untied the ribbon and unrolled the paper. Thomas's face smiled back at her.

"When did you buy it?" she asked.

"Yesterday, as we were leaving the boat landing. You were walking ahead, not paying attention. I'd given the artist a generous tip, so she said I could take it. The person who had it drawn hadn't wanted it, and she didn't need it for anything."

"Why did you do that?"

"I thought it might make you happy. You spent such a long time looking at it."

"No, seriously, tell me why you bought it."

Anthony took a seat on the sofa and looked into his daughter's eyes.

"Because we need to talk. I had always hoped that we'd never have to, and I admit that I never wanted to broach the subject. I never imagined that our time together would lead to such a thing, or be ruined by it, since I can already see how you're going to react... But the signs, as you call them, seem to be showing the way, and the time has come when I must tell you something."

"Cut the drama and get to the point," she said abruptly.

"Julia, I have reason to believe that Thomas is not exactly dead."

*

Adam was livid. He had made a point of traveling without luggage so he could leave the airport more quickly, but the passengers from a 747 from Japan were clogging up the customs counters. He glanced at his watch. The line of people that stretched before him would mean another twenty minutes of waiting before he could jump in a taxi.

Suddenly a word sprang from the depths of his memory. "*Sumimasen!*" His work contact at a Japanese publishing house had used the word so often Adam had thought that apologizing must be Japan's national pastime. "*Sumimasen!* Excuse me!" he repeated over and over, weaving through the people ahead of him. Ten "*sumimasens*" later, Adam finally reached the front of the line and presented his passport to the Canadian customs officer, who stamped it and gave it back to him. Ignoring the rule against using cell phones in the baggage-claim area, he took his phone from his coat pocket, turned it on, and dialed Julia's number.

*

"I think I hear your phone ringing. You must have left it in your room," said Anthony sheepishly.

"Don't try to change the subject. What do you mean by 'not exactly dead'?"

"I suppose it would be equally accurate to describe him as alive…"

"Thomas is alive?" said Julia, growing visibly unsteady.

Anthony nodded.

"How do you know?"

"Because of the letter he sent. Normally dead people aren't able to write letters. Except for me, of course… I hadn't thought of that."

"What letter?" asked Julia.

"The one you received from him six months after his accident. It was sent from Berlin. His name was on the back of the envelope."

"I never got any letter from Thomas. You've got to be kidding."

"You couldn't have gotten it, because you'd left the house, and I couldn't forward it to you, because I didn't have your address. I suppose it's another good item to add to your list."

"What list?"

"The list of reasons you hated me."

Julia pushed back the breakfast table and stood up.

"I thought we agreed on using present tense. Don't you remember? You can go ahead and put that last sentence in the present!" she shouted, stalking out of the room.

Her bedroom door slammed behind her. Anthony, alone in the middle of the room, sat down in her chair.

"What a waste," he murmured, looking at the basket of pastries.

*

It was impossible to cut to the front of the taxi line. A uniformed woman stood guard, directing each person to their cab. Adam was forced to wait his turn. He dialed Julia's number again.

*

"Pick up or turn it off. It's getting on my nerves," said Anthony as he came into Julia's bedroom.

"Get out of here."

"For God's sake, Julia, it was almost twenty years ago."

"And in almost twenty years you never found the time to tell me?" she screamed.

"In twenty years we haven't had many occasions to talk to each other," he replied firmly. "And even so, I don't know if I would have told you. What good would it have done? At the time, it would have just given you another excuse to cut short the life you were building for yourself. You had your first job in the city, a studio on 42nd Street, a boyfriend who was taking theater classes, if I remember correctly, and another who showed his dreadful paintings in a gallery in Queens. You dumped him after getting a new job and a new hairdo. Or was it the other way around?"

"How do you know all that?"

"Just because you never took any interest in my life doesn't mean that I didn't do my best to find out what was going on in yours."

Anthony looked at his daughter for a long moment and then turned to go. She called him back.

"Did you open it?"

"I never read your mail," he said, turning back to her.

"Did you keep it?"

"It's in your room, or, at least, the room that was yours when you lived at home. I put it in your desk drawer. I thought it was the best place for it."

"Why didn't you say anything about it when I came back to New York?"

"Why did you wait six months before calling me after you came back to New York, Julia? Was it because you knew I had seen you through the window of that drugstore in SoHo? Or was it because, after all those years apart, you finally started to miss me? I wouldn't be so sure that, between the two of us, you were the only one pulling the short stick."

"What, was it all just a silly contest to you?"

Anthony placed an envelope on her bed.

"I'll leave this with you," he added. "I should have said something earlier, but I never had the chance."

"What is it?"

"Our return tickets for New York. I ordered them through the concierge earlier this morning, while you were sleeping. I told you, I had a premonition how you'd react, and I imagine that our time together ends here. Get dressed, pack your bag, and meet me down in the lobby. I'll go settle the bill."

Anthony gently closed the door behind him.

*

Traffic on the highway was bumper to bumper, so the taxi driver opted for Saint Patrick Street, but the traffic turned out to be equally dense there. The driver suggested that they get back on the 720 up ahead and cut across on Boulevard René Lévesque. Adam didn't give a damn about the route, as long as it was fast. The driver sighed. There was no use in being impatient—he could do nothing about the situation. They'd get to Adam's destination in half an hour, maybe less if the traffic was better in the city. To think that some people said taxi drivers were unpleasant... He turned up his radio, to put an end to their exchange.

The tip of a skyscraper in Montreal's financial district was already appearing on the horizon. The hotel wasn't much farther.

*

With her bag hanging from her shoulder, Julia crossed the lobby and marched confidently to the front desk. The concierge left his counter to meet her.

"Madame Walsh!" he exclaimed, spreading his arms wide. "Mr. Walsh is waiting outside. Your car is a little late. Traffic is very heavy today."

"Thank you," Julia replied.

"I'm very sorry, Madame Walsh, to see you leaving us ahead of schedule. I hope that our service was not responsible for your early departure?" he inquired apologetically.

"Your croissants are delicious!" fired back Julia. "And once and for all, I'm mademoiselle, not madame!"

She left the hotel and found Anthony waiting for her on the sidewalk.

"The car should arrive soon," he said. "There it is now."

A black Lincoln pulled up in front of them. The driver popped the trunk before getting out to welcome them. Julia settled into the backseat, while the bellboy attended to their luggage. Anthony walked around the back of the car. A taxi honked and missed hitting him by just a few inches.

*

"People never pay attention to where they're going!" ranted the taxi driver as he double-parked in front of the Hôtel Saint Paul.

Adam handed him a fistful of dollars. Without waiting for change he ran to the revolving door. At the front desk, he introduced himself and asked for Miss Walsh's room.

Outside, the black Town Car was blocked in by the double-parked taxi. The driver was casually counting his money and seemed in no hurry.

"Mr. and Mrs. Walsh have already checked out," the woman receptionist replied apologetically.

"Mr. and Mrs. Walsh?" Adam repeated, emphasizing the word 'mister.'

From his desk next to the receptionist, the concierge overheard everything. He rolled his eyes, before introducing himself.

"May I help you?" he asked twitchily.

"Did my fiancée stay in your hotel last night?"

"Your fiancée?" the concierge asked, looking

over Adam's shoulder at the street outside.

The Town Car had not moved.

"Miss Walsh!"

"Mademoiselle did indeed stay with us last night, but I'm afraid she has already left."

"Alone?"

"I really couldn't say, sir," replied the concierge, growing increasingly uncomfortable.

A chorus of honking horns made Adam turn and look outside.

"Sir?" the concierge intervened, trying to attract Adam's attention away from the street. "Perhaps we could offer you something to eat?"

"Your receptionist just told me that Mr. and Mrs. Walsh just left this hotel. That makes two people. Was she alone or wasn't she?" Adam persisted firmly.

"My colleague must have been mistaken," the concierge interjected, flaying the young woman next to him with his eyes. "We have many clients. Maybe you'd like a coffee? A tea?"

"How long ago did she leave?"

The concierge glanced furtively outside. The black car finally moved forward, and he sighed with relief as it disappeared.

"Quite some time ago, I believe," he replied. "We have excellent fruit juices. Let me show you to the dining room. Breakfast is on us…"

13.

Julia kept her nose glued to the window during the entire flight. They didn't exchange one word.

Every time I was in a plane, I'd watch for your face in the clouds, imagining your features among the forms stretching across the sky. I wrote you a hundred letters and got a hundred back in response, two a week. We promised we'd be together again, as soon as I'd saved enough money. When I wasn't studying, I worked every chance I got so that, one day, I could come back to you. I waited tables, ushered at theaters, handed out flyers. I spent every moment on the job, imagining the morning when I would finally land in Berlin to find you waiting for me at the airport.

I spent countless nights falling asleep thinking of your face, remembering the laughter that overcame us as we walked the streets of that gray city. When I was alone with your grandmother, she used to tell me not to invest too emotionally in you. She said our relationship couldn't last, that there were too many differences between us—me a girl from the West, and you a boy from the East. But every time you came home and took me in your arms, I looked over your shoulder and smiled at her, certain she was wrong. When my father forced me into the car that was waiting in the street below your window, I screamed your name. I wished you could have heard me.

I was working at a restaurant when the evening news spoke of an "incident" in Kabul that had killed four journalists, one of them German. I knew at once it was you. My blood ran cold, and I fainted behind the wooden counter where I'd been drying glasses. The TV anchor said that your car had hit a land mine left behind by Soviet troops. It was as though fate wanted to catch you, to keep you from living in freedom. The newspapers didn't give any details, just four deaths. That was enough for their viewers. What did their names matter, let alone their lives and those they left behind? In my heart I knew you were the German journalist they were talking about. It took me two days to get a message to Knapp. During those two days I couldn't eat a thing.

When Knapp finally called me back, I knew from his tone of voice that he had lost a friend and I had lost the man I loved. My best friend, he said, over and over again. He felt guilty for having helped you become a reporter. I tried to console him, even though I felt my soul being shredded to pieces. He had offered you a chance to become the person you wanted to be. I told him how frustrated you had been at never having found the right words to thank him. Knapp and I kept talking about you, so that your presence might linger with us a while longer. He said your body would never be identified. An eye-witness had reported that the truck you were riding in had been blown to pieces when it hit the mine. Chunks of sheet metal were scattered across the ground in a hundred-foot perimeter. In the spot where you died, all that remained was a gaping crater and a twisted metal carcass—testimony to the absurdity of men and their cruelty. Knapp couldn't forgive himself for having sent you to Afghanistan. Between sobs he told me you had been a last-minute replacement. If only you hadn't been available when he was looking for a journalist to ship out as soon as possible. I later realized that he had given you the most beautiful gift imaginable. "I'm sorry, I'm sorry," Knapp repeated as he wept. I was incapable of shedding a single tear. Crying would have taken a little more of you away from me. I couldn't even hang up when the conversation was over. I set the receiver on the counter, took off my apron, and wandered out into the street. I walked without knowing where I was headed. Around me, the city continued living as though nothing had happened.

None of the passersby that morning knew that, in the outskirts of Kabul, a thirty-year-old man named Thomas had died. Who would have even suspected? Who would have cared? Who could comprehend that

I would never see you again and that my world would never be the same again?

I didn't eat for two days. Did I tell you that already? It doesn't matter. I'd say everything twice, just to tell you about my life, to hear myself talking about you. Then I collapsed on a street corner.

Thanks to you I met Stanley. We were friends from the minute we met. He came out of the room next to mine and began walking down the hospital corridor. He looked like he was lost. My door was open, and he stopped, looked at me lying in my bed, and smiled. No clown in the world could have smiled so sadly. His lips trembled, and suddenly he murmured the two words I had forbidden myself to say.

Perhaps I was able to confess it to him because I didn't know him. To confide in a stranger isn't the same as confiding in someone you know. The truth still seems reversible. It's just a simple moment of abandon quickly erased by the stranger's ignorance. "He's dead," said Stanley. And I echoed, "Yes, he's dead." He talked to me about his friend, and I talked to him about you. That's how we met each other, Stanley and I, on the day we both lost the one we loved. Edward died from AIDS, and you from another pandemic that continues to ravage the human race. Stanley sat at the foot of my bed and asked me if I'd been able to cry yet. I told him the truth, and he admitted that he hadn't been able to, either. He extended his hand, and I took it in mine. Together

*we shed our first tears, the tears that carried you far
away from me, and Edward from him.*

*

Anthony Walsh refused the drink the flight attendant
offered him. He glanced behind him. The cabin was
nearly empty, but Julia had preferred to sit ten rows
back, next to the window. Her gaze remained lost in
the sky.

*

*When I got out of the hospital, I decided to leave
home. I tied a red ribbon around your hundred letters and left them in the desk drawer of my childhood
bedroom. I didn't need to reread them to remember
them. I packed a suitcase and left without saying
goodbye to my father. I was incapable of forgiving
him for having separated us. I used the money I had
saved to live far away from him. A few months later,
I began my career as an artist, and the beginning of
my life without you.*

    *Stanley and I spent all of our time together. That's
how our friendship grew. He was working in a
Brooklyn flea market at the time. We had a routine
of meeting in the middle of the Brooklyn Bridge,
where we would sometimes stay for hours, leaning
against the guardrail and watching the boats going*

up and down the river. Sometimes we'd walk down the promenade along the river. He'd talk to me about Edward, and I'd tell him about you. When we both went our separate ways, he'd take a little of you with him.

In the mornings, I would search for your shadow among those of the trees extending out across the sidewalks. I looked for the lines of your face in the reflections on the Hudson River. I listened in vain for your voice in the sound of the wind blowing through the city. For two years, I relived every moment we had spent together in Berlin. Sometimes I'd laugh about the way we had been, but I never stopped thinking about you.

I never got your letter, Thomas, the letter that would have told me you were still alive. I don't know what you wrote. That was almost twenty years ago, but I have a strange feeling, as if you sent it yesterday. Maybe after all those months without hearing from me you wrote to say you weren't going to wait for me anymore. Maybe you wrote to tell me that too much time had passed and I had been gone for too long. Or that we had come to a point where your feelings for me had started to wither. Love can fade into autumn when a couple begins to forget one another... Maybe you stopped believing in our love. Maybe I lost you some other way. Almost twenty years is a long time to wait for a response to a letter.

We're not the same people anymore. Would I still take that same trip from Paris to Berlin today? What would happen if our eyes were to meet again, you on one side of a wall, and I on the other? Would you open your arms to me, like you did for Knapp that November evening in 1989? Would we run off through the streets of a town that has gotten younger, while we have only gotten older? Would your lips still feel as soft? Perhaps that letter was supposed to stay in its drawer. Maybe it's better that way.

*

The flight attendant tapped Julia on the shoulder. It was time to fasten her seatbelt. The plane was approaching New York.

*

Adam had to resign himself to spending part of his day in Montreal. The Air Canada representatives had done everything they could, but, unfortunately, the only seat back to New York was on a flight that took off at 4 p.m. He kept trying to reach Julia but only got her voice mail.

*

From another highway, the skyscrapers of another

city, New York, appeared on the horizon. The Lincoln entered the tunnel of the same name.

"I have a funny feeling that I'm no longer welcome in my own daughter's home. Given the choice between your dusty attic and my apartment, I think I'd feel more comfortable at home. I'll come back on Saturday, to get back into my crate before they pick it up. I think it would be better if you called Wallace to make sure he won't be at my place," said Anthony, handing Julia a piece of paper with a telephone number written on it.

"Your secretary still lives in your house?"

"I don't really know what he's doing. I haven't had much time to touch base with him since my death. If you want to avoid giving him a heart attack, it would be wise to make sure he's not there when I arrive. And as long as you have him on the phone, I'd appreciate it if you could find a good reason for him to go to the other side of the world until the end of the week."

Julia dialed Wallace's number. A message explained that, due to the death of his employer, he was taking a month's vacation. It wasn't possible to leave a message. In case of emergency concerning the business affairs of Mr. Walsh, the caller was instructed to contact Walsh's attorney.

"The coast is clear. You can stop worrying," said Julia, putting her phone back in her pocket.

Half an hour later, their car parked along the

sidewalk outside Anthony Walsh's townhouse. Julia looked up at the building, and her gaze was immediately drawn to a window on the third floor. One afternoon, coming home from school, Julia had seen her mother leaning dangerously off the balcony. What would she have done if Julia hadn't shouted her name? When she spotted her daughter, Julia's mother had given her a little wave, as though the gesture might wipe away any traces of the fatal act she had been about to commit.

Anthony opened his briefcase and handed her a set of keys.

"They gave you back your keys?"

"Let's just say that we anticipated the situation where you wouldn't want me to stay in your house but you wouldn't want to turn me off prematurely, either. Could you open the door? We can't have any of the neighbors recognizing me."

"You know your neighbors? That's new."

"Julia!"

"Fine, I get it," she snapped, turning the knob of the heavy, cast-iron door.

Light poured into the hallway. Nothing had changed; the interior matched that of her earliest memories. The black and white tiles of the front-hall floor still spread before her like an enormous chessboard. To the right, a flight of dark wooden stairs traced a gentle curve to the second floor. The burled walnut banister had been carved by a renowned woodworker, as her father had enjoyed telling guests when he gave them a tour of the house. Farther on stood the door to the kitchen and butler's pantry. Together, the two rooms were larger than any of the apartments Julia had lived in since she left home. To the left was the office where her father balanced his personal accounts on the rare nights he was home. Everywhere there were signs of the wealth that had put a distance between Anthony Walsh and the days when he served coffee in a Montreal skyscraper. A portrait of Julia as a child hung on the wall. Did she still have any of the sparkle that the painter captured in those five-year-old eyes? She looked up at the carved wooden ceiling. Just a few spider webs hanging in the corners of the woodwork would have made the decor seem ghostly, but Anthony Walsh's home was impeccably well-kept.

"Remember how to find your bedroom?" asked Anthony as he went into his office. "I'll let you go up alone. I'm sure you still know the way. If you're hungry, there's probably something to eat in the kitchen cupboards…pasta or some canned food. I haven't been dead that long."

He watched Julia climb the stairs, two at a time, sliding her hand along the banister, exactly as she had done when she was a little girl. And just like she had always done as a child, she turned around when she reached the landing to see if anyone was following her.

"What?" she asked, looking down at him from the top of the stairs.

"Nothing," replied Anthony, smiling.

He went into his office.

The hallway extended before her. The first door led to her mother's bedroom. Julia put her hand on the knob. The latch opened slowly and softly… And closed just as softly, as she decided against going in.

A strange, opalescent light filtered in through the sheer curtains. They had been pulled shut and floated above the carpet, the colors of which had not faded. She went over to her bed, sat on the edge, and pressed her face against her pillow, inhaling its perfume. Memories flooded back—the nights spent reading under the covers with a flashlight, the evenings when imaginary characters came to life across the curtains, when the window was left open, familiar shadows that had populated her moments of insomnia. She stretched her legs and looked around. The ceiling lamp looked like a mobile, but it didn't move, even when she would stand on a chair and blow against its black wings. Near the dresser sat the wooden box where she kept her old notebooks, a few photos, and a set of cards printed with the names of magical countries, purchased at the corner store or traded with friends against cards she had doubles of. What good was it to go to the same place twice, with so many new places to discover? Her gaze wandered to the bookshelf where she kept her schoolbooks neatly propped up between two old toys, a red dog and a blue cat. The couple had never made one another's acquaintance. The dark red cover of a history book she hadn't cracked open since junior high brought her thoughts back to the spot where she used to do her homework. She got up from the bed and went over to the desk.

She had spent so many hours at this wooden tabletop scratched by a compass point, doodling, and then conscientiously writing interminable nonsense whenever Wallace knocked at her door to supervise her progress. She had filled entire pages with "I'm bored, I'm bored, I'm bored." The porcelain knob was in the shape of a star. All it took was a gentle tug for the drawer to slide effortlessly open, but she opened it just a tiny crack. A red marker rolled in the bottom of the drawer. Julia squeezed her hand in through the narrow opening and patted around for it but couldn't reach it. She treated the blind search like a game and kept exploring the inside with her hand.

Her thumb recognized a ruler, and her little finger encountered a necklace won at a carnival that was too ugly to wear. Her ring finger hesitated a moment. Was it her frog-shaped pencil sharpener? Her turtle-shaped tape dispenser? Her forefinger brushed up against something made of paper. In the upper right-hand corner, a slight raised area revealed itself to be the perforation of a stamp. Over the years, it had become slightly detached around the edges. She caressed the envelope in the darkened shelter of the drawer, her finger following the lines of ink left behind by a fountain pen, moving blindly, as in the game where one lover traces words on the other's back. Julia recognized Thomas's handwriting.

She pulled the envelope out of the drawer, opened it, and took out the letter.

September 1991

Julia,

I have survived the folly of men. I was the only one to escape from a very sad adventure. As I wrote to you in my last letter, we had finally set off in search of Massoud. But in the thunder of the explosion that still resonates inside of me, I forgot why I ever wanted to meet him in the first place. I forgot about the fervor that possessed me and made me want to film his side of the story. The only thing I could see was the hatred from which I narrowly escaped and which had taken the lives of my companions. The villagers picked me up from the wreckage, twenty yards from the spot where I should have perished. I'll never know why the blast only projected me through the air, while it tore the others to pieces. They had thought I was dead and laid my body on a little cart. If that boy hadn't given in to his temptation to take my watch, and if he hadn't overcome his fear, if my arm hadn't moved and the child hadn't started screaming, they probably would have buried me. But, like I said, I survived the folly of men.

People say that, when death leans in to kiss you, your entire life passes before your eyes. But I can tell you, when death fixes its lips on yours, you see nothing of the sort. In my feverish delirium, I saw only your face. I wish I could make you jealous and tell you that the nurse who took care of me was a beautiful young woman, but he was a man with a long beard, and there was nothing beautiful about him, except his devotion. I spent the last four months on a hospital bed in Kabul. My body is severely burned, but I'm not writing to you to complain.

It's been five months since I've sent you a letter. Five months is a long time, after writing each other twice a week. Five months of silence, almost half a year—it seems even longer because we haven't seen or touched each other in such a long time. It's funny how hard it is to love somebody from a distance, which brings up the question that haunts me each day.

Knapp flew to Kabul as soon as he heard the news. You should have seen him cry when he came into the ward. I have to admit, I cried a little, too. Luckily, my neighbor in the next bed was sleeping *the sleep of the just, otherwise I don't know what he would have thought of the two of us crying like that amid such fearless soldiers. If Knapp didn't call you right away to tell you I was alive, it's because I asked him not to. I knew he had told you I was dead, and I decided it was up to me to tell you I'd survived. Maybe there's another reason why I asked him not to tell you. Perhaps in choosing to write you this letter, I wanted to leave you free to continue mourning our relationship—that is, if you have already started.*

Julia, our love was born out of our differences, and our shared thirst for discovery whetted every morning we woke up at each other's side. Speaking of mornings—you'll never guess the number of hours I spent watching you sleep, watching you smile. Because you smile when you sleep, even if you don't know it. You'll never guess the number of times you curled up against me, speaking words that I never understood. One hundred times, exactly.

Julia, I know that building a life together is another story. I hated your father, so I have tried to understand him. Would I have acted like him in his place, under the same circumstances? If we had a daughter together, and if I was left alone with her, and she ran off with a foreigner who lived in a world where everything was strange to me and terrified me, maybe I would have acted like he did. I never wanted to tell you about all of those years I lived behind the wall. I didn't want to ruin a single second of our time together with memories from that absurd period. You deserved more than sad memories about the worst things that men are capable of. But your father must have known about those things, and they probably didn't figure in the future he had planned for you.

I hated your father for taking you away, for leaving me standing with a bloody face in our bedroom, powerless to hold on to you. I punched the walls where your voice still echoed, but I wanted to understand. How could I tell you that I loved you, without having at least tried?

Forces beyond your control pulled you back to your life. Do you remember how you always talked about the signs that fate sends us? I never believed in such things before, but I've ended up seeing things your way, even if, while writing you this letter tonight, the signs are not good.

I loved you so much just as you were, and I never wanted you to be somebody else. I loved you so much, without really understanding it, convinced that time would make things clear. Maybe in the middle of all that love I sometimes forgot to ask if you loved me enough to accept all of the things that separated us. Maybe you never gave me the opportunity to ask you the question, and maybe you never took the time to ask yourself, either. But the time has come now, whether we like it or not.

I'm going back to Berlin tomorrow. I'll put this letter in the first mailbox I see. It will get to you in a few days, as they always do. If my math is correct, today should be the 16th or the 17th.

You'll find in this envelope a secret I've kept from you. I wish I could send you a photo of myself, but I'm not looking too great right now, and, besides, it would be a little egotistical. So I'm just sending a plane ticket. You don't have to work for months to join me anymore—that is, if you still want to. You see, I was also saving money to bring you back. I took the ticket with me to Kabul, and I meant to send it to you... But, luckily, it's an open ticket.

I'll wait for you at the Berlin airport, the last day of each month, until year's end.

If we find each other again, I solemnly swear to never take the daughter we have one day away from the man she chooses to be with. And no matter our differences, I'll stand by the guy who steals her away from me. I'll stand by my daughter because I'll have loved her mother.

Julia, I'll never be upset with you. I'll respect your choice, whatever it turns out to be. If you don't come, if on the last day of the month I have to leave the airport alone, please know that I understand. This is why I'm writing you this letter, for you to know that I'll understand.

I'll never forget the wonderful person that came into my life that November evening, an evening when hope finally returned and I scaled a wall to fall into your arms, me from the East, and you from the West.

You'll always stay in my memory as the most beautiful thing that has ever happened to me. As I write these words, I am realizing anew how much I love you.

See you soon, maybe. But, anyway, you are there, and you will always be there. Somewhere I know you are breathing, and that means so much.

I love you,

Thomas

A sleeve yellowed with time had been slipped into the envelope. Julia opened it. *Fräulein Julia Walsh, New York–Paris–Berlin, 29 September 1991* had been typed on the red carbon paper of a plane ticket. Julia put it back in the desk drawer. She cracked open the window and lay down on her bed. With her arms behind her head, she stayed that way for a long time, just staring at her bedroom curtains. Upon the two panels of cloth, the shadows of her old friends came back to visit from bygone moments of solitude.

*

As morning shifted into afternoon, Julia left her room and went downstairs to the pantry. She opened the cupboard where Wallace kept the jam, grabbed a package of Melba toast and a jar of honey, and sat down at the kitchen table. She looked at the mark of a spoon left behind in the unctuous jelly. It was a strange indentation, probably left there during Anthony Walsh's last breakfast in this house. She imagined him sitting in the place where she was sitting now, alone in that enormous kitchen with his coffee mug before him, reading his newspaper. What had he been thinking about that day? The mark was a curious testimony from a past that would never return. Why did such a harmless detail make her realize, suddenly, and for the first time, that her father was dead? Sometimes it takes something small, an object or a smell, to bring back the memory of a person who is gone. Suddenly, in the middle of that huge room, for the first time, she missed her childhood, miserable though it had been. She heard her father clearing his throat and looked up to see him standing in the door, smiling at her.

"May I come in?" he said, sitting down across from her.

"Make yourself at home."

"I had that sent from France. It's made from lavender blossoms. Do you still like honey as much as you used to?"

"As you can see, some things never change."

"What did he say in that letter?"

"I don't think that's any of your business."

"Have you made a decision?"

"About what?"

"You know very well. Are you going to write back to him?"

"Twenty years later is a little late, don't you think?"

"Are you asking me or are you asking yourself?"

"Thomas is probably married with children. What right do I have to reappear in his life?"

"A boy? A girl? Twins maybe?"

"What?"

"I'm just wondering if your psychic skills also allow you to know what his charming family looks like. So what is it, a girl or a boy?

"What's your point?"

"Only this morning you thought he was dead. I think you may be jumping to conclusions about what he's done with his life."

"It's been twenty years, for Christ's sake, not six months."

"Seventeen years. Enough to have been divorced several times—that is, unless he switched sides, like your antique-dealer friend. What was his name again? Stanley? That's it, like Stanley."

"You have a lot of nerve to be making jokes."

"Humor is a wonderful defense when reality smacks you in the face. I don't know who said that, but it's true. Let me ask you again. Have you made a decision?"

"There's no decision to make. It's much too late now. You're probably relieved, aren't you?"

"Too late only happens once things are certain. It's too late for me to tell your mother everything that I wanted her to know before she died. It would have made me so happy if she had written me one last letter before she lost touch with reality. As far as you and I are concerned, too late will be Saturday, when I run down like a common battery-operated toy. But Thomas is still alive, and I'm sorry to have to contradict you, but, no, it is most definitely not too late. Think back to how you reacted when you saw that drawing yesterday. That's what brought us back here this morning. Don't hide behind the pretext that it's too late. Find another excuse, if you must."

"What are you getting at?"

"Nothing. You, however, should be looking for Thomas, unless…"

"Unless what?"

"Never mind. Excuse me. I just talk, talk, talk, but you're the one who's right."

"That's the first time I've heard you say I'm right about something. I'm curious to know—what am I right about?"

"Never mind, I said. It's so much easier to just keep whining and complaining about what could have been. I can already hear the usual nonsense: 'Destiny had other things in store for us. That's just the way it is.' Or, better yet: 'Everything is my father's fault. He ruined my entire life.' Just go on living your drama. It's certainly one way of living."

"God, you scared me. For a minute there I thought you were taking me seriously."

"Given the way you've been acting, the risk of that happening is minimal."

"Even if I were dying to write to Thomas, and even if I finally managed to find his address to send him a letter seventeen years after the fact, I would never do a thing like that to Adam. That would be horrible. Don't you think he's had his share of lies for the week?"

"Absolutely," responded Anthony, his voice heavy with sarcasm.

"What's that supposed to mean?"

"You're right. Lying through omission is much better, much more honest. And, besides, that way you'll share something. He won't be the only person you've ever lied to."

"And who would the other person be?"

"Yourself. Every evening that you lie in bed next to him with even the smallest thought of your old friend from the East, there you go, a little lie. A miniscule instant of regret, and there's another little lie. Each time you ask yourself if maybe you should have gone back to Berlin so that you could move on with a clear conscience, you'll lie to yourself again. Let me add it up; I was always strong in math. Let's say you tell yourself three little lies a week, along with two memories from your past and three comparisons made between Thomas and Adam… That's three plus two plus three, which makes eight, multiplied by fifty-two weeks, multiplied by thirty years of marriage—that's optimistic, I know—that makes 12,480 lies. Not bad for one marriage!"

"Bravo. Impressive talent," retorted Julia, applauding cynically.

"Don't you think that living with somebody when you're not sure about your feelings for them is a lie, a betrayal? Do you have the least idea what it's like when life takes a turn and the person you're with becomes a stranger?"

"Because you do?"

"Your mother called me 'sir' for the last three years of her life. When I went into her bedroom, she would show me to the toilet, thinking I was the plumber. Is that clear enough for you?"

"Mom really called you 'sir'?"

"On good days. On bad days she just called the police because a stranger had broken into the house."

"You really wish she had written you before…?"

"Don't be afraid to say it. Before she lost her mind? The answer is yes, but we're not here to talk about your mother."

Anthony looked at his daughter with a long, penetrating gaze.

"So, is the honey good?"

"Yes," she said, biting into a piece of toast.

"A little firmer than usual, don't you think?"

"Yes, a little firmer."

"The bees got lazy when you left home."

"Maybe," she said, smiling. "You want to talk about bees?"

"Why not?"

"Did you miss her?"

"Of course! What a question."

"Was Mom the woman you jumped into the gutter full of water for?"

Anthony fished around in his jacket pocket and pulled out an envelope. He slid it across the table to Julia.

"What's that?"

"Two tickets for Berlin, with a layover in Paris. There's still no direct flight. We take off at 5 p.m. You can go by yourself, not go at all, or I can come with you. It's up to you. That's new, too, isn't it?"

"Why did you do that?"

"What did you do with that piece of paper?"

"What paper?"

"That note from Thomas that you kept with you. It always appeared like magic whenever you emptied your pockets. A little piece of crumpled paper that always reminded me of how I had hurt you."

"I lost it."

"What did it say? Did you really lose it?"

"That's what I just said."

"I don't believe you. Those kinds of things never disappear entirely. They come back one day, at the bottom of your heart. Go on, go pack your bag."

Anthony got up to leave. On his way out the door, he turned around.

"Hurry up! You don't need to go back to your place. If you need something, we'll buy it over there. We don't have much time. I'll wait for you outside. I've already called the car. Huh, I just had a feeling of déjà vu when I said that."

Julia heard her father's footsteps in the front hall.

She held her head and sighed. Through her fingers, she looked at the jar of honey sitting on the table. She should go to Berlin, not to find Thomas, but to take one last trip with her father. She swore to herself, as sincerely as possible, that it wasn't a pretext or an excuse. Adam would certainly understand one day.

Back in her room, as she was picking up the bag she had left at the foot of her bed, her eyes fell on the bookshelf. The history book with the red cover sat farther out on the shelf than the others. She hesitated a moment, then picked it up, and pulled out a blue envelope hidden inside its cover. She put the envelope in her bag, shut the window, and left the room.

*

Anthony and Julia arrived at the airport just as the
check-in for their flight was closing. The woman behind the counter gave them their boarding passes and
advised them to hurry. At this late hour, she couldn't
guarantee that they'd arrive at the gate before the
final boarding call.

"It's hopeless with my leg," declared Anthony,
looking upset.

"Do you have difficulty walking, sir?" asked the
young woman worriedly.

"At my age, it's unfortunately one problem
among many," he replied proudly, presenting the
certificate for his pacemaker.

"Wait right here," she said, picking up her phone.

A few moments later, an electric golf cart drove
them to the boarding gate for their flight to Paris.
With an escort from the airline, getting through security was a cinch.

"Are you malfunctioning again?" Julia asked as
they sped down the long corridors of the airport terminal.

"Keep it down, for God's sake. You'll give us
away!" hissed Anthony. "There's nothing wrong
with my leg."

He picked up his conversation with the driver as
though he were truly fascinated by the minutiae of
the airport employee's life. Barely ten minutes later,

Anthony and his daughter were the first to board.

While two flight attendants helped Anthony Walsh get comfortable—one placing cushions behind his back, the other offering him a blanket—Julia went back to the door of the airplane. She told the flight attendant that she had one last phone call to make. Her father was on board, and she'd be back in a few moments. She ran back up the gangway and took out her cell phone.

"So how's our mysterious Canadian journey coming along?" asked Stanley as he picked up.

"I'm at the airport."

"You're coming back already?"

"No, I'm leaving again."

"Sorry, princess, I seem to have lost you a few moves back."

"I came back to the city this morning but didn't have the time to come see you. I swear to God I really needed to see you."

"And where might we be headed on the next leg of our adventures? Oklahoma? Exotic Nebraska?"

"Stanley, if you found an unopened letter from Edward written just before he died, would you read it?"

"I've told you, Julia, he used his last words to say he loved me. What more could I need to know? Other excuses? More regrets? Those few words meant more than all of the things we forgot to tell each other."

"So you would just put the letter back where you found it?"

"I think so. But I've never found any letters from Edward in our apartment. He didn't write much, you know, not even a grocery list. I always wrote the grocery list. You can't imagine how mad it made me back then, and yet, twenty years later, I still buy his favorite brand of yogurt every time I go to the supermarket. It's idiotic to remember that kind of thing so long after the fact, isn't it?"

"Maybe not…"

"You found a letter from Thomas, is that it? You always ask me about Edward when you're thinking about him. Open it!"

"Why? Because you wouldn't?"

"It's a pity that, after twenty years of friendship, you still haven't realized I am anything but a good example. Open that letter today. Read it tomorrow, if you'd rather. But don't you dare destroy it. I think I lied to you just now. If Edward had left me a letter, I'd have read it a hundred times, for hours on end, just to be sure I understood every word. Even though I know full well that he would never have taken the time to write me one. Can you tell me where you're going? I'm dying to know what area code I'll be able to reach you at this evening."

"You'll have to wait until tomorrow. And dial 011 first."

"You're going abroad?"

"To Germany. Berlin."

There was a moment of silence. Stanley took a deep breath, before continuing with their conversation.

"What did you learn from the letter, which you obviously have already opened."

"He's still alive!"

"Of course…" sighed Stanley. "And now you're calling me from the airport to ask me if you're right to be setting off in search of him?"

"I'm calling you from the gateway to the plane… And I think you just answered my question."

"Well, then hurry up, silly! Don't miss that plane!"

"Stanley?"

"What now?"

"Are you mad at me?"

"No, of course not. I just hate thinking of you being so far away, that's all. Do you have any more stupid questions?"

"How do you…"

"Answer your questions before you ask them? Local gossips would tell you that it's because I'm a better woman than you are. But you have the right to know it's because I'm your best friend. Now get out of here before I realize how much I miss you."

"I'll call you when I get there. I promise."

"Sure, sure."

The flight attendant motioned to Julia that it was

time to get on the plane. The crew was waiting for her so they could close the cabin door. By the time Stanley remembered to ask what to say to Adam if he called, Julia had already hung up.

14.

After the meal trays had been cleared away, the flight attendant lowered the lights, plunging the cabin into semidarkness. Since the beginning of their borrowed time together, Julia had never seen her father touch a piece of food or sleep. She hadn't even seen him resting. It was probably normal for a machine, but it was a strange idea to get used to, especially since these were the details that reminded her they had only a few days to make up for lost time. Most of the passengers slept; a few watched movies on the little seat-back screens. In the last row, a man did paperwork by the glow of his overhead light. Anthony leafed through a newspaper, and Julia looked out her window at the silvery reflection of the moon on the wing of the airplane, and the ocean below, rippling in the blue night.

*

That spring, I decided not to go back to art school or to Paris. You did everything you could to dissuade me, but my decision was made. Like you, I would become a journalist. And, like you, I set out the next morning in search of work, even though it was a hopeless cause for an American girl. A few days before, the streetcar lines had been restored, linking both sides of the city, as they had in the past. Everything around us was changing. People talked about the reunification of your country, that it might be whole again, like before, when everything in life hadn't revolved around the Cold War. Those who had worked for the secret police seemed to have evaporated overnight, taking their archives with them. A few months earlier, they had tried to destroy all of the compromising paperwork, the files that had been created about you and millions of your fellow citizens. You were among the first to protest, in an attempt to stop them from doing so.

Did you also have a number on a file? Does it still lie in a secret archive, hiding photos of you stolen in the street or at work, the names of your friends, the name of your grandmother? Could your childhood years really have stirred the authorities' suspicion? I wonder how we could have let it all happen, after all of the painful lessons learned in the last war. Was it the only way for our world to get its revenge? You and I, we were born far too late to hate each other. We had too much to invent together. In the evening, when we walked around your neighborhood, I saw that you were often still afraid. Your fear gripped you every time you saw a uniform or a car that drove too slowly for your liking. "Come on, let's not stay here," you'd say, and you'd take me to the shelter of the first side street, the first staircase where we could escape, throwing an invisible enemy off our scent. When I made fun of you, you'd become angry and tell me that I didn't understand anything, that I had no idea what they had been capable of. So many times I caught you examining the faces of the people eating in a restaurant where I'd taken you. So many times you said we had to leave—a somber face in the dining room had reminded you of your disquieting past. Forgive me, Thomas, you were right. I never knew what it was to be afraid. Forgive me for giggling when you forced me to hide under the pilings of that bridge with you because a military truck was crossing the river. I never knew; I could never understand. No one in my life before you could have either.

When you'd point at somebody in the streetcar, I knew from your eyes that you had recognized a former member of the secret police.

Stripped of their uniforms, without their authority and arrogance, the former Stasi melted into the city and became accustomed to the banal lives of those they had once followed, spied on, judged, and even tortured, sometimes for years. After the wall came down, most of them invented a past for themselves, so they would not be identified. Others quietly continued their careers. For many, any sense of remorse they might once have had evaporated as the months passed and the memory of the crimes they had committed faded away.

I remember an evening when we went to see Knapp. The three of us took a walk in the park, and Knapp wouldn't stop asking you questions, not realizing how difficult it was for you to answer them. He believed the wall had cast its shadow on the West, where he was, but you cried out that the shadow fell on the East, where you had been a prisoner of its concrete. How did you get used to living like that, he kept asking. You smiled and asked him if he had really forgotten everything. Knapp persisted, and you finally capitulated, answering his questions. Patiently, you talked to him about a time when everything was organized, secure, when nobody had to take responsibility, when the risk of doing something wrong was very remote. "We had zero percent unemployment, and the state was omnipresent," you said with a shrug. "That's how a dictatorship works," Knapp concluded.

It was convenient for a lot of people. Freedom is a huge risk, and while most men aspire to freedom, they don't know how to use it. I can still remember you telling us, in that café in West Berlin, that behind the wall in the East everyone found a way of reinventing their lives inside their cozy apartments. Knapp tainted the exchange by asking how many people you thought had collaborated with the secret police during the dark years. The two of you never agreed on a number. Knapp imagined thirty percent, at most. You said you had no idea, justifying your ignorance by the fact that you had never worked for the Stasi.

Forgive me, Thomas, you were right. It has taken me until now, until this journey back toward you, for me to finally know fear.

*

"Why didn't you invite me to your wedding?" asked Anthony Walsh, lowering his newspaper to his lap.

Julia jumped, startled.

"I'm sorry. I didn't mean to scare you. Were you lost in your thoughts?"

"No, I was just looking outside, that's all."

"There's nothing out there but the night," replied Anthony, after leaning over to peer through the little window.

"But there's a full moon."

"We're a little too high to jump in the water and make our wishes come true, don't you think?"

"I sent you an invitation."

"Just like the one you sent to two hundred other people. That isn't exactly what I call inviting your father. I'm the one who was supposed to walk you to the altar. We might have needed to talk about it in person beforehand."

"What have you and I talked about during the past twenty years? Not much. I was waiting for you to call me. I was hoping you would ask me to introduce you to my future husband."

"I thought I'd already met him."

"A chance encounter on an escalator at Bloomingdale's is not what I'd call a real introduction. It certainly wasn't enough to know whether you had any interest in him or in my life in general."

"The three of us went and had tea together, if I remember correctly."

"Because I suggested it, and because he wanted to get to know you. It lasted all of twenty minutes, during which you monopolized the conversation."

"He wasn't very talkative. He was practically autistic. I thought he was mute."

"Did you take the time to ask him a single question?"

"And you, Julia, have you ever asked any questions? Have you ever asked me for my advice?"

"What good would it do? I don't need to hear you tell me what you did at my age or what you thought I was supposed to be doing. I could stay silent to the end of time if it meant I might finally make you understand that I never wanted to be like you."

"Maybe you should try to get some sleep," said

Anthony Walsh. "Tomorrow will be a long day. As soon as we land in Paris, we'll have to take another plane to Berlin."

He tucked Julia's blanket around her shoulders and went back to his newspaper.

*

Their plane had just landed on the runway at Charles de Gaulle Airport. Anthony set his watch to Paris time.

"We have two hours to catch our connecting flight. That should be plenty."

Anthony was not aware that their plane, which was supposed to arrive in Terminal E, had been directed to a gate in Terminal F, which did not have a jet way compatible with their particular jet. For that reason, the flight attendant explained, a bus would be coming to pick them up and take them to Terminal B.

Anthony raised his hand and motioned to the chief of the cabin crew to come see him.

"Terminal E!" he corrected.

"Excuse me?" the flight attendant replied.

"In the announcement, you just said we'd be taken by bus to Terminal B, but from what I understood we're currently at Terminal E.

"It's entirely possible," he responded. "We get lost ourselves sometimes."

"Reassure me, we are at de Gaulle, right?"

"Three different terminals, no gangway, and the bus still hasn't arrived—where else could we be?!"

Forty-five minutes after landing, they finally left the airplane. They still had to pass through immigration and find the gate for their flight to Berlin.

Two immigration officers were responsible for checking the passports of passengers arriving on three different flights. Anthony looked at the time on the display board.

"With two hundred people ahead of us in line, we'll never make it in time."

"We'll just take the next flight," replied Julia.

With the passport check finally behind them, they ran through an interminable series of hallways and rolling walkways.

"We could have come by foot from New York," groaned Anthony.

Just after the sentence left his mouth, he collapsed.

Julia tried to catch him, but his fall was so sudden there was nothing she could do. The conveyor belt continued moving, dragging Anthony along with it.

"Daddy, Daddy! Wake up!" she screamed, frightened and shaking him.

Another traveler hurried over to help Julia. They lifted up Anthony's body and set him down a little farther on. The man took off his coat and slid it under Anthony's head. He still wasn't moving. The man suggested they call a doctor.

"No, certainly not," insisted Julia. "It's nothing. He's just dizzy. It happens sometimes. I'm used to it."

"Are you sure? Your husband doesn't look very well."

"He's my father! He's diabetic," Julia lied. "Daddy, wake up," she said, shaking him again.

"Let me take his pulse."

"Don't touch him!" shouted Julia in a panic.

Anthony opened an eye.

"Where are we?" he asked, trying to sit up.

The man who had come to their rescue helped him to his feet. Anthony put a hand out against the wall while he found his balance.

"What time is it?"

"Are you sure he's okay? He doesn't seem to be very with it."

"I beg your pardon!" retorted Anthony, suddenly regaining his strength.

The good Samaritan picked up his coat and left.

"You could have at least thanked him," Julia reproached her father.

"For what? Dragging me a few miserable feet and then feigning a little first aid?"

"You're impossible, you know that? You scared me to death."

"Come on, it was nothing. What could happen to me? I'm already dead!" Anthony chided.

"Do you know what happened?"

"A faulty contact in one of my switchboards, I guess, or some kind of interference. We should tell the manufacturer. It's going to be tedious if my system starts shutting down every time somebody plays with their iPhone."

"I'll never be able to explain this to anyone else."

"Was I dreaming, or did you call me Daddy just a few minutes ago?"

"Certainly dreaming!" she replied, leading him toward their gate.

They had only fifteen minutes to get through security.

"Damn it!" said Anthony, after opening his passport.

"What is it now?"

"The certificate showing I have a pacemaker is gone. I can't find it anymore."

"It must be in one of your pockets."

"I just checked them all. It's nowhere."

Vexed, he looked at the metal detectors up ahead of him.

"If I walk through those, I'll have the security officers all over me."

"So keep looking for that letter," Julia said impatiently.

"I told you, I've lost it. It must have fallen out in the plane when I gave my suit jacket to the flight attendant. I'm sorry, but I really don't know what we can do."

"We didn't come all this way just to turn around and go back to New York. And, besides, how would we even do that?"

Anthony suggested they get a hotel room for the night. "Let's rent a car and drive into the city. I'll figure something out by the time we get there. In two hours, people in New York will be awake. You can just call my doctor and have him fax you a duplicate."

"Doesn't he know that you're dead?"

"God, how stupid of me! I forgot to tell him!"

"Why don't we just take a taxi?" she asked.

"A taxi in Paris? You really don't know this town."

"You have an opinion about everything, don't you?"

"I don't think now is the time for a fight. I can see the rental counters from here. A little car will be fine… Except, no, we really should have a sedan… It's a question of comfort."

Julia ceded to his wishes. Just past noon, she was driving down a ramp onto highway A1 into Paris. Anthony leaned forward, attentively watching the signs along the highway.

"Turn right," he ordered.

"Paris is to the left. It's marked in capital letters."

"Thank you very much. I can still read. Do what I tell you!" railed Anthony, reaching over her and forcing her to turn the steering wheel.

"Are you out of your mind? What the hell are you doing!" she screamed as their car swerved dangerously.

It was now too late for them to change lanes. Amid a concert of angry honking, Julia found herself driving north.

"Great. Now we're headed to Brussels. Paris is behind us."

"I know. And if you're not too tired to drive straight through, 370 miles past Brussels comes Berlin. We'll make it in nine hours, if my calculations are correct. At worst, we'll take a break along the way so you can sleep a bit. There's no security checkpoint on the highway, so it solves our first problem. We don't have a lot of time left. We have only four days before we have to go back, if I don't break down before then."

"You had this all planned before we rented the car. That's why you insisted on a sedan, isn't it?"

"Do you want to see Thomas again, or not? Then drive. I don't have to give you directions, do I? You ought to remember!"

Julia turned the volume on the radio up as far as it would go and accelerated.

*

Twenty years later, the highway route had been altered, and the scenery along the way had changed.

In two hours, they reached Brussels. Anthony wasn't very talkative. From time to time he would grumble under his breath while gazing out at the landscape. Julia took advantage of his distracted state to tilt the rearview mirror toward him so she could watch him unnoticed. Anthony turned down the radio.

"Were you happy in art school?" he asked, breaking the silence.

"I didn't stay there very long, but I loved where I lived. The view from my room was incredible. My desk looked out over the roof of the observatory."

"I loved Paris, too. I have a lot of memories there. I'd even say it's the town where I would have liked to die."

Julia coughed.

"What?" asked Anthony. "You have a very strange look on your face. Have I said something I shouldn't have again?"

"No, no…"

"Yes I have. I can see you're bothered."

"It's just that… It's not easy to say. It's so bizarre…"

"Don't make me beg. Tell me."

"You did die in Paris, Daddy."

"Really? I did?" exclaimed Anthony with surprise. "I hadn't the slightest idea."

"You don't remember anything?"

"The program that transferred my memory stops at my departure for Europe. After that it's just a blackout. I suppose it's better that way. It's probably not very fun to remember one's own death. I'm beginning to realize that the limited lifespan of this machine isn't just necessary because of the families…"

"I know," replied Julia uncomfortably.

"I highly doubt it. Believe me, this situation isn't strange just for you. As more and more time passes, it gets unnerving for me as well. What day is it today, again?"

"Wednesday."

"Three days… Do you know how loud the ticking is when the second hand is literally turning inside your head? You know how I am…"

"It was a heart attack at a stoplight."

"At least it wasn't green… I could have caused an accident."

"It was green."

"Shit. Of course it was."

"You didn't cause an accident, if that's any comfort."

"To be completely honest, it doesn't comfort me in the least. Did I suffer?"

"No. They said you died instantly."

"Yeah, they always tell the family that, to console them. And what does it really matter in the end? It's over and done with. Who remembers the way that people die? It's already something to be remembered for the way you lived."

"Can we talk about something else?" begged Julia.

"Whatever you like. I think it's a trip to talk to someone about my own death."

"The 'someone' in question here is your daughter, and, frankly, you don't seem to be having much fun."

"Don't start being right about things…not now."

An hour later, the car crossed into the Netherlands. Germany was only forty-five miles away.

"It's crazy how things work between the countries here now," Anthony continued. "No more borders… You'd almost think you were free. If you were so happy in Paris, why did you leave?"

"It was just a spur-of-the-moment thing, in the middle of the night. I thought I'd be gone a couple of days. In the beginning, it was just a road trip with some friends."

"Had you known them for long?"

"Ten minutes."

"I might have known. And what did these old friends of yours do?"

"They were students like me, except they were at the Sorbonne."

"Okay. And why did you decide to go to Germany? Spain or Italy would have been more fun, don't you think?"

"We wanted to see a revolution. Antoine and Mathias had a feeling that the wall was going to come down. We knew that something important was taking place, though maybe not the full extent of it, and we wanted to be there to see it happen."

"What did I do wrong in raising you that you wanted to see a revolution?" asked Anthony, tapping his knee.

"I wouldn't be too concerned, if I were you. It's probably the only thing you did right."

"That's one way of looking at it," muttered Anthony, turning back toward his window.

"Why are you asking me all this now?"

"Because you never ask me anything! I loved Paris because it was there that I kissed your mother for the first time. And I can tell you, it wasn't easy."

"I'm not sure I need to know the details."

"If you only knew how pretty she was then. We were just twenty-five years old."

"How did you manage to go to Paris? I thought you were completely broke when you were young."

"When I was drafted, in 1959, I served on a military base in Europe."

"Where was that?"

"Berlin. I don't have the fondest memory of it, either."

Anthony turned his gaze back to the passing landscape.

"You don't have to look at my reflection in the window, you know. I'm sitting right next to you," said Julia.

"Well, then you can also put your rearview mirror back where it belongs, so the next time you pass a truck you can see the cars behind you."

"You met Mom in Paris?"

"No, we really only crossed paths in France. When I finished my service, I took a train to Paris. I wanted to see the Eiffel Tower before I went home to the States."

"And it was love at first sight."

"It's not bad... Not as tall as the Empire State, though."

"I was talking about Mom."

"She was a dancer in a big cabaret revue—the perfect cliché of a homesick American GI's fantasies."

"Mom was a dancer?"

"She was a Bluebell Girl! Her troupe had a special, limited engagement show at the Lido on the Champs-Elysées. A friend of mine got us tickets. Your mother was the lead dancer. You should have seen her tap-dancing up there onstage—she put Ginger Rogers to shame."

"Why didn't she ever say anything about it?"

"We're not a very chatty family. That's at least one trait you seem to have inherited."

"How did you meet her?"

"I thought you didn't want to hear the details. If you slow down a little, I'll tell you."

"I'm not driving fast," Julia replied as the speedometer's needle flirted with 85 miles per hour.

"That's a matter of opinion. I'm more accustomed

to American highways, where we have time to watch the scenery. If you keep driving this fast, you'll need a monkey wrench to remove my fingers from the door handle."

Julia took her foot off of the accelerator. Anthony breathed more easily.

"I had a table right up against the stage. The show played ten nights in a row, and I didn't miss a single one, including the extra Sunday matinee. I bribed an usher with a generous tip so I'd always be seated in the same place."

Julia turned off the radio.

"For the last time, straighten that mirror and watch the highway!" commanded Anthony.

Julia did so without protesting.

"By the sixth day, your mother had figured out what was going on. In later years, she swore that she'd noticed on the fourth day, but I'm sure it wasn't until the sixth. Anyway, I'd caught her looking at me several times during the show. I don't mean to brag, but she almost missed a step. Your mother always insisted it was some other distraction and that it had nothing to do with me. Refusing to admit the truth was your mother's way of flirting. So I sent flowers to her dressing room, where she'd find them after the show. Every evening I sent the same little bouquet of old-fashioned roses, but never with a card."

"Why?"

"I'll tell you if you stop interrupting me. After the last show, I went to wait for her at the stage door. I wore a boutonniere—a simple rose, the same kind as the ones I'd sent her."

"I can't believe you did that!" Julia blurted out, bursting into laughter.

Anthony turned away and was silent.

"And then?" Julia insisted.

"No, that's all. End of story."

"What do you mean, 'end of story'?"

"You'll just keep making fun of me. I'm done."

"I wasn't making fun of you!"

"Then what was that idiotic giggling?"

"Exactly the opposite of what you thought it was. I just never imagined you as a hopeless romantic."

"Stop at the next service station. I'll walk to Berlin alone," said Anthony, grumpily crossing his arms.

"Finish the story or I'll drive faster."

"Your mother was used to admirers waiting for her after the show. There was a guard who escorted the dancers to the bus that took them back to the hotel. And, like I said, after the last show, I waited for her, standing in the way. He pushed me aside a little too roughly, and it set me off, so I punched him."

Julia couldn't help herself and broke into peals of laughter.

"Fine! If that's how it's going to be, you're not getting another word."

"I'm sorry, Daddy," she said breathlessly. "Please, I can't help myself."

Anthony turned and looked at her attentively.

"That time I wasn't dreaming. Did you just call me Daddy?"

"Maybe I did," said Julia, drying her eyes. "Go on!"

"I'm warning you, Julia, if you even so much as smile, it's over. Do you understand?"

"I promise," she said, lifting her right hand.

"Your mother got involved, and she took me aside, telling the bus driver to wait for her a moment. She asked me what I was doing there at every show, sitting at the same table. I think that, at that moment, she still hadn't noticed the old-fashioned white rose I was wearing, so I gave it to her. She was stunned when she realized that I was the one who had been sending the same flowers every night, so I took advantage of the pause and asked her a question."

"What did you ask her?"

"I asked her to marry me."

Julia turned and looked at her father, who told her to concentrate on the road.

"Your mother started laughing, making the same sound you do when you're making fun of me. When she realized I was serious, she told the driver to leave without her and suggested I begin by taking her to dinner. We walked to a brasserie on the

Champs-Elysées. I can't tell you how proud I was to be walking down the most beautiful avenue in the world by her side. You should have seen the way everybody looked at her. We talked the whole dinner long, but at the end of the meal, I found myself in a terrible situation and thought that all my hopes would evaporate on the spot."

"I can't imagine what could be worse, after already having proposed to her."

"I didn't have any money to pay for dinner. It was so embarrassing. I checked my pockets as discreetly as possible, but I didn't have a penny. My savings from the army had all gone to pay for tickets to the Lido and old-fashioned roses."

"What did you do?"

"I ordered a seventh cup of coffee. The brasserie was closing, and your mother left the table to powder her face. I called over the waiter. I'd decided to confess that I didn't have any money. I was ready to beg him not to make a scene and to give him my watch and passport in security, promising that I'd pay the bill as soon as possible, the end of the week at the latest. He handed me a little tray, instead of the bill, and on it there was a note from your mother."

"What did it say?"

Anthony opened his wallet and took out a yellowed scrap of paper, which he unfolded and read in a subdued voice.

I've never been good at goodbyes, and I'm sure you're not, either. Thank you for a wonderful evening. Old-fashioned roses are my favorite. We'll be performing in Manchester at the end of February, and I would be thrilled to see your face in the audience. If you can make it, I'll let you pay for our next dinner.

"See?" Anthony concluded by showing the scrap to Julia. "It's signed with your mother's name."

"That's impressive!" Julia said with a whistle. "Why did she do that?"

"Because your mother understood the situation I was in."

"How's that?"

"She knew what it meant when a guy drinks seven cups of coffee at two in the morning and can't find anything to say when the restaurant lights start to go out."

"Did you go to Manchester?"

"First, I worked for a while, to earn some money. I had three jobs, one after another. At five in the morning, I started by unloading trucks in the market. When I was done there, I went to a café in the neighborhood and waited tables. At noon, I took off my apron and put on a clerk's uniform, to work in a grocery store. I lost ten pounds, but I earned enough money to go to England and buy a ticket to the theater where your mother was dancing, and, most of all, to buy her a real meal afterward. Against all odds, I managed to get a seat in the front row again. As soon as the curtains rose, she smiled at me.

"After the show, we met in an old pub. I was exhausted. I'm ashamed just thinking of it, but I fell asleep at one point, and I know that your mother noticed. We hardly talked at all that evening. We exchanged silences, not conversation. When I asked the waiter to bring the check, your mother looked at me and said simply, 'Yes.' I looked back at her, curious, and she repeated that 'yes' with a voice so clear that I can still hear it. 'Yes, I'd like to marry you.'

"The revue was supposed to stay in Manchester for two months. Your mother said goodbye to her friends, and we took a boat back to the States and got married as soon as we arrived. There was just the priest and two witnesses we'd found in the waiting room. None of our family had come. My father never forgave me for marrying a dancer."

With care, Anthony put the dog-eared scrap of paper back in its place.

"Look! I found my pacemaker letter. I'm such an idiot. Instead of putting it back in my passport, I put it in my wallet."

Julia nodded absently.

"Going to Berlin was just your way of extending our time together, wasn't it?"

"You know me so little you need to ask?"

"And the rental car and the lost pacemaker

certificate, you did all that on purpose, so that we'd have this drive together?"

"Even if I planned it all, it's not such a bad thing, is it?"

A sign up ahead indicated they were entering Germany. Her face grown somber, Julia adjusted the rearview mirror.

"What's wrong? Why aren't you talking anymore?" asked Anthony.

"The day before you turned up in our room and punched Thomas in the face, we had decided to get married. It never happened, though. My father couldn't stand the idea of me marrying a man who wasn't from his world."

Anthony turned back to the window.

15.

They hadn't spoken a word to each other since entering Germany. From time to time Julia would turn up the volume on the radio, only to have Anthony turn it down just as quickly. A pine forest appeared on the horizon. At the forest's edge, a wall of concrete blocks cut off access to a road that was once a detour. In the distance, Julia recognized the gloomy, hulking forms of the former Marienborn border inspection buildings, which had since been converted into a memorial.

"How did you and your friends get across the border?" asked Anthony, gazing at the abandoned watchtowers rolling past on their right.

"By the seat of our pants. One of the guys I was traveling with was a diplomat's son, and we said we were going to visit his parents, who were posted in West Berlin."

Anthony laughed.

"Particularly ironic for you, no? Run away from your real father to visit an imaginary one in Berlin?"

He rested his hands on his knees.

"I'm sorry I didn't give you that letter earlier," he continued.

"Do you mean that?"

"I don't know. I feel better for having said it, though. Could we take a break sometime soon?"

"Why?"

"It would be a good idea for you to get some rest. I'd also like to stretch my legs."

A sign indicated the next rest area was in ten miles. Julia promised to stop when they got there.

"Why did you and Mom move to Montreal?"

"We didn't have much money, especially me... Your mother had some savings, but we went through that pretty quickly. Life in New York kept getting more and more difficult. We were happy in Montreal, you know. I think those were even our best years."

"You're proud of it, aren't you?" asked Julia, her voice bittersweet.

"Proud of what?"

"Of having come from nothing and finding success."

"Aren't you? Aren't you proud of your daring? Don't you feel a sense of satisfaction when you see a kid playing with a stuffed animal that came from your imagination? You must feel proud when you see a poster hanging outside a movie theater for a film whose story you came up with."

"I'm just thankful to be happy. That's enough for me."

Julia turned into the rest area and pulled up along the sidewalk at the edge of a broad lawn. Anthony opened his door and ruffled his daughter's hair before getting out.

"You drive me crazy, Julia!" he said as he walked away.

She turned off the car and rested her head on the steering wheel.

"What on earth am I doing here?"

Anthony crossed the playground, passed a sign that read "for children only," and entered the service station. A few moments later, he came out carrying a bag of snacks and drinks, opened the back door, and put his purchases on the seat.

"Go get some air. I bought everything you'll need to recharge. I'll watch the car while you're gone."

Julia obeyed. She walked around the swing set, avoiding the sandbox, and also went into the service station. When she came back out again, Anthony was stretched out on the bottom of the playground slide, looking at the sky.

"Are you okay?" she asked him, worried.

"Do you think I'm up there somewhere?"

Thrown off by his question, Julia sat down in the grass by his side. Her gaze also wandered skyward.

"I don't know. I searched for Thomas among the clouds for a long time. I was sure I'd seen him on several occasions, and yet he's still alive."

"Your mother didn't believe in God, but I do.

Do you think I'm in heaven?"

"I'm sorry, I can't answer that question. I just can't."

"You can't believe in God?"

"I can't accept the idea that you're not here next to me, that I'm talking to you, even though you're..."

"Even though I'm dead. I told you, you have to learn not to be afraid of words. Finding the right word is important. For example, if you had told me earlier, 'Daddy, you're a bastard and an idiot who has never understood a thing about me. You're a self-centered father who has always wanted to shape me in his own image. You hurt me and told me that it was for my own good, when it was just for your own benefit,' maybe I would have heard you. Maybe we wouldn't have lost all of that time, and we would have been friends. Admit it, it would have been nice to be friends."

Julia remained silent.

"See, that's what I meant about choosing the right words. Instead of having been a good father, I would have liked to have been your friend."

"We should get back on the road," Julia said, her voice fragile.

"Let's wait a while. I think my energy reserve isn't as deep as the manufacturers promised. If I keep on going this way, our time together won't be as long as we planned."

"We can take as much time as we need. Berlin isn't that far. After twenty years, we're just a few hours away."

"Seventeen years, Julia, not twenty."

"Big difference."

"Three years of life? Yes, it is a big difference. Believe me, I know what I'm talking about."

Father and daughter lay motionless, with their hands behind their heads, she in the grass, he on the bottom of the slide, both of them scanning the sky.

An hour went by. Julia had dozed off, and Anthony was watching her sleep. Her dreams seemed peaceful. From time to time she frowned, tickled by wind blowing across her face. Anthony hesitantly pushed back a lock of her hair. When Julia finally opened her eyes, the sky was already colored by the shadows of dusk. Anthony had left her side. She looked around and recognized his silhouette seated in the front seat of their car. She put on her shoes, though she couldn't remember taking them off, and walked across the parking lot.

"Did I sleep long?" she asked, starting the car.

"Two hours, maybe a little longer. I wasn't paying attention."

"What were you doing?"

"I was waiting."

Julia drove out of the rest area and back onto the highway. Potsdam was only fifty miles away.

"It'll be dark by the time we arrive," she said.

"I have no idea how to find Thomas. I don't even know if he still lives in Berlin. After all, you basically dragged me here on a whim. Who's to say he's still around?"

"True, anything is possible. Between the rising cost of real estate, the triplets, and his in-laws moving in, they might have decided to move to a cozy little house in the country."

Julia glared at her father, who once again motioned for her to watch the road.

"It's fascinating how fear can inhibit our minds," he continued.

"What are you trying to insinuate?"

"Nothing, just thinking out loud. Speaking of which, I know it's not my business, but shouldn't you let Adam know you're alive? Do it for me, if not for him—I never want to hear Gloria Gaynor again. She was caterwauling in your purse the entire time you were asleep."

Anthony began singing a frenzied parody of "I Will Survive." Julia did her best to keep a straight face, but the louder he sang, the more she giggled. As they crossed into the outskirts of Berlin, the two of them were roaring with laughter.

Anthony gave Julia directions to the Brandenburger Hof Hotel. Upon their arrival, a bellboy welcomed them, greeting Mr. Walsh as he got out of the car. "Good evening, Mr. Walsh," said the doorman, giving the revolving door a shove. Anthony crossed the hotel lobby to the front desk, where the concierge welcomed him, also by name. At this time of year, the hotel was full, but even though Anthony didn't have a reservation, the concierge assured him that two of their very best rooms would be at his disposal. To the concierge's regret, however, they would not be on the same floor. Anthony thanked him and said it wasn't important. Giving their keys to the bellboy, the concierge asked Anthony if he wanted to make a reservation for the hotel restaurant that evening.

"Would you like to eat here?" asked Anthony, turning toward Julia. "Otherwise," he went on, "I know a great restaurant just a few minutes from here. Do you still like Chinese food as much as you used to?"

Since Julia said nothing, Anthony asked the concierge to reserve a table for two on the terrace at China Garden.

After freshening up, Julia and her father walked to the restaurant together.

"Are you in a bad mood?"

"I can't believe how much everything here has changed," Julia responded distractedly.

"Did you talk to Adam?"

"Yes, I called him from my room."

"And what did he say?"

"That he misses me, that he doesn't understand why I left like I did, or what I'm chasing. He came to look for me in Montreal, but he missed us by an hour."

"Can you imagine the look on his face if he'd seen us together?"

"He made me promise at least four times that I was alone."

"And?"

"I lied four times."

Anthony opened the restaurant door for his daughter.

"You'll end up enjoying it if you keep it up," he said, laughing.

"I don't see what's so funny about it."

"What's funny is that we're in Berlin together, looking for your first love, and you feel guilty for not telling your fiancé that you were in Montreal with your father. Maybe I'm way off the mark, but I think that's ballsy. Feminine, yet ballsy."

Anthony took advantage of the time they spent at dinner to come up with a plan. When they woke up the next morning, they would go to the offices of the press syndicate to find out if a certain Thomas Meyer was still in possession of a press pass.

On the way back from dinner, Julia led her father to the Tiergarten.

"I used to take naps there," she said, pointing to a huge tree in the distance. "It's crazy. I feel like it was just yesterday."

Anthony gave his daughter a mischievous look

and bent over, motioning for her to step into his hands for a boost over the fence.

"What are you doing?"

"Making you a stepladder. Go on, hurry up. Nobody's watching. Let's do it."

Julia didn't make him ask twice. She stepped up and climbed over the fence.

"What about you?" she asked, standing up on the other side and dusting herself off.

"I'll go through the gate," he said, pointing to an entrance just a bit farther on. "The park doesn't close until midnight. It's simpler at my age."

As soon as he rejoined Julia, he led her across the lawn, and they sat at the foot of the enormous linden tree she had shown him.

"It's funny, but I also took a few naps under this tree during my time in Germany. It was my favorite spot. Every time I was allowed a few hours of free time, I came here with a book and watched the girls walk by. At the same age, we were both in the same place, only separated by a few decades. Along with the skyscraper in Montreal, that makes two places where we have shared memories. I'm glad."

"This is where Thomas and I always came," said Julia.

"I'm beginning to like this guy more and more."

An elephant could be heard trumpeting in the distance. The Berlin Zoo was just a few yards behind them, along the edge of the park.

Anthony got up and gestured for his daughter to join him.

"You hated zoos when you were a little girl. You didn't like that the animals were in cages. Back then you wanted to become a veterinarian. You've probably forgotten it, but for your sixth birthday I gave you a big stuffed animal, an otter, if I remember correctly. I must have chosen badly, because she was always sick. You spent all of your time caring for her and trying to make her better."

"Are you trying to suggest that it's thanks to you that I drew Tilly?"

"Of course not! What role could childhood experiences possibly play in our adult lives? Given all the things you blame me for, a proven connection would only worsen my standing."

Anthony confided that he felt his strength fading at a worrisome pace. The time had come to go back. They took a taxi.

Back at the hotel, Anthony bid Julia goodnight as she stepped out of the elevator to go to her room. He stayed inside and continued on to the top floor.

Julia lay on her bed for a long while, scrolling through the numbers on the screen of her cell phone. She decided to call Adam back, but when she got his voice mail, she hung up and called Stanley.

"Have you found what you're looking for yet?" asked her friend.

"Not yet. I just got here."

"Did you take a rickshaw or something?"

"I drove from Paris. It's a long story."

"Do you miss me?" he asked.

"You don't think I'm just calling to talk about myself, do you?"

Stanley admitted that he had walked past her apartment on his way home from work. It wasn't really on his way, but his feet had unconsciously led him to the corner of Horatio and Greenwich Streets.

"It's a sad place when you're not around."

"You're just saying that to make me feel better."

"I ran into your neighbor with the shoe store."

"You talk to Mr. Zimoure?"

"Since we decided to make peace with him, yes… He was standing outside, and he waved, so I waved back."

"I can't even leave you alone for a few days, can I? You're already starting to hang out with unsavory characters."

"You know, he's really not so bad…"

"Stanley, are you trying to tell me something?"

"What?"

"I know you better than anyone. When you meet somebody and don't dislike the person from the outset, I'm already suspicious. A 'not so bad' rating for Zimoure makes me think I should come home tomorrow."

"You'll need a better excuse than that, princess. We said hello to each other, that's all. Also, Adam stopped by to see me."

"The two of you are becoming inseparable."

"He's just lonely. It's not my fault he lives two blocks from my store. And in case you're still interested, he isn't holding up very well. Just dropping by my place is already a sign that something is wrong. He misses you, Julia. He's worried, and I think you've given him good reason to be."

"I swear to God, Stanley, it's not like that at all. In fact, it's the very opposite."

"You don't have to swear anything. Would you just listen to what I'm telling you?"

"Of course," she replied without hesitation.

"You drive me crazy. Do you even know where this mysterious journey is supposed to take you?"

"No," Julia murmured into the phone.

"Well, then how can you possibly expect Adam to understand? I have to go now. It's seven here. I have a dinner to get ready for."

"With who?"

"And with whom did you dine this evening?"

"By myself…"

"You know how lies make me itch. I'm going to hang up now. Call me tomorrow. Kisses."

Julia didn't have time to respond. She heard a click and knew that Stanley was gone, probably headed in the direction of his walk-in closet.

*

A ringing sound woke Julia from her slumber. She stretched to pick up the phone but heard only a dial tone. She got up, crossed the room, and then realized she was naked. She picked up the bathrobe she had abandoned at the foot of her bed the night before, slipping into it on her way to the door.

A waiter stood patiently outside. When Julia opened the door, he pushed in a cart laden with a continental breakfast and two soft-boiled eggs.

"I didn't order anything," she said as the young man began setting up her breakfast on the coffee table.

"Three-and-a-half-minute eggs, isn't that you?"

"Yes, exactly," replied Julia, ruffling her hair.

"That's precisely what Mr. Walsh told us."

"But I'm not hungry," she added, watching the waiter carefully cut the tops off of the eggs.

"Mr. Walsh also told us you would say you weren't hungry. One last thing before I leave—he'll meet you in the front lobby at eight o'clock. That's in thirty-seven minutes," he said, consulting his watch. "Have a good day, Miss Walsh. The weather is gorgeous today. You should have a very pleasant stay in Berlin."

The waiter left Julia staring in disbelief.

She looked at the table and its spread of orange juice, cereal, and fresh bread—nothing was missing. She had made up her mind to ignore breakfast and started to walk to the bathroom but then turned and sat down on the sofa. She dipped a finger into an egg to taste it and ended up eating almost everything on the tray.

After a quick shower, she got dressed. She pulled on a pair of shoes while drying her hair at the same time, hopping around on one foot. She left her room at precisely eight o'clock.

Anthony was waiting for her near the reception desk.

"You're late!" he said as she came out of the elevator.

"Three and a half minutes?" she said in response, looking skeptical.

"That's how you like your eggs, isn't it? Let's move. We have a meeting in half an hour, and with the traffic jams, we'll barely make it."

"Where and with whom do we have a meeting?"

"At the headquarters of the German press syndicate. We have to begin somewhere, don't we?"

Anthony walked through the revolving door and hailed a taxi.

"How did we get this appointment?" she asked, taking a seat next to him in the back of the tan Mercedes.

"I called first thing this morning, while you were still asleep."

"You speak German?"

"One of the technological miracles I come equipped with is that I now fluently speak fifteen different languages. If you'd prefer, you could also attribute my German to the few years that I spent stationed here, if you haven't forgotten about that already. I still remember some of the basics of the language. It allows me to make myself understood when needed. And you? You who wanted to spend the rest of your life here, do you still speak any German?"

"I forgot it all."

The taxi went down Stülerstrasse, turned left, and crossed the park. The giant linden tree cast a long shadow across the lush grass.

The car followed the recently built-up banks of the Spree. On both sides of the river, buildings each more modern than the last rivaled each other in scale and innovation. Architecture for architecture's sake, they were a sign of changing times. The sinister wall had once stood on the edge of the neighborhood they drove through, but not a trace of it had been left behind. Before them now was an enormous structure that housed a conference center under its glass frame. A little farther on, an even bigger complex sprawled over both sides of the river. The building was accessed by an airy white footbridge.

They went through the doors and followed the signs that led to the offices of the press syndicate. A representative received them at the front desk. In more than adequate German, Anthony explained that he was trying to get in contact with a certain Thomas Meyer.

"Regarding what subject?" asked the employee without raising his head from his book.

"I have some very important information for Mr. Meyer, which only he is authorized to receive," replied Anthony, his tone gentle.

Since he seemed to have gotten the receptionist's attention, he added that he would be very appreciative to the syndicate if they might give him an address where he could reach Mr. Meyer. Not his personal information, of course, just his work address.

The receptionist asked him to wait a moment and went to get his supervisor.

The assistant director came and led Anthony and Julia to his office. Comfortably installed on a sofa below an enormous wall-sized photograph of their host holding a massive trophy fish, Anthony repeated his speech word for word. The man sized Anthony up with a steady gaze.

"And what kind of information do you plan on passing along to Thomas Meyer?" he asked, pulling at his mustache.

"I'm not at liberty to tell you, but rest assured that it is essential he receive it," Anthony promised sincerely.

"I don't recall having read any major articles written by a person of that name," the assistant director said doubtfully.

"That's precisely what might change if you help us find a way to get in touch with him."

"And what role does your companion play in this story?" asked the assistant director, pivoting in his desk chair to face the window.

Anthony turned to Julia, who had not spoken a single word since their arrival.

"None whatsoever. Miss Julia is my assistant."

"I'm not authorized to give you any information about the members of our association," concluded the assistant director as he rose to his feet.

Anthony stood and came to meet him, placing his hand on the man's shoulder.

"I can pass this information to Thomas Meyer, and to him alone," he insisted with an authoritative tone. "It could change his life for the better. I refuse to believe that a competent administrator such as yourself would want to obstruct the spectacular career advancement of one of your members. If that's the case, I have no problem going public to denounce your scandalous behavior."

The man rubbed his mustache and sat back down. He tapped away at his keyboard and then turned his computer screen toward Anthony.

"Look. There's no one by the name of Thomas Meyer in our database. I'm very sorry. I'm afraid that if he's not listed here, he doesn't have a press card, and you won't find him in the directory of affiliated journalists. You can check for yourself. Now, if you'll excuse me, I have work to do. If there's no-body besides this Mr. Meyer who can receive your precious information, I'll kindly ask that you leave me to my duties."

Anthony rose and motioned for Julia to follow him. He warmly thanked the administrator for his valuable time and left the building.

"You were probably right," he grumbled, walking back along the sidewalk.

"Your assistant?" asked Julia with a smirk.

"Give me a break. Don't give me that look. I had to come up with something."

"Miss Julia. What next?"

Anthony hailed a taxi coming down the other side of the street.

"Maybe your Thomas has a new line of work."

"I really don't think so. Being a journalist was more than a job for Thomas—it was his calling. I can't imagine him doing anything else."

"Maybe he could! Remind me again the name of that depressing street where the two of you lived?" he asked his daughter.

"Comeniusplatz. It's behind Karl Marx Avenue."

"But of course!"

"What do you mean, 'but of course'?"

"Oh nothing. It just brings back so many good memories, doesn't it?"

Anthony gave the address to the taxi driver.

Their car crossed the city. There were no more

checkpoints, no traces of the wall, nothing to remind people of where the West had ended and the East had begun. They drove past the television tower, a sculptural ball atop an arrow that pointed skyward. The farther they drove, the more the city around them had clearly changed. When they arrived at their destination, Julia recognized nothing of the neighborhood where she had once lived. Everything looked so different that her memory seemed to be from another life.

"It was in these magnificent surroundings that you experienced the most beautiful moments of your life as a young woman?" Anthony asked sarcastically. "I must admit, it has its charms."

"That's enough!" shouted Julia.

Anthony was surprised by his daughter's sudden outburst.

"What did I say?"

"Please be quiet."

The old buildings and houses that had once stood on the street were gone, replaced by recently constructed apartment blocks. Nothing from Julia's memories remained, apart from the public square.

She walked to number 2, where there used to stand a fragile house, and behind a green door, an old wooden staircase that led to the second floor. Julia used to help Thomas's grandmother climb the last few steps. She closed her eyes and remembered it. The odor of wax when she went near the dresser.

The drapes that were always pulled, allowing some light to filter through but protecting the interior from prying eyes. The table in the dining room covered with an ancient oilcloth and surrounded by three chairs. The threadbare sofa sat across from an old black-and-white television set. Thomas's grandmother had not turned it on since it began broadcasting only the news that the government wanted people to hear. And just behind, the thin divider that separated the living room from their bedroom. How many times had Thomas nearly suffocated her with the pillow, trying to muffle her laughter elicited by his clumsy caresses?

"Your hair was longer back then," said Anthony, pulling Julia from her daydream.

"What?" she asked, turning around.

"When you were eighteen, your hair was much longer."

Anthony's gaze swept across the city's horizon.

"There's not much left, is there?"

"You mean there's nothing left," she stammered.

"Come on, let's sit down. You're pale. You need to regain your strength."

They took a seat on a bench situated near a patch of grass yellowed by the repeated passage of children's feet.

Julia was silent. Anthony lifted his arm as though he wanted to put it around her shoulder, but his hand ended up resting on the back of the bench.

"There used to be other houses here, you know. They needed paint, and they were falling down, but inside they were cozy. It was…"

"Better in your memories. That's often the way it is," said Anthony reassuringly. "Memory is a strange artist. It alters the colors of our lives, erases the boring moments, and leaves only the pretty lines, the most enchanting curves."

"At the end of the street, where that god-awful library is now, there was a little café. I'd never seen anything so seedy. The room was painted gray, it was lit with fluorescent lights, and the tables were all in Formica, with booths huddled against the walls. But we had such a wonderful time there. We were so happy. You could only buy vodka and bad beer. I used to help out the owner when the place got busy. I'd put on an apron and wait tables. It was just over there." Julia pointed to the library that had replaced the café.

Anthony coughed.

"Are you sure it wasn't on the other side of the street? From here I can see a little bar that's the spitting image of the place you're describing."

Julia turned her head. On the corner of the boulevard, across from the place she had just indicated, a neon sign flickered out in front of a rundown old bar.

Julia stood up abruptly, and Anthony followed her. She started down the street, moving faster and faster, until finally she was running. She sprinted the last few endless feet. Gasping for breath, she pushed open the bar's door and went inside.

The room had been repainted, and two ceiling lamps had replaced the fluorescent tubes, but the Formica tables were the same, and they gave the place a pleasant retro atmosphere. A man with white hair stood behind the unchanged bar. He recognized her.

A single customer sat at the back of the room. From behind he seemed to be reading a newspaper. Holding her breath, Julia walked up to him.

"Thomas?"

16.

In Rome, the head of the Italian government had just handed in his resignation. The press conference over, he submitted to the demands of the photographers one last time. Hundreds of flashbulbs sparkled, lighting up the stage. At the back of the conference room, a man leaning against a radiator was packing up his equipment.

"You're not going to capture the scene?" asked the young woman at his side.

"No, Marina, taking the same photo as fifty other people doesn't serve any purpose. It's not my idea of journalism."

"With such a bad attitude, it's a good thing you have a pretty face to balance things out."

"That's one way of admitting I'm right. How about I take you to lunch, instead of listening to you lecture me?"

"Do you have a place in mind?" she asked.

"No, but I'm sure you must."

An RAI journalist walked past and kissed Marina's hand before slipping away.

"Who was that?"

"An asshole," replied Marina.

"He's an asshole who seems to think you're not half bad."

"Exactly. Shall we go?"

"Let's grab our passports and get out of here."

Arm in arm, they left the large hall where the press conference had taken place and walked down a corridor to the building's exit.

"What are your plans?" Marina asked as she presented her press pass to the security guard.

"I'm waiting for news from my editors. I've been working on empty projects like this one for three weeks, waiting for the go-ahead for Somalia."

"That's a fine way to talk about me!"

He, in turn, showed his press pass, so that the security officer would return his ID, something every visitor to the Palazzo Montecitorio was obligated to hand over before entering the building.

"Mr. Ullmann?" asked the puzzled officer.

"Yes, I know, the name I use as a journalist is different from the one on my passport. If you look at the first name and the photo on my press card, you can see they're the same."

The officer verified the faces were indeed the same and surrendered the passport to its owner without any further questions.

"Where did you get the idea to sign your articles with a pseudonym? Some sort of celebrity caprice?"

"It's more complicated than that," replied the reporter, wrapping his arm around Marina's waist.

Under a blazing sun they crossed the Piazza Colonna, where hordes of tourists were clutching ice-cream cones.

"Thankfully you kept your first name."

"What difference does that make?"

"I like the name Thomas. It suits you. You look like a Thomas."

"Oh really? Names have faces now? What a strange idea."

"No, they do. You couldn't have another name. I can't imagine you as a Massimo or an Alfredo. Not even Karl. Thomas is exactly the name you were meant to have."

"You're crazy. Where are we going?"

"This heat and everyone parading around with ice cream makes me crave a granita. Let's go to the Tazza d'oro, by the Pantheon. It's not very far from here."

Thomas stopped at the foot of the Column of Marcus Aurelius. He opened his bag, chose a camera, attached a lens, and took a picture of Marina inspecting the bas-reliefs sculpted to glorify the column's namesake.

"Isn't that a photo already taken by fifty others?" she asked, laughing.

"I didn't know you had so many other admirers," smiled Thomas, clicking the shutter again to take a picture with a narrower frame.

"I'm talking about the column! You're taking a picture of me?"

"This looks just like the Victory Column in Berlin, but you're the only Marina I know."

"Like I said, all of your charm hangs from your pretty face—you're a pathetic flirt, Thomas. You wouldn't stand a chance here in Italy. Come on, let's go. It's too hot here."

Marina took Thomas's hand, and they left the column behind them.

*

Julia's gaze ran up and down the Victory Column thrusting into the sky over Berlin. Sitting at its base, Anthony shrugged at her.

"It's not like we were going to find him on the first day," he sighed. "You realize how strange it would have been if that guy in the bar had turned out to be your Thomas?"

"I know. I got it wrong, that's all."

"Maybe it's just because you wanted it to be him."

"From behind he looked the same. He had the same haircut and was reading his newspaper the way Thomas used to, from back to front."

"Why did the owner of the bar make that face when we asked if he remembered him? He seemed pleasant enough when you were reminiscing about the old times."

"Well, it was nice of him to say I haven't changed. I can't believe he even recognized me."

"Who could forget you, my dear Julia?"

Julia gave her father a friendly jab in the ribs with her elbow.

"I'm sure he was just lying and remembered your Thomas perfectly. His face closed up as soon as you mentioned his name."

"Stop calling him 'my Thomas.' I don't even know what we're doing here. What's the point of all this?"

"Thank you for reminding me what a good decision it was to die last week."

"Will you give it up? If you think I'm going to leave Adam to chase a ghost, you're sadly mistaken."

"My little girl, at the risk of aggravating you even further, allow me to observe that I'm the only ghost in your life. You've reminded me of the fact often enough. Please don't strip me of that honor in the present circumstances."

"You're not funny at all."

"Fine, I'm not funny. Every time I open my mouth you cut me off. I'm not funny, and you don't want to hear what I have to say, but judging by your reaction in that café, when you thought you'd seen Thomas, I wouldn't like to be in Adam's place. Now go ahead, tell me I've got it all wrong, that it's not like that."

"You're wrong!"

"Well, that's one bad habit I'm not giving up," Anthony retorted, crossing his arms.

Julia smiled.

"What have I done now?"

"Nothing, nothing," said Julia.

"Oh come on, tell me."

"You have a little old-fashioned side that I didn't know about."

"Don't be so hard on me," replied Anthony as he got up. "Come on, I'll take you to lunch. It's already three, and you haven't eaten anything since this morning."

*

Adam stopped by the liquor store on his way to work. The wine specialist suggested a Californian vintage with excellent tannins, a nice body, and slightly high alcohol content. It sounded enticing to Adam, but he was looking for something a little more refined, something a little more in the image of the person for whom the bottle was intended. Immediately understanding his customer's request, the salesman went to the back of the store and brought out an excellent Bordeaux. It was a very difficult year to find and was not at all in the same price range as the Californian wine, but did excellence have a price?

Julia had told Adam that her best friend couldn't resist the lure of a good vintage. She said that, when a wine was exceptional, Stanley completely forgot his limits. Two bottles should be enough to get him drunk, and whether he liked it or not, he'd finish by leaking Julia's whereabouts.

*

"Let's review our strategy from the beginning," said Anthony, seated on the outdoor terrace of a sandwich shop. "We tried the press syndicate, and his name wasn't on their lists. You're convinced he's still a journalist. Let's trust your instinct, despite the evidence to the contrary. We went back to where he used to live, and the building is no longer there. That, my dear Julia, is what they call making a clean break with one's past. I can't help but wonder if it isn't all intentional."

"What exactly are you getting at? That Thomas has severed all ties with anything from when the two of us were together? So what are we doing here? Let's go home, if that's really what you think," said Julia, her frustration getting the better of her. She gestured impatiently for the waiter to take away the cappuccino he had just served her.

Anthony motioned for him to leave the cup on the table.

"I know you don't like coffee, but it's very good this way."

"Why does it bother you so much that I simply prefer tea?"

"It doesn't bother me. It's just that I'd be happy if you made an effort. I'm not asking much."

Julia swallowed a sip with much grimacing.

"Stop acting like you think it's disgusting. I get it. But I'm telling you, one day you'll get past the bitterness and come to appreciate the flavor of things. And if you really believe that your friend tried to cut off all ties to his past with you, you're overreacting. Maybe he just needed a fresh start, a break from his past in general, not necessarily the one you shared with him. I don't know if you realize how much of a struggle it must have been to get used to a world where everything was different from the world he knew growing up. Every new liberty was acquired at the price of his childhood values."

"Now you're taking his side?"

"Only idiots never admit they're wrong. The airport is just half an hour's drive from here. We could stop by the hotel, grab our things, and catch the next flight. You could sleep in your stunning New York apartment this evening, if you like. At the risk of repeating myself, only idiots never admit they're wrong, and you'd do well to think about that before it's too late. Now, do you want to go home, or would you rather we continue our search?"

Julia stood up. She drank her cappuccino in one

smooth gulp and wiped her mouth with the back of her hand.

"So, Sherlock, do you have a new lead?"

Anthony left a few coins on the table and rose to his feet.

"Didn't you once tell me about a close friend of Thomas's who spent a lot of time with the two of you?"

"Knapp? He was his best friend, but I don't remember ever saying anything about him to you."

"Let's just say my memory is keener than yours. What did Knapp do for a living, again? Wasn't he a journalist?"

"Yes, of course."

"Wouldn't it have been a good idea to mention his name when we had access to that list of all the journalists in Germany this morning?"

"I never gave it the slightest thought."

"See? It's like I was saying. You're going stupid. Let's go!"

"Back to the syndicate?"

"No," said Anthony, rolling his eyes. "I somehow doubt that we'd be welcomed with open arms."

"Where then?"

"A man of my age has to introduce the miracles of the Internet to a young woman who spends her life glued to a computer screen? It's pathetic. Let's find a cybercafé. And could you pull back your hair? In this wind I can't even see your face."

*

Marina insisted on paying for Thomas. After all, they were in her country, and when she came to Berlin, he always picked up the check. Thomas didn't see the need to argue over two iced coffees.

"Do you have work today?" he asked her.

"Did you even notice how late it is? The afternoon is almost over! Besides, you're my work right now. No photos, no articles."

"So what should we do?"

"While I'm waiting for this evening, I'd like to take a walk. It's finally getting cooler, and we're in the middle of the city—let's make the most of it."

"I have to call Knapp before he leaves the office."

Marina passed her hand over Thomas's cheek.

"I know you'd do anything to get away from me as soon as possible, but don't be so anxious. You'll make it to Somalia. Knapp needs you there. You explained it to me a hundred times; I know the story by heart. He's shooting for the job of editorial director, you're his best reporter, and your work is essential to his promotion. Give him time to get things ready."

"He's been getting things ready for three damned weeks!"

"He's just being careful because you're his friend. You can't begrudge him that! Come on, take me for a walk."

"You're not reversing our roles, by any chance, are you?"

"Yes, but I love switching roles with you!"

"And now you're making fun of me?"

"Absolutely," replied Marina, bursting into laughter.

She led him toward the Piazza di Spagna and the Spanish Steps, pointing to the twin bell towers of Trinità dei Monti.

"Is there a more beautiful place on earth than this?" asked Marina.

"Berlin!" Thomas replied without the slightest hesitation.

"Sacrilege. If you promise to stop spouting nonsense, I'll take you to Café Greco. Have one of their cappuccinos and then tell me if they serve them like that in Berlin."

*

His eyes glued to the computer screen, Anthony tried to decode the text that appeared before him.

"I thought you spoke German fluently," said Julia.

"Speak, yes. Reading and writing is another story. But this is a technological problem, not a linguistic one. I don't understand anything about this machine."

"Let me try," ordered Julia, taking command of the keyboard.

She tapped away, and a search engine appeared on the screen. She typed "Knapp" in the designated space and then suddenly stopped.

"What is it?"

"To tell you the truth, I can't exactly remember his name. I don't even know if Knapp was his first or last name. We just always called him by the one name."

"Let me try," said Anthony. Next to "Knapp" he typed the word "journalist."

A list of eleven names appeared—seven men and four women with the name Knapp, and all of them practiced the same profession.

"That's him," exclaimed Anthony, pointing to a Jürgen Knapp on the third line.

"How do you know it's that one?"

"Because it says he's managing editor, and if I recall the way you talked about that young man, I imagine that he must have been sufficiently intelligent to be successful at his chosen profession by the age of forty. If not, he would surely have switched careers, like your Thomas. You should congratulate me on my insight, instead of getting on your high horse."

"I don't see when I would have spoken to you about Knapp, and even less how that would have allowed you to create a psychological profile," replied Julia, stupefied.

"Do you really want to bring up the accuracy of

your memory? Would you tell me again on which side of the street stood the café where you had so many good times? The Knapp you're looking for works as an editor at the *Tagesspiegel,* on the international news desk. Shall we go pay him a visit, or would you rather we just kept chatting in this café?"

*

It was rush hour, and it took them a long time to cross Berlin, its streets clogged with cars. The taxi dropped them off at the Brandenburg Gate. After having faced the traffic, they now had to blaze a trail through the dense crowd of locals returning home from work and the swarms of tourists who had come to see the famous monuments. It was here that Reagan had once called upon Gorbachev to "tear down this wall" and help bring peace to the world. The concrete borderline used to rise behind the columns of the huge gate. For once, two world leaders had listened to each other and worked together to reunite East and West.

Julia picked up her pace, and Anthony began to have trouble keeping up with her. He called out her name several times, sure he'd lost track of her, but he always spotted her outline amid the crowd of people that flooded onto the Pariserplatz.

She waited for him at the building's front door. Together they presented themselves at reception.

Anthony asked if he could see Jürgen Knapp. The receptionist was on the phone, but she put the call on hold and asked if they had an appointment.

"No, but I'm sure he'd be delighted to see us," promised Anthony.

"Who should I say it is?" asked the receptionist, admiring the scarf tied around the hair of the woman leaning on her desk.

"Julia Walsh," she replied.

Seated behind his desk on the third floor, Jürgen Knapp asked the receptionist to please repeat the name that she had just said. He asked her to hold the line, muffled the receiver in the palm of his hand, and walked over to the plunging glass facade that overlooked the glass ceiling of the lobby below.

From here he had a commanding view of the front hall and, in particular, the front desk. He saw a woman remove a scarf from her head and run her fingers through her hair. Even though her hair was shorter than he remembered, this elegant woman pacing underneath his window was, without a doubt, the same woman he first met eighteen years ago.

He picked up the phone again.

"Tell her I'm not here, that I'm traveling this week. Tell her that I won't be back until the end of the month. And, please, be convincing!"

"Very well," answered the receptionist, carefully avoiding the name of the person she was speaking with. "I also have somebody on the line for you.

Shall I connect them?"

"Who is it?"

"I didn't have the time to ask."

"Yes, go ahead and put through the call."

The receptionist hung up and acted her role to perfection.

*

"Jürgen?"

"May I ask who is calling?"

"It's Thomas. Don't you recognize my voice?"

"Of course I do. Excuse me, I was distracted."

"I've been on hold for at least five minutes. I'm calling from abroad. Were you talking to a minister or something? Why did you make me wait so long?"

"I'm sorry, it wasn't anything important. I have good news for you, though. I was going to tell you this evening. I got the green light; you're going to Somalia."

"Great!" exclaimed Thomas. "I'll come back to Berlin and head out as soon as possible."

"There's no need for that. Stay in Rome. I'll order you a plane ticket, and we'll express mail you all of the necessary documents. You'll have them by morning."

"Are you sure it wouldn't be better for me to stop by the office and see you first?"

"No. Trust me. We've waited long enough to get

the necessary authorizations. There's no time to lose. Your flight for Africa leaves Fiumicino Airport late tomorrow afternoon. I'll call you tomorrow morning with the details."

"Are you okay?" asked Thomas. "Your voice sounds strange."

"Everything's fine. You know me. It's just that I would have liked to be with you to celebrate this moment."

"I don't know how I can thank you, Jürgen. I'll win a Pulitzer and get you that promotion to editor in chief!"

Thomas hung up. Knapp watched Julia and the man she was with walk across the lobby and out the door.

He turned to his desk and put the receiver back on the hook.

17.

Thomas joined Marina, who sat waiting for him at the top of the Spanish Steps. The Piazza di Spagna was crowded with tourists.

"So did you get through to him?" Marina asked.

"Come on, there are too many people here. I can barely breathe. Let's do a little window-shopping. If you find the store where you saw that multicolored scarf you liked, I'll buy it for you."

Marina slid her sunglasses to the tip of her nose and stood without saying a word.

"That's not the direction of the store," shouted Thomas after her, as she suddenly headed down the steps toward the fountain.

"It's the opposite direction. I don't want your scarf."

Thomas ran after her, catching up with her at the bottom of the steps.

"You were in love with it yesterday!"

"Like you say, that was yesterday. Today I don't want it anymore. Women are fickle like that. And men are idiots."

"What's the problem?" asked Thomas.

"The problem is that if you really wanted to give me a present, you should have chosen it yourself, wrapped it up nicely, and hidden it as a surprise. That's what it means to be attentive. It's a rare quality that women are very fond of, though I can tell you, it takes more than that to get a woman to marry you."

"I'm sorry. I thought it would make you happy."

"Well, it did exactly the opposite. I don't want a present if it's just a bribe to forgive you."

"But I haven't done anything you should forgive me for!"

"Oh no? Your nose is growing as we speak! Let's celebrate your departure for Somalia, instead of fighting. Isn't that what Knapp told you on the phone? You better find a nice restaurant to take me to this evening."

Marina started walking again, without waiting for Thomas's reply.

*

Julia got out of the taxi. She and Anthony went through the hotel's revolving door.

"There's got to be a solution. Your Thomas can't have just vanished into thin air. He's out there somewhere, and we'll find him. It's simply a matter of patience."

"In twenty-four hours? We only have tomorrow, and then Saturday we fly back. Or had you forgotten?"

"I'm the one whose days are numbered, Julia. You have your whole life ahead of you. If you want to take this adventure to its logical conclusion, you'll come back to Berlin alone. At least this trip has helped us make peace with the city. That's not half bad, is it?"

"That's why you dragged me all the way here? So my conscience would be clear?"

"It's up to you if you want to see it that way. I can't make you forgive me for something that, under the same circumstances, I would probably do again. But let's make an effort for once. Let's not fight about it. You can still get a lot done in a day, believe me."

Julia looked away. Her hand brushed up against Anthony's. He hesitated a moment, then walked across the lobby to the elevators.

"I'm afraid I can't go out with you this evening," he told his daughter as they stood waiting for the elevator to arrive. "Don't be mad at me, but I'm tired. I think it would be wise to rest my batteries for tomorrow. I never thought I would say that and mean it literally…"

"Go get some rest. I'm exhausted, too. I think I'll just order room service. We can meet up at breakfast. I'll come have it in your room, if you like."

"That sounds wonderful," said Anthony with a smile.

The elevator took them upstairs. Julia got out first and waved to her father as the doors started to close. Standing in the hallway, she watched as the red numbers counted up on the screen above the elevator.

As soon as she got back to her room, Julia ran a steaming hot bath, into which she emptied two little bottles of bath oil that had been left on the edge of the tub. She returned to the bedroom and ordered a bowl of cereal and a fruit salad from room service. While she was there, she turned on the plasma TV hanging on the wall across from the bed. She left her clothes in the bedroom and went into the bathroom.

*

Knapp inspected himself in the mirror. He adjusted his tie and gave himself one last glance before leaving the bathroom. At eight o'clock sharp, the photo exhibition he had organized under the direction of the Cultural Ministry would open at the Berlin Museum of Photography. The project had demanded a considerable amount of extra work, but the time invested was worth it; the exhibition would contribute to the advancement of his career and hopefully land him the promotion to editor in chief. If the evening was a success, if his colleagues in the written press gave the exhibition good reviews the next day, it wouldn't be long before he moved into the large glass office at the entrance to the newsroom. Knapp looked at the clock in the front hall of the building. He had fifteen minutes, more than enough time to cross Pariserplatz on foot and place himself at the bottom of the steps in order to welcome the minister and the television cameras onto the red carpet.

*

Adam rolled up the cellophane wrapper from his sandwich and aimed for a trashcan attached to one of the park's lampposts. He missed his shot and got up to pick up the greasy ball. As he neared the lawn, a squirrel lifted its head and stood on its hind legs.

"Sorry pal," said Adam, "I don't have any peanuts in my pockets, and Julia's out of town. We've both been dumped."

The little animal looked at him, bobbing its head to each word that Adam spoke.

"I don't think squirrels like cold cuts," he said, launching a morsel of ham that had flopped out from between the two pieces of bread.

The rodent snubbed Adam's offering and scampered up a tree. A woman jogging past stopped in front of Adam.

"Do you talk to the squirrels, too? I love it when they come up to you and wiggle their sweet little faces."

"It's strange. Women can't resist squirrels, even though they're basically rodents," grumbled Adam.

He threw his sandwich in the trashcan and walked away with his hands shoved in his pockets.

*

There was a knock at the door. Julia grabbed a wash-cloth and wiped off her facemask. She stepped out of the tub and slipped on the robe hooked to the back of the bathroom door. She walked across the bed-room to let the waiter in and asked him to put the tray on the bed. She took some money from her purse, slid it into the bill, which she signed, and handed it back to him. As soon as he was gone, she got under the covers and started picking at the ce-real. Remote control in one hand, she channel surfed, searching for a show that was not in German.

She flipped past three Spanish channels, a Swiss, and two French channels. She gave up watching the war coverage on CNN (too violent), the stock-mar-ket report on Bloomberg (she was terrible at math), and a game show on RAI (the hostess was vulgar). She started over at the beginning.

*

Knapp stood on tiptoe to watch the motorcade pull up. The man standing next to him tried to step in front of him, but Knapp gave him an elbow and put him back in his place. The guy should have arrived earlier if he wanted to be in front. A bodyguard opened the car door, and the minister stepped out, welcomed by a swarm of cameras. Alongside the exhibition's curator, Knapp stepped forward and bowed to welcome the high-ranking government representative, before escorting him along the red carpet.

*

Julia browsed the room-service menu. A single raisin and two seeds were all that was left of her cereal and fruit salad. She couldn't decide between a piece of chocolate cake, a strudel, pancakes, or a club sandwich. She carefully inspected her stomach and hips, then threw the menu across the room. The news report was coming to an end and showing images of a glamorous art opening. Celebrities in evening wear walked down a red carpet under a shimmer of flashbulbs. A long, elegant gown worn by a famous actress or singer, probably from Berlin, attracted Julia's attention. None of the faces among the assembly of beautiful people looked familiar... And then suddenly one did.

She got up with a start, knocking over the room-service tray in the process, and stared at the television screen. She was sure she recognized the man who had just entered the building, smiling at the camera that zoomed in on him, only to pan away toward the columns of the Brandenburg Gate.

"That handsome son of a bitch!" exclaimed Julia as she ran to the bathroom.

*

The concierge assured her that the art opening in question couldn't be anywhere other than at the Brandenburger Stiftung. It was among the most recently built of Berlin's latest architectural wonders. The front steps had a perfect view of the Brandenburg Gate. The *Tagesspiegel* had undoubtedly organized the gala Julia had seen on television. Miss Walsh had no need to hurry, though. The large exhibition of photographic journalism would last until the anniversary of the fall of the Berlin Wall, which was still five months away. If Miss Walsh wished, he could easily procure her two invitations tomorrow morning. But what Julia wanted was a way to get an evening dress on the spot.

"It's almost nine o'clock, Miss Walsh!"

Julia dumped the contents of her purse on the counter and started frantically sorting. There were dollars, euros, spare coins, even an old German mark that she had always kept. She took off her watch and pushed the entire pile forward with both hands, like a gambling addict desperate to stay in the game.

"I don't care if it's red, purple, or yellow. It doesn't matter. But I beg you, find me a long dress!"

The concierge looked at her, perplexed. He raised his left eyebrow. But his sense of duty spurred him on; he couldn't abandon Mr. Walsh's daughter in a difficult situation. Then he had an idea.

"Sweep that mess back into your purse and follow me," he said, leading Julia to a storage room.

Even in the dim light, the gown he presented her with looked magnificent. It belonged to a client who was staying in suite 1206. The concierge explained that the designer had delivered it too late for them to disturb the countess. It went without saying that damage of any sort was out of the question. Like Cinderella, Julia would have to bring the dress back to him before the twelfth stroke of midnight.

He left her alone in the room, suggesting she leave her clothes on the hanger.

Julia undressed and slid into the delicate fabric as carefully as she could. There was no mirror for her to see how she looked. She tried to see her reflection in the side of a metal support pillar, but the cylinder deformed the picture beyond recognition. She let down her hair and blindly applied her makeup. She abandoned her purse, along with her pants and sweater, and headed back through the shadowy hallway to the lobby.

The concierge motioned for her to come closer. Julia silently obeyed. A mirror hung on the wall behind him, but as soon as Julia tried to see herself in it, he stopped her, blocking her view.

"No, no, no," he said, as Julia ducked and bobbed, trying to see around him. "Just hold still."

He took a tissue from his drawer and corrected her lipstick.

"Now go ahead and admire yourself," he concluded, standing aside.

Julia had never seen such a magnificent dress. It was far more beautiful than any of the haute couture she lusted after while window-shopping in New York.

"I don't know how to thank you!" she murmured, dumbstruck.

"You do its creator honor. I'm sure it looks a hundred times better on you than it does on the countess," he said, smiling. "I've called you a car. It will wait for you at the exhibition and bring you back to the hotel."

"I could have taken a taxi."

"Wearing a gown like that? I hope you're joking. Think of it as your carriage, and my insurance policy. Don't forget, just like Cinderella! Have a good evening, Miss Walsh," said the concierge as he accompanied her to the limousine.

When they were outside, Julia stood on tiptoe to kiss the concierge on his cheek.

"Just one last favor, Miss Walsh."

"Anything!"

"We're very lucky that this dress is long, very

long. I beg you, don't pick it up like that again. Your espadrilles are not even remotely appropriate."

*

The waiter set a plate of antipasti on the table. Thomas served Marina a few grilled vegetables.

"Could you tell me why you're wearing sunglasses in a restaurant where the light is so low that I can't even read the menu?"

"Because," answered Marina.

"That's a response that could stand some clarification," replied Thomas mockingly.

"Because I don't want you to see the look in my eyes."

"What look?"

"*The* look."

"Oh. I'm sorry, but I don't understand a word of what you're saying."

"I'm talking about the look that you men see in our eyes when we're comfortable around you."

"I didn't know there was a specific look for that."

"There is. You know it full well—you're a man like any other."

"If you say so. And why shouldn't I see this look that betrays once and for all that you're comfortable around me?"

"Because, if you saw it, you'd begin thinking about the best way to dump me."

"What are you talking about?"

"Thomas, most men who decide to bring an end to their solitude through a simple no-strings-attached relationship do so with romantic words, but never 'I love you.' Men like that fear the day that the woman they pass their time with starts giving them *the* look."

"But what is the look, really?"

"The one that makes you think we've fallen madly in love with you, that we want more from you. Stupid things, like vacation plans, or any plans at all! And if we make the mistake of smiling when there's a baby carriage in the vicinity, things are over for sure."

"And if I took off your sunglasses, I would find the look behind them?"

"You're full of yourself. My eyes hurt, that's all. What did you think?"

"Why did you say all that, Marina?"

"When are you going to finally tell me that you're leaving for Somalia? Before or after your tiramisu?"

"Who said I was going to order tiramisu?"

"In the two years since I've known you and worked with you, I've observed your habits."

Marina pushed her sunglasses down to the tip of her nose and let them fall into her plate.

"Fine. I'm leaving tomorrow. But I just found out."

"You're going back to Berlin tomorrow?"

"No, Knapp prefers that I leave for Mogadishu from here."

"You've been waiting to leave for three months. And now, after three months, he snaps his fingers and you obey?"

"It's a matter of gaining a day. We've already lost enough time as it is."

"He's the one who made you lose time, and you're the one doing him a favor. He needs your work for his precious promotion, but you don't need him to do great journalism. With your talent, you could win a prize photographing a dog pissing on a fire hydrant."

"What's your point?"

"Stand up for yourself, Thomas! Stop spending your life running from the people who love you, instead of confronting them. Take me, for instance. Just tell me I'm boring you with my conversation, that we're just lovers, and that it's not my place to lecture you. And Knapp—tell him that you can't just go to Somalia without first going home, packing a suitcase, and hugging your friends goodbye. Especially since you don't know when you'll be back!"

"Maybe you're right."

Thomas picked up his cell phone.

"What are you doing?"

"I'm sending a text message to Knapp, telling him to buy me a ticket that leaves from Berlin on Saturday."

"I'll believe it when the message is in your out-box!"

"Then will you let me see *the* look?"

"Maybe… If you're lucky."

*

The limousine pulled to a halt at the end of the red carpet. Julia contorted herself to hide her shoes as she stepped out of the car. She walked up the steps, and a group of photographers started taking her picture when she reached the top.

"I'm nobody," she said to a television camera-man, who didn't understand English anyway. At the entrance, the doorkeeper admired Julia's incredible gown. As he was blinded by the bright lights of the television crew filming her entry, he decided it was useless to ask for her invitation.

The hall was immense. Julia's eyes swept over the faces of the crowd. Cocktails in hand, the guests loitered in front of the gigantic photographs. Julia smiled in response to greetings from complete strangers. Farther on, a harpist on a slightly elevated platform was playing Mozart. Weaving her way through the surreal ballet, Julia stalked her prey.

A ten-foot-high photograph caught her eye. The shot had been taken in the mountains of Kandahar or Tajikistan. Or was it the border with Pakistan? The uniform of the soldier lying in a ditch didn't help identify his nationality. The barefoot child at his side looked like all of the lost children in the world.

A hand touched her shoulder, and Julia jumped.

"You haven't changed a bit," Knapp declared. "What are you doing here? I didn't know you were on the list of invitees. What a wonderful surprise. Are you in town for long?"

"And you, what are you doing here? I thought you were traveling until the end of the month. At least, that's what I was told when I came to your office this afternoon. Didn't you get my message?"

"I came back early. I came here directly from the airport."

"You're a very bad liar, Knapp. And I know from experience. I've gained a certain amount of expertise in the field these past few days."

"How was I to know that it was you who was asking for me? I haven't heard from you in twenty years."

"Eighteen. Do you know another Julia Walsh?"

"I'd forgotten your last name, Julia. Not your first name, of course, but I didn't put two and two together. I'm a very busy man, and there are so many people coming to see me, trying to sell their useless stories that I'm obliged to screen my calls."

"Thanks for the compliment."

"What brings you to Berlin?"

Her eyes returned to the photograph. A certain T. Ullmann had taken it.

"Thomas could have taken that photo. It looks like his work," said Julia sadly.

"But Thomas hasn't taken a picture in years! He doesn't even live in Germany anymore. He left all that behind him."

Julia tried to hide how the news hit her, forcing herself to show no emotion.

Knapp continued, "He lives abroad now."

"Where?"

"In Italy, with his wife. We don't talk to each other very often. Once a year maybe, and not even every year."

"Did the two of you have a fight?"

"No, not at all. Our lives just went their separate ways. I did my best to help him realize his dream of becoming a journalist, but when he returned from Afghanistan, he was a changed man. Then again, you know better than I, don't you? He decided to do something else with his life."

"No, I don't know anything about it!" retorted Julia, her jaw tightening.

"The last I heard, he was in Rome running a restaurant with his wife. Now, if you'll excuse me, I have some guests that I need to attend to. I'm glad to have seen you again. I'm sorry this was so brief. Are you leaving soon?"

"Tomorrow morning," replied Julia.

"You still haven't told me what brought you back to Berlin. Business?"

"Goodbye, Knapp."

Julia left without looking back. She quickened her step as soon as she was past the glass doors and ran down the red carpet to the waiting car.

Back at the hotel, Julia crossed the lobby in haste and took the unmarked door that led to the storage room. She slipped out of the gown, put it back on its hanger, and pulled on her jeans and sweater. She heard a cough behind her.

"Are you decent?" asked the concierge, covering his eyes with one hand and holding out a box of Kleenex in the other.

"No," sobbed Julia.

The concierge pulled out a tissue and offered it blindly.

"Thank you," she replied.

"I thought that your makeup looked splotchy when I saw you run past just now. Didn't your evening live up to expectations?"

"That's the least you could say," responded Julia, sniffling.

"It happens to the best of us. The unexpected is treacherous."

"But for God's sake, none of this was expected. Not this trip, not this hotel, not this city, and definitely not this useless running around. My life was perfect. It was just what I wanted. So why…?"

The concierge stepped toward her, and that step

was all it took for Julia to throw herself on his shoulder. He delicately patted her back and did his best to console her.

"I don't know what has made you so terribly sad, but if you'd allow me to suggest it, you ought to share your feelings with your father. He'd probably be a great comfort to you. You're lucky to still have him in your life, and the two of you seem so close. I'm sure that a man like him knows how to listen."

"If you only knew how wrong you are. My father and I close? Him listen to other people? We must not be talking about the same man."

"I've had the pleasure of serving your father on many occasions, Miss Walsh, and I can assure you he has always been a perfect gentleman."

"I can't think of a ruder person!"

"You're right, we must not be talking about the same person. The man I know has always been benevolent. He describes you as his one success in life."

Julia was speechless.

"Go on, go see your father. I'm sure he'll listen to your problems."

"Nothing in my life is what it once seemed. And he's sleeping now. He was exhausted."

"He must have gotten a second wind, because I just sent up a meal tray."

"My father ordered something to eat?"

"That's what I said, Miss."

Julia slid on her shoes and thanked the concierge, kissing him on the cheek.

"I can count on you to keep our conversation a secret, can't I?" he said.

"I've never seen you before," promised Julia.

"And I can put that gown back in its garment bag without worrying that it might be stained?"

Julia lifted her right hand and smiled at the concierge, who told her to hurry along.

She went back across the lobby and took the elevator to the sixth floor. She hesitated a moment and then pushed the button for the top floor.

She heard the television from the hall. Julia knocked on the door, and her father answered immediately.

"You were sublime in that gown," he said, lying back down on the bed.

Julia looked up and saw that the evening news was rebroadcasting shots from the exhibition's opening.

"It would have been impossible to miss such a beautiful vision. I've never seen you look so elegant. It confirms what I've always thought—it's high time you left your ripped jeans behind you. If I had known what you had planned, I would have come along. I would have been very proud to be at your side."

"I didn't have any plan. I was watching the same channel as you, and I saw Knapp on the red carpet, so I went."

"Interesting," said Anthony, standing back up. "For somebody who was supposedly out of town until the end of the month... Either he was lying or he's capable of being in two places at once. I won't even ask how your meeting with him went. You seem all worked up."

"I was right—Thomas is married. And you were right—he's not a journalist anymore," Julia explained, collapsing into an armchair. She eyed the meal tray on the coffee table in front of her.

"You ordered food?"

"I ordered that meal for you."

"You knew I would come knock on your door?"

"I know more than you might imagine. Seeing you on television, and knowing how little you enjoy glitzy events, I suspected something was up. I thought that Thomas must have reappeared for you to run off like that in the middle of the night. At least that's what I thought when the concierge called to ask my permission to order you a limousine. And I thought I'd order you a bit of comfort food if your evening didn't turn out like you expected it would. Go on, pick up the cover. It's just pancakes. They can't replace love, but with a little bit of maple syrup, they'll chase away the blues."

*

In the suite next door, a certain countess was also

watching the evening news. She asked her husband to remind her to call Karl the next day and congratulate him. But she planned to let him know that the next time he created a design exclusively for her it would be better to make sure it was really one of a kind so that she wouldn't see it being worn by another, younger woman, who, to make things worse, had a better figure than her. Karl would certainly understand that she would be sending the gown back to him. Although sumptuous, it no longer held any interest for her.

*

Julia told her father all about her evening. She told him about her unexpected departure for the cursed exhibition, about her conversation with Knapp, and her pathetic return, without understanding or admitting to herself why such a strong wave of emotion had overtaken her. It wasn't hearing that Thomas was living his life. She had suspected that from the beginning—how could he do otherwise? The worst part, and she couldn't explain why, was hearing that he had given up journalism. Anthony listened to her without interrupting or making the slightest commentary. Swallowing her last bite of pancake, she thanked her father for the surprise snack, which, though it hadn't put her mind in order, would certainly help her gain a couple pounds. There was no point in staying in Berlin. Signs or not, there was nothing more to find. She just wanted to put some order back in her life. She'd pack her bag before going to bed, and the two of them could take the plane first thing tomorrow morning. This time it was she who felt a sense of déjà vu—too much déjà vu for her liking.

In the hall, she kicked off her shoes and took the service stairs back down to her room.

Anthony picked up the telephone as soon as Julia left his room. It was 4 p.m. in San Francisco, where the person he was calling picked up after the first ring.

"Pilguez speaking."

"Is this a bad time? It's Anthony Walsh."

"It's never a bad time for old friends. To what do I owe the pleasure of hearing your voice, after such a long time?"

"I have a favor to ask, a little investigation, if you're still up for it."

"I've been so bored since I retired… If you called to tell me you'd lost your keys, I'd be on the case immediately."

"Do you still have your contacts with the border police? Somebody in immigration or visas that could do a little research for us?"

"I still have some influence, if that's what you're asking."

"Well, I'll need you to use that influence to its maximum. Here's the story…"

The conversation between old friends lasted a good half hour. Inspector Pilguez promised to get Anthony the information he wanted as soon as possible.

*

It was 8 p.m. in New York. A little sign on the door of the antique shop indicated it was closed until tomorrow. Inside, Stanley was decorating the shelves of a late-nineteenth-century bookcase he had gotten just that afternoon. Adam knocked on the window.

"What a leech!" Stanley muttered, trying to hide behind a sideboard buffet.

"Stanley, it's me, Adam! I know you're in there!"

Stanley crouched, holding his breath.

"I have two bottles of Château-Lafite!"

Stanley slowly lifted his head.

"1989!" cried Adam from the street.

Stanley opened the door.

"I'm sorry, I was working on a display and didn't hear you," he said, letting his visitor in. "Have you already eaten?"

18.

Thomas stretched and slid out of bed, careful not to wake Marina, who was sleeping next to him. He went down the spiral staircase and crossed the living room of the duplex apartment. Behind the counter of the bar, he placed a cup under the nozzle of the coffee machine, which he covered with a towel to muffle the noise, before pressing the button. He slid open the glass doors and walked out onto the patio to soak in the first rays of sunlight that were already caressing Rome's rooftops. He walked over to the railing and looked down into the street. A deliveryman unloaded cases of fruits and vegetables in front of the little grocery store next door to Marina's building.

A volley of Italian curses followed a strong odor of burning toast. Marina appeared wearing a dressing gown and a sullen face.

"Two things," she said. "First of all, you're butt naked. I doubt that my neighbors across the street want that kind of entertainment during breakfast."

"And the second?" asked Thomas without turning around.

"We'll be having our breakfast downstairs. There's nothing left to eat."

"Didn't we buy some bread last night?" asked Thomas teasingly.

"Get dressed," responded Marina, going back inside.

"Good morning to you, too!" grumbled Thomas.

An old woman watering her plants gave Thomas a friendly wave from her balcony on the other side of the narrow street. Thomas smiled at her and left the terrace.

It wasn't even eight, but the air was already hot. The owner of the trattoria downstairs from Marina's apartment was setting up his terrace, and Thomas helped him bring the umbrellas out onto the sidewalk. Marina sat down and grabbed a croissant from a basket filled with pastries.

"What are you going to do with your day?" asked Thomas, helping himself to the pastries. "Are you mad because I'm leaving?"

"What I love about you is your knack for always saying sensitive things at the right moment."

The trattoria owner set two steaming cappuccinos on their table. He looked at the sky, prayed for a storm before the end of the day, and complimented Marina on her early-morning beauty. He winked at Thomas and went back inside.

"How about we try not to ruin this morning," continued Thomas.

"Great idea. Finish your croissant. We'll go upstairs, and you can jump me. You can take a shower in my bathroom while I play idiot maid and pack your bag. A quick kiss on the doorstep, and you disappear for two or three months, maybe forever. Don't say anything. Whatever you say will be pointless."

"Come with me!"

"I'm a writer, not a reporter."

"We could spend the evening in Berlin together, and tomorrow when I fly to Mogadishu, you come back to Rome."

Marina turned to signal to the café owner to bring her another cappuccino.

"You're right. Goodbyes at the airport are much better. A little drama can't hurt…"

"And it wouldn't hurt for you to come and show your face in the newsroom in Berlin," Thomas added.

"Drink your coffee while it's hot."

"If you say yes, instead of moping, I'll get you a ticket."

*

An envelope appeared underneath the door. Anthony winced as he bent over to pick it up. He ripped it open and read the fax.

I'm sorry. I still haven't finished, but I'm not giving up. I hope to get some results soon.

The message was signed *GP,* the initials of George Pilguez.

Anthony Walsh sat down at the desk in his suite and scribbled a note to Julia. He called the concierge and ordered a car and driver. He left his room and made a quick trip to the sixth floor. Walking on tip-toe to his daughter's bedroom, he slid the note under the door and left without waiting.

"Thirty-one Karl Liebknecht Strasse, please," he told his chauffeur.

The sedan drove off.

*

After a quick cup of tea, Julia grabbed her bag from the closet shelf and began folding her clothes, only to end up throwing the whole pile in without any further fuss. She stopped in the middle of her preparations and walked over to the window. A misty rain fell on the city. In the street below, a sedan drove away from the hotel.

*

"Bring me your dopp kit, if you want it in your bag," called Marina from the bedroom.

Thomas stuck his head out of the bathroom.

"I can pack my own bag, you know."

"Certainly. You can do it yourself, but you do it

badly, and I won't be there in Somalia to iron all of your clothes for you."

"Because you just did?" asked Thomas, almost concerned.

"No, but I could have!"

"Have you made a decision?"

"About whether I dump you today or tomorrow? You're a lucky bastard. I decided it would be good for my career if I went to say hello to our future editorial director. It's good news for you, and although it has no correlation with your departure from Berlin, it means you'll get to spend another evening in my company."

"I'm thrilled," smiled Thomas.

"Really?" continued Marina, zipping his bag shut. "We have to leave Rome by noon. Are you going to spend the entire morning in the bathroom?"

"I thought I was the one who did all the moaning and groaning."

"You're rubbing off on me, amigo. It's not my fault."

Marina pushed Thomas aside to get into the bathroom. She untied the sash on her dressing gown and led him under the shower.

*

The black Mercedes turned and parked in front of a row of large gray buildings. Anthony asked the driver to wait for him. He hoped he would be back within an hour.

He walked up a few stairs sheltered by an awning and entered the building that currently housed the Stasi archives.

Anthony presented himself to the receptionist and asked for directions.

He was directed down a hallway that was bone-chilling. Here and there display cases held different models of microphones, video cameras, and photo-graphic tools. There were steamers for opening mail and gluers for sealing it back up after it was read, copied, and archived, along with all kinds of other equipment used to spy on the day-to-day lives of a population held prisoner by a police state. There were pamphlets, propaganda manuals, and an array of systems for eavesdropping, which grew increas-ingly sophisticated as the years passed. Millions of people had been spied on, judged, and catalogued to assure the totalitarian state's security. Lost in his thoughts, Anthony stopped before a photograph of an interrogation room.

I know I was wrong. Once the wall had fallen, the process was irreversible. But who was to know for sure, Julia? The people who lived through the Prague Spring? Our Western democracies, which let so many crimes and injustices go unnoticed? Who could have promised that today's Russia would be free of its despotic leaders? Yes, I was afraid. I was terrified that the dictatorship would close the doors that had just cracked open to allow freedom, and imprison you in its totalitarian stranglehold. I was afraid of being a father forever separated from his daughter, not because she chose it, but because a government had decided for her. I know that you'll always hate me for it, but if things had turned out differently, I would have never forgiven myself for not coming and getting you out. I have to admit that part of me is happy I was wrong.

"Can I help you?" asked a voice from the end of the corridor.

"I'm looking for the archives," Anthony stammered.

"They're here, sir. What can I do for you?"

A few days after the collapse of the wall, the employees of the East German political police, faced with the inevitable defeat of their regime, began to destroy everything that might be considered evidence of their actions. But they couldn't just rip up millions of pages of personal information collected during nearly forty years of totalitarianism. Beginning in December 1989, the populace caught wind of what the former Stasi was up to and took over their offices. In every East German city, citizens occupied those offices and prevented the destruction of what represented over a hundred miles of reports of all kinds, documents that were now open to the public.

Anthony asked to see the dossier of a certain Thomas Meyer, who used to live at number 2, Comeniusplatz, in East Berlin.

"Unfortunately, I can't fulfill your request, sir," apologized the official in charge.

"I thought the law guaranteed public access to the archives."

"It does, but the law is also meant to protect our citizens against any intrusion into their private lives that might be caused by the use of their personal information," replied the employee as though reciting a speech he knew by heart.

"I think it's the interpretation of the law that's most important. If I'm correct, the main point of the law we're both talking about is to facilitate access to Stasi files in order to clarify the influence that the state's secret police had over the private lives of individuals, no?" continued Anthony, repeating verbatim the text engraved on a plaque hung at the entrance to the archives.

"Yes, of course," admitted the employee, who didn't understand what his visitor was trying to get at.

"Thomas Meyer is my son-in-law," Anthony lied with unwavering aplomb. "Today he lives in the United States. I'm happy to report that soon I'll be a grandfather. As you can imagine, it's important that he one day be able to have a frank conversation with his children about his past. Who wouldn't want to? Do you have children, Mr.…?"

"Hans Dietrich," replied the official. "I have two adorable little girls, Emma and Anna. They're five and seven."

"How wonderful!" exclaimed Anthony, clasping his hands together. "You must be so happy."

"I'm spoiled, really."

"Poor Thomas. The memories of his tragic adolescence are still too vivid for him to come to do this research himself. I came a very long way, in his name, to give him the chance to reconcile himself with his past and, maybe even one day, find the strength to come here with his daughter (between you and me, I just know he's going to have a little girl!). To come back here with her, to the country of his ancestors, and allow her to find her roots. Please, Hans," continued Anthony solemnly, "as a future grandfather talking to the father of two adorable little girls, I ask you to help me. Help the daughter of your compatriot Thomas Meyer. Be the one who, through his generous understanding, gives her the happiness we all dream she might have."

Overwhelmed, Hans Dietrich didn't know what to think. His visitor's teary eyes finally conquered him. He offered Anthony a tissue.

"Thomas Meyer, you said?"

"That's the name," replied Anthony.

"Take a seat in the reading room. I'll see if we have anything on him."

Fifteen minutes later, Hans Dietrich placed a metal binder on the desk where Anthony Walsh was waiting.

"I think I found your son-in-law's file," he announced, his face radiant. "We're lucky that it wasn't among the papers that were destroyed. The reconstruction of the ripped-up files is far from being finished. We're still waiting on the necessary funding."

Anthony warmly thanked him and then feigned the need for a bit of privacy to study his son-in-law's past. Hans left him alone, and Anthony dove into the voluminous file. It began in 1980. The young man had been spied on for nine years. Page after page listed his actions and gestures, the people and places he frequented, his skills, his literary preferences, written accounts of what he said in private and in public, his opinions, and his attachment to the values of the state. It listed his ambitions, his hopes, his first blush of love, and his romantic experiences and disappointments. Nothing that contributed to the formation of Thomas's character seemed to have been left out. Lacking a mastery of the German language, Anthony had to ask for the help of Hans Dietrich to interpret the final page of analysis, at the end of the file, updated the last time on October 9, 1989.

Thomas Meyer, orphan, was a student with

suspicious ties. His best friend and neighbor from an early age had managed to escape to the West. Jürgen Knapp had probably hidden beneath the backseat of a car. He had never come back to the East. There was no proof to confirm that Thomas Meyer had played a role in J. Knapp's escape, and the candor with which he discussed his friend's plans with the Stasi informant indicated his probable innocence. The informant for the dossier had discovered preparations for the escape, but too late, unfortunately, to lead to the arrest of Jürgen Knapp. Nevertheless, the close ties between Thomas and the traitor, along with the fact that he did not denounce his friend's plans to defect, made it impossible to consider him as a promising element for the future of the Democratic Republic. Given the facts cited in the dossier, it was not advocated that charges be pressed against him, but it was out of the question for any important position in the service of the state to be entrusted to him. The report recommended keeping him under surveillance to assure that he did not have contact with his former friend or any other person residing in the West. A probation period lasting until his thirtieth birthday was recommended, before any further alteration of his status or closing of his file.

Hans Dietrich finished his translation. Stupefied, he read and reread the name of the informant who had provided the information, to make sure that he wasn't wrong. He was unable to hide his unease.

"Who could imagine such a thing," said Anthony, his eyes fixed on the name at the bottom of the page. "How awful."

Hans Dietrich agreed. He was equally appalled.

Anthony thanked his host for the precious aid he had given him. Distracted by a detail, the archival official hesitated a moment before revealing what he had just discovered.

"I think you should know, given the context of your research, that your son-in-law has made the same awful discovery that we have. A note on the tab of the file shows that he has consulted it himself."

Anthony thanked Dietrich again, assuring him of his gratitude. He would make his own humble contribution to the financing of the archives' reconstruction. He realized today better than he ever had how much understanding the past can help men navigate their futures.

As he left the building, Anthony felt the need for some fresh air, to recover his strength. He went and sat in a little park near the parking lot for a few minutes.

Thinking back to the information Dietrich had confided to him, he rolled his eyes and exclaimed, "Why didn't I think of that earlier!"

He got up and went to the car. As soon as he was inside, he took his cell phone and called San Francisco.

"Did I wake you up?"

"Of course not, it's only three in the morning!"

"Sorry. I think I have some important information."

George Pilguez turned on the lamp on his bedside table and looked for something to write with.

"I'm listening," he said.

"I think I know why our man wanted to change his family name, or at least to use it as little as possible."

"Why?"

"It's a long story…"

"Do you have any idea about his new identity?"

"I haven't the foggiest."

"Wonderful. You call me in the middle of the night, and that's all the information you have to help my investigation move forward?" retorted Pilguez sarcastically. He hung up.

He turned out the light, crossed his arms behind his head, and tried to go back to sleep. Half an hour later, his wife told him to get to work. It didn't matter that the sun had not yet risen. She couldn't stand him wiggling around in bed next to her, and she fully intended to sleep some more.

George Pilguez put on a robe and stumbled into the kitchen, grumbling. He started to make himself a sandwich. He liberally buttered two slices of bread, taking advantage of the fact that Natalia was not standing next to him to lecture about his cholesterol.

He took his meal to his desk. Some agencies never closed, so he picked up the phone and called a friend who worked in immigration.

"If a person who has legally changed their name visited our country, would their original name still show up in our files?"

"What nationality?" asked the person on the other end of the line.

"German…born in the East."

"In that case, yes. To receive a visa from our consulate they would need to use their original name. There is probably a trace somewhere."

"Do you have something to write with?" asked George.

"I'm in front of my keyboard, buddy," replied his friend, Rick Bram, immigration officer at JFK Airport.

*

The Mercedes drove back to the hotel. Anthony Walsh gazed out his window, watching the city pass by. The flashing sign outside of a pharmacy intermittently displayed the date, the time, and the temperature. It was almost noon in Berlin and 21 degrees Celsius.

"Only two days left," murmured Anthony Walsh.

*

Julia paced in the lobby, her luggage at her feet.

"I assure you, Miss Walsh, I haven't the faintest idea where your father went. He called for a car early this morning without giving any other information, and he hasn't been back since. I tried to call, but his driver's phone is turned off."

The concierge looked at Julia's bag.

"Mr. Walsh also didn't ask me to change your travel reservations. He didn't tell me that you'd be leaving today. Are you sure he's made a decision?"

"I'm the one who made a decision! I told him to meet me this morning. The plane leaves at 3 p.m. It's the last flight possible if we're to catch our connecting flight to New York, in Paris."

"You could always fly through Amsterdam... That would buy you some time. I'd be happy to arrange it for you."

"Yes, please, could you do that right away?" said Julia, searching her pockets.

To the concierge's astonishment, she gave up and put her head on the counter in front of him.

"Is something wrong, miss?"

"My father has the tickets."

"Don't worry, I'm sure he'll be back soon. There's still time if you absolutely have to be in New York by this evening."

A black sedan pulled up in front of the hotel. Anthony Walsh got out of it and came through the revolving door.

"Where have you been?" asked Julia, running up to meet him. "I was worried sick."

"That's the first time I've ever seen you concerned about my whereabouts and well-being! What a wonderful day!"

"I was worried because we were going to miss our flight."

"What flight?"

"We agreed last night that we'd go back today. Don't you remember?"

The concierge interrupted their conversation to hand Anthony a message that had just been faxed to him. He opened the envelope, looking at Julia from time to time as he read through the fax.

"Yes, but that was last night," he replied jovially.

He glanced at Julia's bag and asked the bellboy to take it back up to his daughter's room.

"Come on, I'll take you to lunch. We have to talk."

"About what?" she asked worriedly.

"About me! Oh, come on now. Don't make that face. I was kidding."

They sat down at a table on the terrace.

*

The alarm clock woke Stanley in the middle of a bad dream. As though in punishment for his wine-soaked evening, a splitting migraine gripped his head in a vise as soon as he opened his eyes. He got up and staggered to the bathroom.

After seeing his face in the mirror, he swore to abstain from consuming any alcohol until the end of the month. It seemed reasonable, since it was already the 29th. Aside from the jackhammer at work on his temples, the day looked as though it would be quite pleasant. At lunchtime, he'd offer to collect Julia at her office for a walk along the river. Frowning, he remembered in quick succession that his friend was not in town and that he had not heard from her the night before. He also couldn't remember a word of the conversation during his boozy dinner. It was only a little while later, after having drunk a large cup of tea, that he began to wonder whether the word "Berlin" had crossed his lips during his evening with Adam. Stepping out of the shower, he weighed the necessity of informing Julia of his growing doubt. Maybe he should call her? Then again, maybe not...

*

"A man who lies once will probably lie again," began Anthony as he handed a menu to Julia.

"Is that for my benefit?"

"The world does not revolve around you, my dear Julia! I was referring to your friend Knapp."

Julia put down the menu and shooed away the waiter coming toward them.

"What are you talking about?"

"What do you expect me to talk about in your company at a restaurant in Berlin?"

"What have you found out?"

"Thomas Meyer, a.k.a. Thomas Ullmann, is a reporter for the *Tagesspiegel*. I know without a doubt that he works every day with the little bastard who told us all those lies."

"Why would Knapp lie to us?"

"You should ask him yourself. I imagine he has his reasons."

"How did you find out?"

"I have superpowers. It's one of the advantages of being reduced to being a machine."

Julia looked perplexedly at her father.

"Why not?" continued Anthony. "You invent animals that talk to children. Don't I have the right to a few supernatural powers in the eyes of my own daughter?"

Anthony moved his hand toward Julia's but thought twice and picked up a glass instead, raising it to his lips.

"That's water!" screamed Julia.

Anthony jumped.

"I don't think it would be very good for your circuits," she whispered, embarrassed at the curious looks from the neighboring diners.

Anthony's eyes widened.

"I think you just saved my life," he said, setting

the glass back down. "In a manner of speaking, of course."

"So how did you find out?" asked Julia a second time.

Anthony looked at his daughter for a long time and decided to say nothing of his morning visit to the Stasi archives. After all, the important news was the result of his research.

"You can sign an article with a pseudonym, but crossing a border is another matter. We found that drawing in Montreal, which means that he went there, and from there I imagined that, with a little luck, he also went to the U.S."

"So you really do have superpowers."

"Actually, I have an old friend who used to work for the police."

"Thank you," murmured Julia.

"What's your plan now?"

"I have no idea. I'm just glad that Thomas became what he always dreamed of becoming."

"What do you know about that?"

"He always wanted to be a reporter."

"Do you think that was his only dream? Do you really think that, when he looks back at his life, he'll want to be looking through a scrapbook of faded newspaper clippings? Many men realize in times of solitude that, in achieving success they have only distanced themselves from their loved ones, and from themselves."

Julia looked at her father, guessing at the sadness that he hid with a smile.

"Let me ask you again, Julia. What's your plan now?"

"Going back to Berlin would probably be the wise thing to do."

"I believe that's what they call a Freudian slip. Don't you mean New York?"

"I just got mixed up."

"Funny, just yesterday you would have called that a sign."

"Like you said, that was yesterday."

"Don't be wrong on this one, Julia. You can't thrive when your life is full of memories that feel like regrets. The foundation of a happy life requires a few important certitudes. It's up to you to choose now. I won't be there to decide for you. In fact, I haven't decided anything for you in a long time. Watch out for solitude, Julia. It's a dangerous companion."

"You've known a lot of solitude?"

"I'm very familiar with it, yes. I was alone for many long years, if you really want to know, but I only had to think of you to chase the solitude away. Let's just say I became aware of certain truths a bit too late. Still, I can't complain. Most jerks like me don't get a second chance like this one, even if it has lasted only a few days. And there's one more truth I should tell you: I missed you, Julia, but I can't do anything to get back those lost years. I foolishly let them slip past—because I had to work, because I had other obligations, because I thought I had an important role to play when the only thing in life that mattered was you. But enough of my rambling. It's not our style to blather on, you and I.

"I'd have liked to come along and watch you give Knapp a piece of your mind, maybe even kick his ass, but I'm too tired now. Besides, I told you, it's your life."

Anthony leaned over to take a newspaper off of a nearby table. He opened its pages and began to flip through them.

"I thought you didn't read German," said Julia, with a lump in her throat.

"You're still there?" retorted Anthony, turning a page.

Julia folded her napkin, pushed back her chair, and rose to her feet.

"I'll call you as soon as I've talked to him," she said as she walked away.

"They're forecasting thunderstorms early this evening!" replied Anthony, watching her go.

But Julia was already hailing a taxi and was too far away to hear. Anthony folded the newspaper and sighed.

*

The car stopped outside the main terminal at

Rome-Fiumicino Airport. Thomas paid the driver and walked around to open Marina's door. A short while later, they were checked in, with the security screening behind them. Thomas, bag hanging off his shoulder, glanced at his watch. Their flight took off in an hour. Marina loitered in front of the shop windows. He took her by the hand and led her to a bar.

"What do you want to do tonight?" he asked, ordering two coffees at the counter.

"Visit your apartment. Ever since I've known you, I've been wondering what it's like."

"One big room with a work table by the window and a bed shoved up against the opposite wall."

"Sounds good to me. No need for anything else," said Marina.

*

Julia pushed open the front door at the *Tagesspiegel* building and gave her name at the reception desk. She asked to see Jürgen Knapp. The receptionist picked up her phone.

"And tell him that I'll wait in the lobby until he comes down, even if it means I have to waste the entire afternoon."

Leaning against the glass wall of the elevator cabin that slowly descended to the first floor, Knapp's eyes remained fixed on his visitor. Julia paced back and forth in front of the windows, where the pages of that day's edition were hung.

The elevator doors opened, and Knapp crossed the lobby.

"What can I do for you, Julia?"

"You can start by telling me why you lied to me."

"Follow me. Let's go somewhere a bit more quiet."

Knapp led her toward the staircase. He motioned for her to sit in a little room near the cafeteria, while he searched his pockets for loose change.

"Coffee? Tea?" he asked, walking over to the beverage machine.

"Nothing for me."

"Why did you come to Berlin, Julia?"

"Are you really that stupid?"

"We haven't seen each other for twenty years. How am I supposed to know why you're here?"

"For Thomas!"

"After all these years?!"

"Where is he?"

"I already told you, in Italy."

"With his wife and children, and he's given up journalism, I know. I know that at least some of your touching story is invented. He changed his name, but he's still a reporter."

"If you already know all that, why are you wasting your time here?"

"Answer me first, why did you hide the truth from me?"

"You want to start asking real questions? I have a few questions myself. Did you ever stop to wonder if Thomas even wants to see you again? What right do you have to reappear in his life like this? Is it just because you decided it was the right moment? Did the desire to see him just pop into your head, and here you are, straight out of another decade? I'm afraid there's no wall left to knock down, no more revolution to stir up, no more excitement or wonder... None of that craziness. All that's left is a little good sense. It's the good sense of adults who are doing their best to get by and to build their careers. Get out of here, Julia. Leave Berlin and go home. You've done enough damage already."

"You can't speak to me that way. You have no right!" replied Julia, her lips trembling.

"You think I'm out of line? Well I have a few other questions for you, while we're at it. Where were you when Thomas hit that land mine? Were you waiting for him at the gate in the airport when he arrived, injured from Kabul? Did you take him to his physical therapy every morning? Were you there to console him when he felt helpless?

"Don't even answer. I know what you'll say. Your absence devastated him. Do you have the least idea of the pain you caused him? Do you know how long it lasted? Do you realize how that idiot, his heart broken, still came to your defense even though I did everything to allow him to finally hate you?"

Though the tears flowed down Julia's cheeks, nothing could stop Knapp now.

"Can you tell me how many years it took him to accept the truth and turn the page? How long it took him to get over you? Every corner of Berlin reminded him of a memory the two of you shared, and he told me about them outside of cafés, on park benches, along the banks of canals. Do you know how many new people he met in vain, how many women tried to love him, only to run up against your perfume or the stupid things you had said that made him laugh?

"I know everything about you, the feeling of your skin, your bad temper in the morning, which he thought was cute—I'll never understand why—what you ate for breakfast, the way you pulled your hair back, the way you put on your makeup, the clothes you liked to wear, the side of the bed you slept on. A thousand times I had to hear the pieces you learned at your Wednesday piano lessons, because, his soul shredded to pieces, he continued to play them, week after week, year after year. I had to look at all of your drawings and watercolors of those stupid animals that he knew by name. I can't count the number of shop windows we stopped in front of because you would have liked a certain dress, painting, bouquet, and I don't know what else. Can you imagine how many times I wondered what you'd done to him to make him miss you so much?

"And when he finally started getting over you, I feared that we'd run into somebody who looked like you, some ghost that would send him reeling back in time and erase all the progress he'd made. It was a long road for him. You wanted to know why I lied to you? I hope now you understand."

"I never meant to hurt him, Knapp, never," Julia sobbed, overwhelmed with emotion.

Knapp picked up a paper napkin and handed it to her.

"Why are you crying? Where are you in your life, Julia? Married? Divorced maybe? Children? A recent transfer to Berlin?"

"You don't have to be so cruel."

"You, of all people, aren't going to lecture me about cruelty, now are you?"

"You don't understand…"

"But I can imagine. You changed your mind after twenty years, is that it? It's too late. He wrote you when he came back from Kabul. Don't tell me he didn't, because I helped him find the right words. I was there when he came back crestfallen from the airport the last day of every month. You made a choice, and he respected it without reproach. Is that what you came to find out? Well, you can leave in peace."

"I never made a choice, Knapp. Thomas's letter… I only got it two days ago."

*

The plane flew over the Alps. Marina had dozed off, her head resting on Thomas's shoulder. He lowered the shade on the window and closed his eyes in an attempt to sleep. They would land in Berlin in an hour.

*

Julia told her story, and Knapp didn't interrupt her a single time. She too had taken a long time to mourn the disappearance of a man she had thought was dead. When she finished telling her tale, she got up and apologized again for the pain she had unknowingly and unwittingly caused. She said goodbye to Knapp and made him swear never to tell Thomas about her visit to Berlin. Knapp watched her walk down the hallway to the stairs. As she set her foot on the first step, he called out her name. Julia turned around.

"I can't keep that promise. I don't want to lose my best friend. Thomas is on a plane coming from Rome. He lands in forty-five minutes."

19.

The taxi driver told her that the trip to the airport typically took about thirty-five minutes. She promised him she'd double his price if he got her there in time. At the second stoplight, she suddenly opened her door and got into the front seat, next to him, just as the light turned green.

"Passengers have to sit in the back!" the driver exclaimed.

"Be that as it may, the mirror I need is up here," she said, lowering the sun visor. "Go on, drive! *Schnell, schnell!*"

She didn't like what she saw in the mirror. Her eyes were swollen, and the tip of her nose was still red from her crying fit. She hadn't waited twenty years to fall into Thomas's arms just to show up looking like an albino rabbit. She gave a loud sigh of frustration—they might as well turn around! A sharp turn ruined her first attempt at applying her mascara. Julia grumbled at the driver, who, in turn, retorted that they could arrive in the next fifteen minutes or they could stop on the shoulder for Julia to finish daubing at her face.

"Just keep driving!" she shouted with urgency, returning to her mascara.

The highway was clogged with traffic. She begged the driver to pass on the right, despite the solid line forbidding it. He could lose his license for that kind of infraction, he said. Julia promised that, if they got pulled over, she'd pretend to be giving birth. The driver pointed out that she didn't have the belly of a pregnant woman. In response Julia stuck out her stomach and began moaning and wailing, hands at the small of her back. "Fine, fine," said the driver, pressing his foot on the accelerator.

"I've gained a little weight, haven't I?" Julia said, worriedly inspecting her waist.

At 6:22 p.m., she leapt out onto the sidewalk before the taxi had come to a complete stop. The entire length of the terminal stretched before her.

Julia wondered where the international arrivals could be found. A passing steward pointed her to the far western end of the building. Breathless after her harrowing run, she scanned the arrivals screen. No flights from Rome were listed. Julia took off her shoes and began to race in the opposite direction. She blazed a trail into a crowd surrounding the exit door for arriving passengers, wiggling through the mass of people to a vantage point just behind the railing. The first wave of passengers came through the exit, the sliding doors opening and closing with each group of passengers that left the baggage-claim area. Tourists, vacationers, salesmen, businessmen and women…all of them dressed according to their function. People waved their hands in the air, some ran forward to hug each other, others were happy to just say hello. Here she heard French, there some Spanish… A little later, English.

With the fourth wave of people, she finally heard Italian. Two hunched-over university students with backpacks walked arm-in-arm, looking like tortoises. A priest clutching his missal resembled a magpie. A copilot and flight attendant exchanging addresses had surely been giraffes in a past life. A conference delegate with a face like an owl looked for his group, stretching out his neck. A little butterfly of a girl ran to her mother's waiting arms. A father bear was reunited with his wife. Suddenly, in the middle of a hundred other faces, Thomas's appeared, just as it had twenty years before.

There were a few lines around his eyes, the dimple in his chin was more pronounced, and he hadn't shaved in a few days. But his eyes—soft like sand, with that same gaze that had pulled her across the rooftops of Berlin and turned her knees to jelly under the full moon in the Tiergarten—his eyes were the same. Julia held her breath, stood on her toes, and leaned out over the barrier. Just as she was raising her arm, Thomas turned to talk to a young woman holding him by the waist. As they passed in front of her, Julia's heels and heart sank to the ground.

The couple left the terminal and disappeared.

*

"Do you want to stop by my place first?" asked Thomas as he closed the taxi door.

"I'll see your apartment soon enough. We should probably go to the office. It's late, and Knapp may have gone already. It's important for my career that he see me. Wasn't that the pretext you came up with so I'd accompany you to Berlin?"

"Potsdamerstrasse," Thomas told the chauffeur.

Ten cars behind them, a woman got into another taxi and headed for her hotel.

*

The concierge told Julia that her father was waiting for her in the bar. She found him sitting at a table near the window.

"It doesn't look like it went very well," he said, getting up to greet her.

Julia let her weight fall into an armchair.

"Nothing went well. Knapp hadn't lied about everything."

"You saw Thomas?"

"At the airport. He was arriving from Rome…in the company of his wife."

"Did you talk to each other?"

"He didn't see me."

Anthony called to the waiter.

"Do you want something to drink?"

"I'd like to go home."

"Were they wearing rings?"

"She had her arm around his waist. I didn't ask them for a marriage certificate."

"Just a few days ago, you had somebody's arm around your waist, too. I wasn't there to see it, because it was my funeral, but still, I was present in a way…" Anthony said, letting out a laugh. "I'm sorry, but it does make me laugh to say so."

"I really don't see what there is to laugh about. We were supposed to get married that day. Our absurd trip together is over tomorrow, and it's probably for the best. Knapp was right. What right do I have to reappear in his life?"

"The right to a second chance, maybe?"

"For him, for you, or for me? It was a selfish act and destined to fail from the start."

"What do you plan on doing now?"

"Packing my bag and going to bed."

"I meant once we get back."

"I'll take stock of my life and try to glue together the pieces of all of the things I've broken. I'll try to forget everything and start living my old life again. I don't have any other choice this time."

"Of course you do. You have the choice to follow this through and leave Berlin with a clear conscience."

"You're one to be giving lectures on love."

Anthony looked at his daughter attentively and scooted his chair toward hers.

"Do you remember what you did every night when you were a little girl, until you finally collapsed from exhaustion?"

"I'd read under the covers with a flashlight."

"Why didn't you just turn on your lamp?"

"To make you think that I was sleeping. I was reading in secret..."

"Did you ever wonder whether your flashlight was magical?"

"No, should I have?"

"Did it ever go out a single time during all those years?"

"No," replied Julia, confused.

"And yet you never had to change the batteries? Or did you? My dear, what do you know about love? You only ever loved those who reflected you in a positive light. Look me in the face and talk to me about your marriage, about your plans for the future. Swear to me that, aside from this unexpected journey, nothing else could have interfered with your love for Adam.

"How could you know the first thing about Thomas's feelings or where his life is headed, when you don't have the slightest idea of the direction you're going in? Is it just because a woman had her arm around his waist?

"Let's be frank with one another. I'd like to ask you a question, and I want you to promise to answer me sincerely. How long did your longest relationship last? I'm not talking about Thomas, or feelings you might have once dreamed about, but a real relationship. Two, three, four years, maybe five? It's not important, but some people say love lasts seven years. Go on, be honest and tell me. Would you be capable of giving yourself without reserve for seven years, without holding back or being afraid or doubting, all the while knowing that the person you love more than anything in the world will one day forget almost everything that you've experienced together?

"Would you be willing to accept the fact that your care, your love will one day be erased from their memory and that nature, detesting empty space, would fill that emptiness with reproaches and regrets? If you knew all that was inevitable, would you still find the strength to get up in the middle of the night, when the person you love is thirsty or has a nightmare? Would you still want to make their breakfast every morning? Would you find a way to fill up their days, to entertain them? Would you tell her stories when she gets bored, sing her songs, take her out because she needs fresh air, even when it's cold? And in the evening, would you ignore your exhaustion and come to sit at the foot of her bed and chase away her fears, to talk to her about a future that would certainly take her far away from you? If your response to all of these questions is yes, then excuse me for misjudging you. You really do know what it means to love somebody."

"Are you talking about Mom?"

"No, my dear child, I'm talking about you. The love I just described is that of a father or a mother for their child. Can you imagine how many days and nights we spent watching over you, protecting you from the least little danger, looking at you, helping you grow up, drying your tears, making you laugh? Do you know how many times we took you to the park in the middle of winter, and how many times we toted bags full of toys to the beach in the summer, the miles and miles we covered, words repeated until you learned them? And yet, how old are you in your earliest childhood memory?

"Imagine how much you have to love a child to learn to live only for them, all the while knowing that they'll remember nothing of those first years, and that in the years that follow, they'll suffer from the things that weren't done right, only to one day, inevitably, leave us, proud of their freedom.

"I know that you're angry at me for not being there enough when you were young. Do you know how hard it is the day your children leave home? Have you ever thought of how that rupture affects a parent? Let me tell you what happens. You stand like a fool on the doorstep, watching them leave, trying to convince yourself that their departure is necessary and that you should cherish the carelessness that pushes you away, dispossessing you of your own flesh and blood.

"When your children close that door behind you, we parents have to learn everything over again. We have to learn how to furnish empty rooms, to stop listening for the sound of footsteps and the reassuring creak of the stairs when you came home late, knowing that we could finally sleep soundly. When you left, I sought sleep in vain, knowing you weren't going to come home anymore. You see, my dear Julia, even though no father or mother ever wins a prize for it, that's what it means to love somebody, and we have no alternative, because *God, how we love our children*. You'll always be mad at me for taking you away from Thomas. One last time, I ask you to please forgive me for not giving you that letter."

Anthony raised his arm and asked the waiter to bring them some water. Sweat pearled on his forehead. He took a handkerchief from his pocket.

"Forgive me," he repeated, his arm still in the air. "Forgive me, forgive me, forgive me."

"What's wrong?" asked Julia, worriedly.

"Forgive me," Anthony repeated three times in a row.

"Daddy?"

"Forgive me, forgive me…"

He stood, staggered, and fell back into the armchair.

Julia called the waiter for help. Anthony made a reassuring gesture, insisting it was unnecessary.

"Where are we?" he asked in a daze.

"In Berlin, in the hotel bar."

"But where are we now? What day is it? What am I doing here?"

"Stop it!" begged Julia in a panic. "It's Friday. We came here together. We left New York four days ago to find Thomas, don't you remember? It was because of that stupid drawing I saw on the pier in Montreal. You gave it to me and wanted to come here. Tell me you remember it. You're tired, that's all. You have to conserve your batteries. I know that it's ridiculous, but you're the one who said it first. You wanted us to talk about everything, but we've only talked about me. You have to find your wits. We still have two days left, just for the two of us, to say all those things we never said. I want to hear about everything that I've forgotten about. I want to hear the stories you used to tell me. Like the one about the pilot stranded on the banks of the Amazon when his plane ran out of fuel. And the otter that showed him the way and served as his guide. I remember the otter's fur was blue, a blue only you could describe…"

Julia took her father by the arm and led him back to his room.

"You don't look well. Sleep. You'll have more energy tomorrow."

Anthony refused to lie down on the bed. The armchair near the window would do very well.

"You know," he said, sitting down. "It's funny how we always find a good reason not to love—fear of suffering or fear of being abandoned—and yet you never appreciate how much you love life until you realize that it will leave you one day."

"Don't say that…"

"Stop projecting yourself into an imaginary future, Julia. There are no broken pieces to glue together. There is simply your life to live, and that never turns out like you expect it will. And I can tell you, it goes by at a blinding speed. What are you doing with me here in this room? Go walk in the footsteps of your memories. You wanted to take stock, so go on. Do it. You were here twenty years ago. Now go and find those years you missed while there's still time. Thomas is in the same city as you this evening. What does it matter whether you see him or not? You're both breathing the same air. You know he's there, closer to you than he'll ever be again. Go out and stop under every window where a light is lit. Pick up your head and ask yourself what you'd feel if you thought you recognized his silhouette on the other side of the curtains. And if you think it's him, shout his name from the street. He'll hear you and maybe come outside. He'll tell you he loves you, or he'll tell you to get out of his life forever. At least you'll have a clear heart."

He asked Julia to leave him alone. She moved closer, and Anthony smiled.

"I'm sorry I scared you in the bar earlier. I shouldn't have done that," he said with a guilty look.

"You didn't just pretend to malfunction…did you?"

"Don't you think I missed your mother when she started to lose her mind? You're not the only one who lost her. I spent four years living by her side without her having the slightest idea of who I was. Go on now! It's your last night in Berlin!"

Julia went back to her room and stretched out on the bed. There was nothing on television, and the magazines on the coffee table were all in German. She got up and decided to get some fresh air. What good was it to stay in her room? She might as well wander around the city and take advantage of her last moments in Berlin. She fished around in her suitcase in search of a sweater. Toward the bottom, her hand brushed up against the blue envelope she'd always hidden between the pages of a history book on a shelf in her childhood bedroom. She looked at the handwriting on the front and put the letter in her pocket.

Before leaving the hotel, she went to the top floor and knocked on the door of the suite where her father was resting.

"Did you forget something?" asked Anthony as

he opened the door.

Julia didn't respond.

"I don't know where you're going, and it's probably better that way, but don't forget, tomorrow at eight o'clock, I'll be waiting for you in the lobby. I called a car for us. We can't miss that plane. You have to take me back to New York."

"Do you think that love ever stops hurting?" asked Julia, still standing in his door.

"Never, if you're lucky."

"Well, then it's my turn to ask for forgiveness. I should have shared this with you much sooner. It's mine, and I wanted to keep it all to myself, but it concerns you as well."

"What is it?"

"The last letter Mom wrote to me."

She handed it to her father and left.

Anthony watched his daughter walk away. He looked at the envelope that she had given him and immediately recognized his wife's handwriting. He took a deep breath. His shoulders drooped. He sat down in an armchair to read.

Julia,

You come into this room, and your silhouette stands out against the light flooding in through the door. I hear your footsteps coming toward me. I know your face, and I manage to find your name.

I know your familiar scent; it's a comfort to me. Only that rare fragrance saves me from the worrying that has strangled me for such a long time. You must be the girl who often comes in the evening, and I know that evening is near when you arrive at my bedside. Your words are soft, more peaceful than those of the man who comes at noon. I also trust him when he tells me he loves me, because he seems to wish me well. His gestures are gentle. Sometimes he gets up and goes toward the other light, which shines beyond the trees outside the window. Sometimes he lowers his head and cries from some heartache that I don't understand. He calls me by a name that I don't recognize but that I take as mine each time he says it, just to make him happy. I must admit to you that, when I smile at him, hearing the name that he gives me, I feel lighter.

You are sitting nearby, on the edge of the bed. My eyes follow your fingers delicately caressing my forehead. I'm not afraid. You never stop calling to me, and I see in your eyes that you also want me to give you a name. There's no sadness left in you. That's why I enjoy your visits. I close my eyes when your wrist passes over my nose. The smell of your skin reminds me of my childhood—or does it remind me of yours? You are my daughter, my love, and I know that now and for a few moments longer. I have so many things to tell you and so little time. I would like you to laugh, my love, for you to run and tell your father, who hides by the window when he cries, that he should stop crying, that I recognize him sometimes. Tell him I know who he is. Tell him that I remember how we loved each other, because I also love him all over again each time he comes to visit me.

Goodnight, my love. I'm sleeping now, waiting for you.

Your mother

20.

Knapp was waiting at the front desk. Thomas had called as he left the airport to tell him they had arrived. After greeting Marina and hugging his friend, he took them to his office.

"It's a good thing that you're here," he said to Marina. "You'll be able to help me out of a pinch. Your prime minister is coming to Berlin this evening, and the journalist that was supposed to cover the event and the gala dinner in his honor has fallen terribly ill. We have three columns reserved in tomorrow's edition. You have to get changed and leave right away. I'll need your copy before two a.m., so that there's time to send it to the proofreaders. Everything needs to hit the press before three. I'm sorry to interfere with any plans you may have made for this evening, but it's urgent. The newspaper has to come first."

Marina rose, said goodbye to Knapp, planted a kiss on Thomas's forehead, and whispered, "Arrivederci, my idiot," in his ear before slipping away.

Thomas took leave from Knapp and ran down the hall after her.

"You're not going to just up and obey him like that, are you? What about our dinner together?"

"And you? Aren't you at his beck and call, too? Remind me again, what time is your flight for Mogadishu? Thomas, you've told me a hundred times, career always comes first, before everything else. You won't be here tomorrow, and who knows how long you'll be gone. Take care of yourself. God willing, we might meet again in one town or another."

"At least take the keys to my place. Come write your article at my apartment."

"I'll be more comfortable in a hotel. I think it would be too difficult to concentrate at your place. The temptation to explore your palace would be irresistible."

"There's only one room, you know. The tour won't last long."

"You really are my favorite idiot. I was talking about jumping in bed with you, silly. That will have to wait for next time. If I change my mind, I'll come give myself a treat and wake you up with your doorbell. See you soon!"

Marina threw him a carefree "ciao" and walked away.

*

"Are you okay?" asked Knapp when Thomas came back, slamming the door behind him.

"You're a pain in the ass! I came back for one night in Berlin with Marina. It's the last night before I leave, and you manage to take her away from me. Do you really think I believe you had nobody else to cover that story? What's your problem anyway? Are you jealous or something? Do you like her? You've become such an ambitious bastard that nothing besides this newspaper matters to you anymore."

"Are you done?" asked Knapp, sitting back down behind his desk.

"Admit it, you're a real pain in the ass," continued Thomas furiously.

"Take a chair. I have something important to tell you that I think you should hear from a seated position."

*

The Tiergarten glowed in the evening light. Two old streetlamps spread their yellow haloes across the footpath along the canal. On the lake, the boatmen were tying their crafts to one another. Julia followed the path to the edge of the zoo. A little farther on was a lookout point over the river. She cut through the woods, unafraid of getting lost, as though each tree were familiar to her. The Victory Column stood before her. She walked through the roundabout, and her feet led her past the Brandenburg Gate. Suddenly, she realized where she was. She stopped.

There, almost twenty years before, at the end of this row of trees had once stood a wall. It was there that, for the first time, she had seen Thomas. Today a bench sat in that spot under a linden tree, welcoming the passersby.

"I was sure I'd find you here," said a voice behind her. "You still have the same way of walking."

Julia jumped, startled. Her chest tightened.

"Thomas?" she whispered breathlessly without turning around.

"I don't know what you're supposed to do in a situation like this. Shake hands? Hug?" he said hesitantly.

"I don't know either," she said, still too afraid to turn and face him.

"When Knapp told me that you were in Berlin, I didn't know how I could find you. I first thought to call all of the youth hostels, but there are so many now... Then I imagined that, with a little luck, you'd come back here."

"Your voice is the same, a little deeper," she said, turning to face him with a fragile smile.

He took a step closer to her and lowered his voice.

"If you'd like, I could climb that tree and jump from a branch. It's almost as high as the first time I fell on top of you."

Thomas closed the distance between them and took Julia in his arms.

"Time passes so quickly and so slowly, all at

once," he said, holding her tightly against him.

"Are you crying?" asked Julia, gently caressing his cheek.

"No, it's a gnat that flew in my eye. And you?"

"Your gnat's twin sister. It's funny, there must have been only two..."

"Close your eyes," whispered Thomas, his lips warm against her ear.

Then, as though nothing had ever separated them, Thomas did as he had done every morning they woke up together. He lightly brushed Julia's lips with his fingertips, before kissing each of her eyelids.

"It was the prettiest way of saying good morning," she said when he was finished.

Julia burrowed her face into the hollow between Thomas's neck and shoulder.

"You still smell the same. I hadn't forgotten."

"Come on, it's cold. You're shivering."

Thomas took Julia by the hand and led her toward the Brandenburg Gate.

"You were at the airport earlier today?"

"Yes. How did you know?"

"Why didn't you wave to me?"

"I didn't really feel like introducing myself to your wife."

"Her name is Marina."

"That's a pretty name."

"She's a friend. We have a…how do you say?… causal relationship."

"I think you mean casual."

"Something like that. I still don't speak English perfectly."

"You get by pretty well."

They left the park and crossed the square. Thomas led her to a café terrace. They sat down and spent a long time just looking at each other in silence, incapable of finding any words.

Thomas finally broke the silence. "It's crazy how little you've changed."

"Oh, I assure you, in twenty years, I've done some changing. If you saw me when I woke up in the morning you'd know just how many years have passed."

"I don't need to do that. I counted every one."

The waiter uncorked the bottle of prosecco and served them two glasses.

"Thomas, about your letter... You should know..."

"Knapp told me everything. Your father really followed through with his convictions!"

He lifted his glass and clinked it against hers delicately. Couples strolled across the square, stopping to admire the beauty of the Brandenburg Gate's pillars.

"Are you happy?"

Julia said nothing.

"Where are you in life?" asked Thomas.

"In Berlin, with you, just as lost as I was twenty years ago."

"Why did you come here?"

"I didn't have an address to send you a response. After twenty years I wasn't about to trust the post office to deliver my thoughts."

"Are you married? Do you have any children?"

"Not yet," responded Julia.

"Not yet for children or for marriage?"

"For both."

"Any plans?"

"You didn't have that scar on your chin before."

"Before, I'd only jumped off of a wall. I hadn't hit a mine."

"You've gained a little weight," said Julia with a smile.

"Thanks a lot."

"No, seriously, it was a compliment. It suits you very well."

"You're a bad liar, but it's true, I've aged. Are you hungry?"

"No," said Julia, lowering her eyes.

"I'm not either. Do you want to take a walk?"

"I feel like everything I say is ridiculous," she murmured.

"No, it's not. But you haven't told me anything about your life yet," said Thomas sadly.

"I went back to our café, you know."

"I've never gone back."

"The owner recognized me."

"See? I said you hadn't changed."

"They knocked down the old building where we used to live and put up a new one. On our street there's nothing left except the little park across the way."

"Maybe it's better like that. I don't have many good memories back there, apart from our time together. I live in the West now. To many that means nothing, but I still see the border when I look out the window."

"Knapp told me about you," continued Julia.

"What did he tell you?"

"That you ran a restaurant in Italy, that you had a horde of children who helped you make your pizzas," Julia responded.

"What an idiot... How did he come up with that?"

"He was remembering all of the pain I caused you."

"I imagine I must have hurt you, too, if you thought I was dead."

Thomas looked at Julia and winced slightly.

"That sounded pretentious, didn't it?"

"Yes, a little, but it's true."

Thomas took Julia's hand in his.

"We both followed our own roads. Life decided that for us. Your father had a lot to do with it, but, in the end, you have to believe that fate didn't want us to be together."

"Maybe destiny was just trying to protect us.

Maybe we would have ended up annoying each other and getting a divorce. You'd have been the man that I hate the most in the world, and we'd have never spent this evening together."

"But maybe we would have been together tonight, fighting over how to raise our children. And then there are couples that break up but stay friends. Do you have a boyfriend? Please don't accuse the question this time."

"Avoid!"

"What?"

"You meant to say 'avoid the question.'"

"I have an idea. Follow me."

The neighboring terrace belonged to a seafood restaurant. Thomas grabbed a table right from under the noses of a couple of waiting tourists.

"You do things like that now?" asked Julia as she sat down. "It's not very polite… You'll get us kicked out!"

"In my line of work, you learn to take care of yourself. Besides, the owner is a friend. We might as well take advantage."

The owner had just waved hello to Thomas from across the restaurant.

"Next time, try to be more discreet. You'll get me in trouble with my clientele!" he whispered to Thomas.

Thomas introduced his friend to Julia.

"What would you recommend for two people who aren't hungry at all?" he asked.

"I'll bring you some shrimp. Your appetite will come back once you start eating."

The owner left. Before going into the kitchen, he turned and gave Thomas a wink and a thumbs up—clearly, to tell Thomas that he thought Julia was a catch.

"I work in animation."

"I know. I like the blue otter a lot."

"You've seen it?"

"I'd be lying if I said that I hadn't missed a single one of your cartoons, but like everything in my profession, I heard the creator's name through the grapevine. One afternoon when I was in Madrid and had some free time, I noticed the movie poster and went into the theater. I have to admit that I didn't understand the words, since Spanish isn't my strong point, but I think I got the general idea of the story. Can I ask you a question?"

"Shoot."

"The bear character isn't based on me, by any chance, is it?"

"Stanley thought you're more like the hedgehog."

"Who's Stanley?"

"My best friend."

"And how would he know if I looked like a hedgehog?"

"He's very intuitive, intelligent, and, most of all, I talk to him about you all of the time."

"Sounds like he's a nice guy. What kind of friend is he exactly?"

"A widower with whom I've shared a lot of difficult moments."

"I'm sorry for him."

"Good times, too, though!"

"I was talking about the fact that he lost his wife. Has she been dead long?"

"It was his boyfriend who died."

"Well, then I'm even sadder for him."

"What? That doesn't make any sense."

"I know, it's stupid, but he seems nicer when I imagine him in love with a man. And who inspired the weasel?"

"My downstairs neighbor. He runs a shoe store. Tell me, the afternoon you went to see my cartoon, how was your day?"

"It was sad when the movie was over."

"I missed you, Thomas."

"I missed you, too, more than you can imagine. But we should change the subject. There aren't any gnats to accuse in this restaurant."

"I think you mean there aren't any gnats to *blame*."

"Whatever. I've lived through a hundred days like the one in Madrid, here and elsewhere… And I sometimes still have days like that. You know, we really have to talk about something else, before you *accuse* me of boring you with my nostalgia."

"And in Rome?"

"You still haven't told me anything about your life, Julia."

"Twenty years take a long time to recount, you know."

"Is somebody waiting for you?"

"Not tonight."

"And tomorrow?"

"Yes. There's somebody in New York." Julia looked down at the table.

"Is it serious?"

"I was supposed to get married…on Saturday."

"Supposed to?"

"We had to cancel the ceremony."

"Because of him or because of you?"

"Because of my father…" she raised her eyes back up, a slight smile on her lips.

"He's obsessed, isn't he? Did he also smash your future husband's face?"

"No, even more inspired than that."

"I'm sorry."

"No, you probably aren't sorry, and I can't blame you."

"Don't get me wrong, I'd love to punch your fi-ancé in the face… No, I'm sorry, that time I really went over the line." Thomas shook his head ruefully.

Julia let out a little giggle, a second, and then couldn't help herself and burst out in a fit of laughter.

"What's so funny?"

"If you had only just seen the look on your face," continued Julia, still laughing. "You looked like a kid caught in the pantry with jam all over his face. I understand now why you inspired so many of my characters. Nobody but you can make faces like that. God, how I've missed you."

"Stop saying that, Julia."

"Why?"

"Because you were supposed to get married last Saturday." Thomas was no longer smiling.

The owner of the restaurant came to their table with a large plate in his arms.

"I found just what the two of you need," he announced cheerfully. "Two exquisite sole, a few grilled vegetables to go with them, and a sauce with fresh herbs—just the ticket for your stubborn stomachs. Shall I prepare them for you?"

"Excuse me," said Thomas to his friend. "I'm afraid we won't be staying. Can you bring me the bill?"

"What's this I hear? I don't know what's been going on here, but it's entirely out of the question that you leave my restaurant without tasting my cooking. So go ahead, have a good fight, say everything that you have on your minds, and I'll go prepare these two little miracles. You can give me the pleasure of making up over my fish. And that's an order, Thomas!"

The owner walked away to prepare the sole on a side table, never taking his eyes off of Thomas and Julia.

"I get the impression we don't have a choice. If

you don't put up with me a little while longer, your friend will be very angry," said Julia.

"I get the same impression," said Thomas, his face softening a bit. "Please forgive me, Julia, I shouldn't have…"

"Stop asking me to forgive you all the time. It doesn't suit you. Let's try to eat, and then you can take me back to my hotel. I feel like walking by your side. Do I have the right to say that?" There was a faint hint of pleading in her voice.

"Yes," Thomas replied with a smile. "How did your father prevent you from getting married this time?"

"Forget about him. Let's talk about you."

Thomas told her about the past twenty years of his life, leaving a lot out. Julia did the same. When they had finished their dinner, the owner insisted that they taste his chocolate soufflé. He had made it especially for them. It was served with two spoons, but Julia and Thomas used only one.

They left the restaurant under the bright moonlight and returned to Julia's hotel through the park. The full moon was reflected in the lake, where a few boats gently rocked, tied to a pontoon.

Julia told Thomas an old Chinese legend about jumping into puddles under the full moon. He told her about all of his travels but said nothing about the wars he had covered. She told him about New York, her job, and her best friend but never spoke of her plans for the future.

They left the park behind and walked through the city. Julia made Thomas stop when they reached a certain square.

"Do you remember?" she asked.

"Yes. This is where I found Knapp in the middle of the crowd. What an incredible night. Whatever happened to your two French friends?"

"I haven't talked to them in a long time. Mathias runs a bookstore in Paris, and Antoine is an architect in London, I think."

"Did they get married?"

"And divorced, last I heard."

"Look," said Thomas, pointing to the darkened window of a café. "That's the place where we always met up with Knapp."

"You know, I found the number that the two of you always bickered about."

"What number?"

"The percentage of East Germans who collaborated with the Stasi by giving them information. I ran across it two years ago in the library, flipping through a journal that published a special edition about the fall of the wall."

"You were still interested in that kind of thing two years ago?"

"Only two percent. See, you can be proud of your fellow citizens."

"My grandmother was part of that two percent, Julia. I went and looked at my file in the archives. I suspected that there would be something on me because of Knapp's defection to the West. My own grandmother informed on me. I read pages upon pages of details about my life, the things I did, who my friends were. It's a funny way to get in touch with your childhood memories."

"If you only knew what I've been through these past few days. She might have done it to protect you, so that you wouldn't be bothered."

"I'll never know."

"Is that why you changed your name?"

"Yes, to put my past behind me and start a new life."

"Was I part of that past you erased?"

"We're back at your hotel, Julia."

She looked up and saw the sign of the Brandenburger Hof Hotel lighting up the face of the building. Thomas took her in his arms and smiled sadly.

"There's no tree here. How can we say goodbye like this?"

"Do you think things would have worked out between us?"

"Who knows."

"I don't know how to say goodbye, Thomas. I don't even know if I want to."

"It was so sweet, so wonderful to see you again. It was like receiving an unexpected gift from life," Thomas whispered.

Julia rested her head on his shoulder.

"Yes, it was wonderfully sweet."

"You still haven't answered the only question that really worries me. Are you happy?"

"Not anymore."

"And you? Do you believe that things would have worked out between us?" asked Thomas.

"Probably."

"Well, then you've changed."

"Why do you say that?"

"Because, back in the old days, with your old sarcastic sense of humor, you would have said our lives together would have turned out to be an utter fiasco, that you would have never been able to watch me grow old, to gain weight...that you wouldn't have liked for me to be traveling for work all the time."

"I've learned to lie since then."

"There's the Julia I recognize. The Julia I never stopped loving."

"I can think of one way of knowing whether we would have had a chance," said Julia breathlessly.

"What's that?"

Julia placed her lips on his. Their kiss lasted a long time. Like two teenagers in love, they were oblivious to the rest of the world. She took him by the hand and led him through the hotel lobby. The concierge dozed behind his desk. Julia pulled Thomas to the elevators. She pushed the button, and their embrace continued to the sixth floor.

Their bodies reunited, just as they had been in

their most intimate memories. Their sweat mingled under the sheets. Julia closed her eyes. His caressing hand slid down her stomach, and she reached up to clasp the nape of his neck. His mouth brushed over her shoulder and down her neck to the curves of her breasts... His lips wandered uncontrollably. She wove her fingers into his hair. His tongue went deeper, lower, and the pleasure rose in waves, bringing back the sensations of their past. Their legs intertwined, their bodies twisted around one another, and nothing could have torn them apart. Their movements hadn't changed. They were sometimes awkward but just as tender as they had always been.

The minutes stretched into hours. Morning light broke over their languid bodies, abandoned in the warmth of the bed.

*

In the distance a church bell struck eight. Thomas stretched and walked over to the window. Julia sat up and dreamily gazed at the play of shadow and light over his body.

"God, you're beautiful," said Thomas as he turned around and saw her.

Julia didn't respond.

"Now what?" he asked with a gentle voice.

"I'm hungry!"

"Is that bag on the chair already packed?"

"I'm leaving…this morning," Julia stammered.

"It took me ten years to put you behind me. I thought I had succeeded. I thought I knew fear on the battlefield, but I had no idea. That was nothing compared to what I'm feeling right now, next to you in this room, faced with the idea of losing you again."

"Thomas…"

"What do you want me to say, Julia? That this was all a mistake? Maybe it was. When Knapp admitted to me that you were in town, I imagined that time might have erased all the differences that once separated us—a girl from the West and a boy from the East. I hoped that age would have at least done us that favor. But our lives are still very different, aren't they?"

"I draw; you're a reporter. We've both become what we'd always dreamed of."

"But that's not important, at least not for me. You still haven't told me why your father caused you to cancel your wedding. Is he going to come into this room and knock me down again?"

"I was only eighteen and didn't have any choice but to follow him. I was hardly an adult. As far as my father is concerned, he's dead now. His burial was the day I was supposed to get married. Now you know why."

"I'm sorry for him. I'm sorry for you, too, if it caused you any suffering."

"There's no need to be sorry, Thomas."

"Why did you come to Berlin?"

"You know very well why. Knapp told you everything. I got your letter a few days ago. I couldn't have come any sooner."

"You didn't want to get married without being sure, is that it?"

"You don't have to be cruel."

Thomas sat at the foot of the bed.

"I learned to tame solitude over the years. It took an incredible amount of patience. I walked through cities all over the world in search of air you might have breathed. They say that the thoughts of two people who love each other always end up coming together. I often wondered, falling asleep at night. I wondered if you ever thought about me when I was thinking about you. I came to New York and walked the streets, dreaming of running into you, but at the same time scared that it might happen. I thought I saw you a hundred times. My heart stopped beating every time I saw a woman who reminded me of you. I swore to never love like that again—it's insanity, you know, an irresponsible sort of self-neglect. Time has passed, and our time has passed as well, don't you think? Didn't you ask yourself that before taking your plane?"

"Stop, Thomas! Don't ruin everything. What do you expect me to say? I stared at the sky day and night convinced that you were watching me from up there. So, no, I never asked myself that question before I got on the plane."

"What are you suggesting, then? That we stay friends? That I call you when I'm in New York and that we have a drink together and reminisce about old times? You'll show me pictures of your children, who aren't our children. I'll tell you that they look like you, while trying to ignore how they also look like their father. While I'm in the bathroom, you'll call your future husband, and I'll let the water run so I don't hear him say, 'Hello, darling.' Does he even know you're in Berlin?"

"Stop it!" shouted Julia.

"What are you going to tell him when you get back?" asked Thomas, turning back to look out the window.

"I don't know. I have no idea."

"See? I'm right. You haven't changed a bit."

"Yes, Thomas, of course I've changed. But all it took was a sign. Fate led me here and made me realize that my feelings haven't changed…"

Anthony Walsh paced in the street below, checking his watch. He was watching his daughter's window, and the impatience on his face could be seen from the sixth floor.

"Remind me again when your father died?" asked Thomas, closing the blinds.

"I already told you. He was buried last Saturday."

"Don't say another word. You were right. We

shouldn't ruin the memory of last night. You can't love somebody and lie to them. You can't. We can't."

"I'm not lying to you…"

"Take your bag and go home," muttered Thomas.

He put on his pants, his shirt, and his coat, not taking the time to tie his shoes. He went over to Julia, took her hand, and pulled her into his arms.

"I'm flying to Mogadishu this evening. I already know that I'll think about you constantly while I'm over there. Don't worry about me, and don't have any regrets. I imagined living this moment so many times I've lost count. It was magnificent, my love. Just being able to call you that one more time, just one more time, was something I hardly dared dream of. You've always been the most beautiful woman of my life, the woman haunting my fondest memories. That's a lot. I'll just ask you to do one thing: Promise me you'll be happy."

Thomas kissed Julia tenderly and left without turning around.

As he exited the hotel, he passed by Anthony, who was still waiting by the car.

"Your daughter shouldn't be much longer," he said, waving goodbye.

21.

Julia and her father said nothing to one another during the flight back to New York, apart from one sentence spoken repeatedly by Anthony: "I think that I messed up again." His daughter never entirely understood what he meant. It was raining when they arrived in Manhattan in the middle of the afternoon.

"Look, Julia, you have to say something eventually!" Anthony protested as they entered her apartment on Horatio Street.

"No," responded Julia, dropping her bag.

"Did you see him last night?"

"No!"

"Tell me what happened. Maybe I can help, give you some advice."

"You? That's rich."

"Don't be so stubborn. You're not five years old anymore. I have only twenty-four hours left."

"I didn't see Thomas. Period. Now I'm going to take a shower."

Anthony stood in the door, blocking his daughter's passage.

"And afterward? Are you planning on staying in the bathroom for the next twenty years?"

"Get out of my way."

"Not until you answer my question."

"You want to know what I'm going to do now? I'm going to try to gather the pieces of my life that you so cleverly scattered to the winds in one short week. I most likely won't be able to put everything back together, because some pieces will certainly be gone forever. Don't make that face like you don't understand. You were apologizing the entire flight."

"I wasn't talking about our trip."

"What then?"

Anthony said nothing.

"That's what I thought," continued Julia. "While I'm waiting for your response, I think I'll go slip on some garters and a push-up bra, call Thomas and try to get laid. If I can lie to him like I've learned to do this past week, maybe he'll still be willing to discuss marriage."

"You said Thomas."

"What?"

"You meant to say Adam. You made another Freudian slip."

"Get out of my way before I kill you."

"You'd be wasting your time; I'm already dead. And if you think you shock me by going on about your sex life, you're far off the mark, my dear."

"As soon as I get to Adam's place," she continued, looking her father up and down, "I'll throw him up against the wall and undress him…"

"That's enough!" shouted Anthony angrily. "I don't need to know all the details," he added, calming down.

"Will you let me take a shower now?"

Anthony rolled his eyes and let her pass. He put his ear up to the door and heard Julia make a phone call.

No, they shouldn't disturb Adam if he is in a meeting. She just wanted to let him know she is back in town. If he is free that evening, he can come and pick her up at eight. She'll be waiting downstairs, outside her building. If he isn't able to make it, he can just call her.

Anthony crept into the living room and sat down on the couch. He picked up the remote to turn on the television and then realized he was holding the wrong one. He looked at the little white button and smiled, putting it down beside him.

Fifteen minutes later, Julia reappeared with a raincoat thrown over her arm.

"You're going somewhere?"

"To work."

"On a Saturday? In this weather?"

"There's always somebody at the office on the weekend, and I have a lot of emails to catch up on."

As she was preparing to leave, Anthony called out to her.

"Julia?"

"What is it now?"

"Before you do something really stupid, I think you should know that Thomas still loves you."

"And how do you know?"

"We crossed paths this morning. He was very civil. He waved to me as he was leaving the hotel. I suppose he must have seen me waiting in the street from your hotel-room window."

Julia glared furiously at her father.

"Get out of here. When I get back, I want you gone."

"Where? To that awful attic?"

"Anywhere but here!" said Julia, slamming the door behind her.

*

Anthony grabbed an umbrella hanging from a hook near the door and went to the balcony overlooking the street. Leaning out over the railing, he watched Julia walk away toward the intersection. As soon as she had disappeared, he went into her bedroom. She had left the cordless phone on her nightstand. He picked it up and pressed redial.

He introduced himself as Julia Walsh's assistant. Of course he realized that Miss Walsh had just called and that Adam was not available. However, it was extremely important to tell Adam that Julia would be waiting for him earlier than planned, at six o'clock, and in her apartment, not out in the street, because it was raining. True, that was only forty-five minutes from now. All things considered, maybe it would be best to interrupt his meeting, to pass along the news. It would be pointless for Adam to call her back, since her phone was out of batteries, and she had stepped out to run some errands. Anthony made the secretary promise twice to deliver the message and then hung up, smiling and feeling particularly satisfied with himself.

*

Julia pivoted in her desk chair and turned on her computer. An endless list of emails extended across the screen. She glanced at her desk and saw her inbox overflowing and the light on her voice mail blinking frenetically.

She took her cell phone out of her raincoat pocket and called her best friend to come to the rescue.

"Do you have any customers?" she asked.

"In this weather? Not even a fish. This afternoon was a complete waste."

"I know. I'm soaking wet."

"You're back!" exclaimed Stanley.

"I got back about an hour ago."

"You should have called sooner!"

"Would you be willing to close your store and meet an old friend at Pastis?"

"Order me a tea, not a cappuccino…or whatever you want. I'll be right there."

Ten minutes later, Stanley joined Julia, who was waiting for him at a table tucked in a back corner of the former brewery.

"You look like a cocker spaniel that fell in a lake," she said, hugging him.

"And you look like the poodle that jumped in to rescue him. What did you order?" asked Stanley as he sat down.

"Croquettes."

"Speaking of which, I have two or three juicy little tidbits about who slept with whom this week, but you go first. I want to know everything. Let me guess, I haven't had any news from you for two days… You must have found Thomas. And judging by your face, things didn't go as you'd hoped they would."

"I wasn't hoping for anything…"

"Liar."

"If you've ever wanted to spend some time in the company of an utter imbecile, get ready, because your moment is now!"

Julia told him almost everything from her trip. She told him about going to the press syndicate, Knapp's lies, the reasons behind Thomas's double identity, the art opening, the last-minute limousine ordered by the concierge to take her there… When she got to the part about the shoes that she'd worn with the dress, Stanley was scandalized. He pushed away his tea and ordered a glass of white wine. The rain outside fell increasingly harder. Julia told him about her visit to East Berlin, the street where all the old buildings had been knocked down, the vintage decor of the bar that had survived the demolitions, her conversation with Thomas's best friend, her crazy ride to the airport, seeing Marina, and, finally, before Stanley nearly fainted, she told him about meeting Thomas in the Tiergarten.

Julia continued, describing the terrace of the best fish restaurant in the world, though she had hardly tasted the food, their nighttime walk around the lake, the hotel room where she had made love the night before, and, last of all, the story of the last breakfast they never had together. When the waiter came back a third time to ask if everything was okay, Stanley threatened to stab him with a fork if he interrupted them again.

"I should have come with you," said Stanley. "If I had known you were leaving on an adventure like that, I never would have let you go alone."

Julia idly swirled a spoon in her tea. He looked at her attentively and put his hand on hers, stopping the spoon's circles.

"Julia, you never take sugar. You're a little lost, aren't you?"

"You can leave out the 'little.'"

"If it reassures you, I have a hard time imagining

him going back to that Marina woman. It seems unlikely, from my experience."

"What experience?" replied Julia, smiling. "Besides, by now Thomas is in an airplane headed for
Mogadishu."

"And we're here in New York under the rain,"
sighed Stanley wistfully, turning to watch the downpour beating against the window.

A few passersby had taken refuge under the
awning on the terrace. An old man held his wife up
against him, to protect her a little better.

"I'm going to put my life back into order, as best
I can," continued Julia. "I suppose it's the only thing
I can do now."

"You're right. I am drinking with a real imbecile.
You have the rare luck to find your life in a mess,
and you want to tidy things up? What a fool you are,
princess. Oh, please, dry those eyes this instant.
There's enough water outside, and now is not the
time to cry. I still have too many questions to ask."

Julia passed the back of her hand over her eyelids
and smiled at her friend.

"What do you plan on telling Adam?" continued
Stanley. "For a while there, I thought I was going to
have to start feeding him twice a day, if you didn't
come home soon. He invited me to go to his parents'
house in the country tomorrow. I'm warning you
now, don't blow my cover. I invented a terrible case
of food poisoning to get out of it."

"I'll tell him the part of the truth that will hurt him the least."

"The thing that causes the most suffering in relationships is cowardice. Are you going to give things with him a second chance or not?"

"It may sound awful to say this, but I don't think I have the courage to be single again."

"Then he's going to suffer. Maybe not now, but sooner or later, he's going to suffer."

"I'll find a way to protect him."

"Can I ask you a personal question?"

"You know I wouldn't hide anything from you."

"Your night with Thomas…how was it?"

"Tender, gentle, magical… And then sad the next morning."

"I was talking about the sex."

"Tender, gentle, magical…"

"And you're trying to make me believe that you don't know what to do?"

"I'm in New York, and so is Adam. Thomas is very far away now."

"Princess, the important thing isn't knowing what city or corner of the world the other person is in, but whether or not you truly love them. Mistakes don't count. There's only the life that we live."

*

Adam got out of a taxi, under the pouring rain. The

gutters were overflowing. He leapt to the sidewalk and pressed insistently on the buzzer. Anthony Walsh got up from his seat.

"Alright, alright already! I'm coming," he grumbled, pressing the button that opened the door downstairs.

He heard steps on the staircase and welcomed his visitor with a broad smile.

"Mr. Walsh?" Adam exclaimed with alarm, taking a step back in horror.

"Adam! To what good fortune do I owe your visit?"

Adam stood speechless on the landing.

"Cat got your tongue?"

"But you're dead!" he stammered.

"Now, then, let's not be disagreeable. I know that we haven't always seen eye to eye, but there's no need to talk about me that way!"

"But I was there in the cemetery the day of your burial," Adam faltered.

"That's enough. You're being rude, pal. But we can't just stand here chatting in the door all night long. Come in... You look pale."

Adam walked into the living room. Anthony suggested he take off his dripping trench coat.

"I'm sorry to insist," he said, hanging his coat on the coat rack, "but you must understand my surprise. My wedding was canceled because of your funeral."

"It was also my daughter's wedding, wasn't it?"

"She couldn't have invented this entire story just to…"

"Leave you? Don't flatter yourself. Our family is known for its fertile imaginations, but if you knew Julia well, you'd also know that she'd never do such a crazy thing. There must be another explanation, and if you'd be quiet for two seconds, I could suggest one or two that might seem plausible."

"Where's Julia?"

"Alas, it's been nearly twenty years since my daughter kept me informed of her whereabouts. To tell you the truth, I thought she'd be with you. We've been back in New York for at least three hours."

"You were traveling with her?"

"Of course. Didn't she tell you?"

"I think it would have been difficult for her to explain. I was there when the plane brought your body back from Europe. I rode in the hearse that drove us to the cemetery."

"How very charming. What else? You might as well flip the switch on the incinerator while you're at it."

"I threw a handful of dirt on your coffin!"

"How considerate of you."

"I don't feel very well," Adam confided, his face turning a funny shade of green.

"Well, then go on and sit, instead of standing there like an idiot."

He gestured to the sofa.

"Yes, there. You still recognize a place to rest your backside, don't you? Or did all of your neurons fizzle when you caught sight of me?"

Adam obeyed. He dropped to the sofa. In doing so, he also sat upon the single button of the white remote control.

Anthony fell silent. His eyes snapped shut, and he fell to the floor like a tree, lying stiffly on the carpet at Adam's feet.

*

"I don't suppose you brought back a photo of him, did you?" asked Stanley. "I'm so curious to see what he looks like. Sorry, I know I'm jabbering like an idiot, but I hate it when you're quiet like this."

"Why?"

"Because I'll never be able to know all of the things that are going through your head."

Their conversation was interrupted. Gloria Gaynor belted "I Will Survive" inside Julia's purse.

She grabbed her cell phone and showed Stanley the caller ID, displaying Adam's name. Stanley shrugged. Julia took the call. She heard her fiancé's terrified voice.

"We have a few things to say to each other, you and me, especially you, but that has to wait. Your father just passed out."

"In other circumstances, I would have thought

that was funny, but given the timing, I think it's rather bad taste."

"I'm in your apartment, Julia…"

"What are you doing in my apartment? You're early!" she replied, paralyzed with fear.

"Your assistant called to tell me that you wanted to meet with me earlier."

"My assistant? What assistant?"

"Who cares? I'm calling you to tell you your father has collapsed and is lying motionless in the middle of your living room. Come as soon as possible! I'm calling an ambulance."

Julia shouted back, making Stanley jump.

"Whatever you do, don't do that! I'll be there immediately."

"Have you gone crazy, Julia? I shook him—he's not moving. I'm calling 911."

"Don't call anybody, you hear me? I'll be there in five minutes," she replied, getting up from the table.

"Where are you?"

"Pastis. I'll cross the street and come up. In the meantime, don't do anything. Don't touch anything, especially not him!"

Stanley had no idea what was going on and murmured that he'd get the check. As she ran out through the restaurant, he shouted after her to call when the fire had been put out.

*

She took the stairs four at a time. Upon entering the apartment, she saw her father's body spread out in the middle of the living-room floor.

"Where's the remote control?" she said as she crashed into the room.

"What?" asked Adam, utterly confused.

"A little box with buttons on it... Only one button in this case. A remote control, don't you know what that is?" she replied, urgently searching the room.

"Your father has fallen unconscious and you want to watch TV? I'm calling 911 and asking for two ambulances."

"Did you touch anything? How did this happen?" asked Julia, opening all of the drawers and cupboards.

"I didn't do anything at all, apart from talking to your father, whom, I might add, we buried last week. It was a singular experience, really."

"You can make your jokes later Adam—this is an emergency."

"I wasn't trying to be funny. Are you going to tell me what the hell is going on here? At least tell me that I'm going to wake up and laugh at this nightmare."

"I thought the same thing in the beginning. Where is it, for God's sake?"

"What are you talking about?"

"Daddy's remote control!"

"I'm calling now," Adam swore, heading toward the kitchen phone.

Arms spread wide, Julia barred his path.

"Don't take another step. Tell me exactly what happened from the moment you arrived."

"I already told you," Adam fumed. "Your father opened the door, I apologized for being so surprised to see him, and he invited me in, promising to explain what he was doing here. He told me to sit down, so I sat down on the couch, and he collapsed midsentence."

"The couch!" shouted Julia, knocking Adam over as she ran across the room.

She frantically looked under all the cushions and sighed with relief when she found the precious remote.

"As I was saying, you've gone completely insane," grumbled Adam, crawling to his feet.

"Please, God, please let it work," begged Julia, holding the little white remote.

"Julia!" shouted Adam. "For the last time, tell me what the hell is going on!"

"Shut up!" she replied on the verge of tears. "I'm just sparing us a useless conversation. You'll understand in a minute. And for you to understand, it has to work…"

She prayed to the heavens, closed her eyes, and pushed the button.

"You see, Adam my boy, things aren't always

what they seem…" continued Anthony as he opened his eyes. He cut himself short when he saw Julia standing in the middle of the room.

He coughed and got up, while Adam collapsed weakly into the welcoming comfort of the armchair.

"Oh…" continued Anthony. "What time is it? Is it already eight o'clock? I didn't notice the time pass." He brushed off his sleeves.

Julia gave him a scorching glare.

"I'll leave the two of you alone. I think it's better that way," he went on, embarrassed. "You must have a lot to say to each other. Listen carefully to what Julia has to say to you, Adam. Be very attentive, and don't interrupt. In the beginning it will seem a bit difficult to believe, but you'll see, if you concentrate, everything will make sense. I'll just find my coat and be out of here…"

Anthony took Adam's raincoat off the coat rack, went back across the room on tiptoe to recover the umbrella he'd abandoned near the window, and went out.

*

Julia first pointed to the shipping crate in the middle of the room and attempted to explain the unbelievable. She, in turn, fell onto the sofa, while Adam paced around.

"What would you have done in my position?"

"I don't know. I don't even know what my position is anymore. You lied to me for a week, and now you expect me to believe this fairy tale."

"Adam, if your father knocked on your door the day after his death, if fate allowed you to spend a few more days with him, six more days to tell each other all the things you'd never said, to revisit your childhood memories, wouldn't you grab the opportunity? Even if it seemed absurd?"

"I thought you hated your father."

"I thought so, too, and yet now I'd like to be able to spend more time with him. I only talked about myself, and there were so many other things I wanted to know about him, about his life. For the first time I was able to see him through the eyes of an adult, free of all my childhood selfishness. I admit my father had his flaws, but so do I. It doesn't mean that I don't love him. On my way home, I realized that, if I knew my children would be tolerant of me, I'd be less afraid of becoming a parent myself one day. I'd be more worthy, as well."

"I cannot believe how naïve you are. Your father orchestrated everything in your life from the day of your birth. Isn't that what you always told me, on the rare occasions you talked about him? If I'm to believe that your absurd explanation is true, he's succeeded in the unlikely feat of continuing his reign of control, even after his death. You share nothing with him, Julia. He's a machine!

Everything that he might have said was prerecorded. How could you fall into such an obvious trap? The two of you had no conversations. It was a monologue.

"You come up with imaginary characters—do you allow children to actually talk to them? Of course not. You just anticipate what they want to hear and invent sentences that will entertain or reassure them. Your father did exactly the same thing. He's manipulated you once again. Your little week of traveling together was a farce, a parody of a reunion. His presence was just a mirage, like it always was, but extended for a few more days. And you, so thirsty for the love you'd never received, you fell right into his trap. Right up to the point of ruining our wedding plans. And it wasn't even the first time he'd succeeded."

"Don't be ridiculous, Adam. My father didn't die just to keep us from getting married."

"Where did the two of you go together, Julia?"

"What does it matter?"

"Don't worry if you can't admit it yourself. Stanley did it for you. Oh, don't be mad at him—he was completely drunk. You're the one who told me that he couldn't resist a good bottle of wine, and I chose one of the best. I would have imported it from France myself to find out where you were, to understand why you'd gone away from me, to know what I should do to make you love me again. I would have waited a hundred years to marry you, Julia. But today I feel nothing but emptiness."

"I can explain, Adam."

"Now you can explain? What about when you came by my office to tell me that you were leaving on a trip? Or when we just missed each other in Montreal the next day? Or all the days afterward when I called you and you never even bothered to pick up your phone or return my messages? You decided to go to Berlin in search of a man from your past, and you told me nothing. What am I to you? A bridge between two periods in your life? A security blanket to hold onto until you're reunited with the man you've really always loved?"

"Please, you don't understand…" begged Julia.

"If he knocked at the door right now, what would you do?"

Julia remained silent.

"How am I supposed to know, if you don't even know yourself?"

Adam headed to the door.

"Tell your father, or his robot, that he can keep my raincoat."

Adam left. Julia counted his footsteps down the stairs and heard the front door slam behind him.

*

Anthony knocked hesitantly before coming in. Julia

was leaning on the windowsill, looking wistfully out into the street.

"Why did you do that?" she murmured.

"I didn't do anything. It was an accident," responded Anthony.

"Adam accidentally came to my place two hours early, you accidentally let him in, and he accidentally sat on your remote control, accidentally causing you to be sprawled across the living-room floor?"

"I admit, it's a series of rather ominous signs... Maybe we should try to understand their meaning."

"Cut the sarcasm. I'm not in the mood for jokes. I'll ask you one more time: Why did you do that?"

"To help you admit the truth to him and to make you confront the truth yourself. Don't you feel like a burden has been lifted from your shoulders? It may seem like you're more alone than you've ever been, but at least you're at peace with yourself."

"I wasn't only talking about the little act you put on this evening."

Anthony took a deep breath.

"Your mother's illness made it so that she didn't know who I was before she died, but I'm sure that, at the bottom of her heart, she hadn't forgotten the way we loved one another. I'll never forget, that's certain. We weren't a perfect couple, and we weren't model parents—far from it. We often didn't know what to do next. We fought, but never, you hear me, never did we doubt the choice we made to be together or the love we felt for you. Winning your mother's heart, loving her, and having a child with her were the most important choices of my life. They were the most beautiful things in my life, as well, even if it's taken me such a long time to find the right words to tell you so."

"Was it in the name of that love that you brought so much chaos into my life? That you caused so much damage?"

"Do you remember that little piece of paper I told you about during our trip? You know, the one a person always keeps near—in a wallet, in their pocket, in their head? Mine was the note your mother left the evening that I couldn't pay our bill in that restaurant on the Champs-Elysées. Maybe you understand now why I dreamed of dying in Paris. Maybe for you it was that old German mark that never left your purse or Thomas's letters that you kept in your bedroom."

"You read them?"

"I would never do such a thing. But I noticed them when I put his last letter in your desk drawer. When I got your wedding invitation, I went up to your old bedroom. Standing in the middle of that little universe brought me closer to you, to all of those things that I remember, that I'll never forget. I couldn't stop wondering what you'd do the day you discovered that letter from Thomas. I wondered if I should destroy it or send it to you, if the best thing

was to give it to you the day of your wedding. I
didn't have much time to decide. But, you see, like
you said, when you pay attention, life sends you
some astonishing signs. In Montreal I found part of
the response to the question I'd been asking myself,
but only part of it. The rest belonged to you. I would
have been happy just to mail you Thomas's letter,
but you'd been so successful at burning your bridges
that, until you invited me to your wedding, I didn't
even know your address. Would you even have
opened a letter if you knew it was from me? Besides,
I didn't know I was going to die!"

"You have an answer to everything, don't you?"

"No, Julia, you face your decisions alone. It's
been that way for longer than you think. You can
turn me off, remember? You just have to push the
button. You were free to refuse to go to Berlin. I left
you alone when you decided to go wait for Thomas
at the airport, and I wasn't there when you walked
back to the place where the two of you first met. I
certainly wasn't there when you brought him back
to the hotel. Julia, you can blame your childhood,
accuse your parents for all of the problems you confront, make them responsible for the trials of your
life, for your weaknesses, for your fears, but, in the
end, we're responsible for our own existence, and
we become who we decide to become. You have to
learn to put your dramas in perspective—there are
always families worse than yours."

"Like whose, for example?"

"Like Thomas's grandmother, who betrayed his every move."

"How do you know about that?"

"No parent can live their child's life for them, but that doesn't keep us from worrying and suffering each time we see you're unhappy. Sometimes it even pushes us to action, to try to show you the way. Sometimes it's better to be wrong and tactless, out of excess love, than to do nothing at all."

"If you intended to show me the way, you've failed. I'm completely lost."

"You may be lost, but you're not blind anymore!"

"Adam was right. We never once had a real conversation during our week together."

"Yes, maybe he's right, Julia. I'm not exactly your father—just what's left of him. But wasn't this machine capable of finding solutions to your problems? Over these past few days, was I ever without a response to any of your questions? Maybe it's because I know you better than you imagined. So perhaps one day you'll realize that I also loved you far more than you ever imagined. And now that you've heard all that, I can let myself die."

Julia looked at her father a long time, then went and sat down next to him. They stayed silent, like that, for a long time.

"Do you really believe what you said about me?" asked Anthony.

"To Adam? Were you listening through the door again?"

"Through the floor, to be precise. I went up to your attic. With the rain outside, I could have caught a short circuit," he said with a smile.

"Why didn't I get to know you sooner?" she asked him.

"It sometimes takes years for parents and children to get to know each other."

"I wish we had a few more days together."

"I believe we just had them, my dear Julia."

"What will happen tomorrow?"

"Don't worry. You're lucky. The death of a father is always a difficult thing to face, but for you it's already in the past."

"I'm not in the mood for jokes."

"Tomorrow is another day. You'll see."

As the night deepened, Anthony's hand inched toward Julia's. Finally, he took her hand in his. Their fingers tightened and stayed like that, intertwined. Later, when Julia fell asleep, her head came to rest on her father's shoulder.

*

The sun hadn't risen yet. Anthony Walsh took every precaution not to wake his daughter as he stood up. He delicately settled her on the sofa and placed a blanket around her shoulders. Julia grumbled in her sleep and rolled over.

After making sure she was still sound asleep, he took a pen and paper, sat down at the kitchen table, and started to write.

Once his letter was finished, he set it out on the table. Then he opened his bag and took out a little package of a hundred other letters, bundled together by a red ribbon. He went into his daughter's bedroom and put them in one of her dresser drawers, careful not to bend the corners of the yellowed photograph of Thomas that accompanied them.

Back in the living room, he walked over to the sofa, took the white remote control, put it in the breast pocket of his coat, and leaned over to plant a kiss on Julia's forehead.

"Sleep, my darling Julia. Have a wonderful life. I love you."

22.

Julia stretched and opened her eyes. The room was empty, and the crate was closed.

"Daddy?"

There was no reply. Silence reigned over her apartment. The kitchen table was set with breakfast for one, and an envelope sat propped up against the jar of honey, between the box of cereal and the milk carton. Julia recognized the handwriting. She sat down.

My darling Julia,

By the time you read this letter, my batteries will have run down. I hope that you won't be mad at me, but I wanted to avoid useless goodbyes. Burying your father once was quite enough. When you finish reading these last words, leave your apartment for a few hours. They'll come and get me, and I'd rather that you weren't here. Don't open the box again. I'm sleeping inside peacefully, thanks to you. Thank you so much for the days you gave me, my dear. I waited for them for such a long time. I'd always dreamed of getting to know the mysterious woman you've become. I've learned one of the great lessons of a parent's life these last few days—the importance of taking time to get to know the adult who has replaced the child, to give that adult their rightful place. I'm sorry for the things you missed during your childhood. I did my best. I wasn't there with you enough, not as much as you would have liked. I wanted to be your friend, your confidant; in the end, I was only your father. But I'll always be your father. No matter where I'm going, I'll always remember an infinite love, the love I hold for you. Do you remember that Chinese legend I shared with you? That lovely story about the power of the full moon's reflection? I was wrong to doubt its truth. It was just a matter of patience. I got my wish in the end—the woman that I had always hoped to have in my life was you.

I can still see you as a little girl, running into my arms. It may sound silly to say, but you're the best thing that ever happened to me. Nothing made me happier than the sound of your laughter and the hugs you gave me when I came home in the evening. I know that, one day, when you're free from your worries, these memories will come back to you, too. I also know that you'll never forget the dreams you told me about when I came and sat at the foot of your bed. Even when I was absent, I was never as far away from you as you thought. Clumsy and awkward though I may be, I love you. I only have one more thing to ask of you: promise me you'll be happy.

Your Daddy

Julia folded up the letter. She walked over to the crate in the middle of the room and caressed its wooden sides, murmuring to her father that she loved him, too. Heavy-hearted, she obeyed his last wishes. Going downstairs, she left a key with her neighbor. She warned Mr. Zimoure that a truck would be coming to pick up a package at her house that morning and asked him to open the door for them. Without giving him time to respond, she headed downtown toward a familiar antiques store.

23.

Fifteen minutes went by, and silence reigned over Julia's apartment once more. A gentle click was followed by the sound of the crate cautiously creaking open. Anthony stepped out, dusted off his shoulders, and walked over to the mirror to adjust his tie. He put the frame holding his photograph back in place on the bookshelf, and looked around the room.

He left the apartment and went downstairs to the street. A car waited for him, parked out in front of the building.

"Good morning, Wallace," he said, settling into the backseat.

"Good to see you again, sir," replied his private secretary.

"Is the shipping company ready?"

"The truck is right behind us."

"Perfect."

"Shall I take you back to the hospital, sir?"

"No, I've already lost enough time as it is. We'll go to the airport. We can stop by the house along the way. I need to change suitcases. You should also pack a bag for yourself. I'm taking you with me. I've lost the taste for traveling alone."

"May I ask where we're going, sir?"

"I'll explain on the way. Don't forget your passport."

The car turned onto Greenwich Street. At the intersection, the window rolled down, and a white remote control landed in the gutter.

24.

New Yorkers couldn't remember a milder October. The Indian summer was one of the most beautiful in collective memory. Like every weekend for the past three months, Stanley and Julia were having brunch together. Today, they had a table waiting for them at Pastis. This Sunday was special, however. Mr. Zimoure had put his stock on sale, and for the first time, Julia knocked at his door without a disaster to report. He agreed to let her shop two hours before his official opening time.

"What do you think?"

"Turn around and let me have a look at you."

"Stanley, you've been looking me up and down for half an hour. I can't stand on this podium a minute longer."

"Do you want my advice or not, princess? Turn around again so I can see the front. Yes…just as I suspected. Kitten heels don't become you at all."

"Stanley!"

"You know I'm allergic to sales."

"You know how expensive this store is! Excuse

me if I don't have any other choice with my paltry income," she whispered.

"Don't start that again!"

"So are you going to take them?" asked Mr. Zimoure, exhausted. "I think I've taken out everything in your size. The two of you alone have managed to ransack my entire store."

"No," replied Stanley, "we still haven't seen those ravishing pumps on that shelf over there. Yes, up on the top shelf, the last one over there…"

"I'm afraid I don't have that in Miss Julia's size."

"What about in the stockroom?" begged Stanley.

"I have to go down and see," sighed Zimoure as he headed down the stairs.

"It's a good thing he's so distinguished and handsome, because with a personality like that…"

"You think he's distinguished and handsome?" Julia laughed incredulously.

"I've had a change of heart these past few months. Maybe we could invite him to dinner at your house sometime."

"Are you kidding me?"

"I'm not the one who's always saying he sells the most exquisite shoes in New York."

"And that makes you want to…"

"I can't remain a widower for the rest of my life. Do you have a problem with that?"

"Of course not, but Mr. Zimoure?"

"Forget Zimoure!" said Stanley, looking out the window into the street.

"Already?"

"Don't turn around, but that man watching us through the window is drop-dead gorgeous!"

"What man?" asked Julia, holding as still as possible.

"The man who's had his face pressed up against the glass for the last ten minutes. He's staring at you like he's seen the Virgin Mary or something. But as far as I know, she doesn't wear three hundred dollar pumps, particularly not ones on sale. Don't turn around! I told you, I saw him first."

Julia lifted her head, and her lips began to tremble.

"Oh, no," she said in a soft voice, "I saw this one long before you."

She abandoned the shoes on the platform, turned the lock on the door, and ran out into the street.

*

When Mr. Zimoure came back upstairs, he found Stanley, sitting alone on the platform, holding a pair of pumps.

"She left?" he asked with alarm.

"Yes," replied Stanley, "but don't worry, she'll come back. Probably not today, but she'll come back."

Zimoure dropped the box of shoes he had been holding. Stanley picked it up and gave it back to him.

"You look so exhausted. Come on, let me help you clean up this mess, and then I'll buy you a coffee. Or a tea, if you'd prefer."

*

Thomas brushed Julia's lips with his fingertips and gently kissed each of her eyelids. She melted into his arms.

"I tried to convince myself I could live without you, but as you can see, I can't," he said, his voice thick with emotion.

"What about your work in Africa? What will Knapp say?"

"What good is it for me to run around the planet reporting the truth about other people if I'm lying to myself? What good is it to jump from country to country when the person I love is right here?"

Julia was standing on her tiptoes, looking deep into his eyes.

They kissed, and their kiss lasted a very long time, like the kiss of two people so blindly in love they've forgotten the rest of the world exists.

"How did you find me?" Julia asked, snuggling into Thomas's arms.

"I searched for you for twenty years. Looking

downstairs from your apartment wasn't much of a stretch."

"Eighteen years. Believe me, that was long enough."

Julia kissed him again.

"And you, Julia? What made you decide to come to Berlin?"

"I told you, it was a sign… I saw your portrait at a street artist's stand."

"But I've never had my portrait drawn."

"Of course you did. It was your face—your eyes, your mouth—she even captured the dimple in your chin."

"And where did you find this picture that looks so much like me?"

"In the Old Port of Montreal."

"But Julia, that's impossible. I've never been to Montreal."

Julia looked skyward and saw a cloud blowing over New York. She smiled as she saw the form it took.

"I'm going to miss him so much."

"Who's that?"

"My father. Come on, let's go for a walk. I'll show you around my town."

"But you're barefoot."

"That really doesn't matter," Julia replied.

Thank you

Emmanuelle Hardouin,
Pauline Lévêque,
Raymond and Danièle Levy,
Louis Levy,
Lorraine.

Susanna Lea and Antoine Audouard.

Léonard Anthony, Marie Garnero, Kerry
Glencorse, Katrin Hodapp, Mark Kessler, Moïna
Macé, Laura Mamelok, Danielle Melconian,
Romain Ruetsch, Lauren Wendelken.

Chris Murray.

Antoine Caro.

Pauline Normand, Marie-Ève Provost,
and Kim McArthur.

Philippe Guez, Éric Brame
and Miguel Courtois.

Yves and Martyn Lévêque,
Charles Veillet-Lavallée.